U0153256

中英論文寫作 第三版
的第一本書
用綱要和體例來教你寫研究計畫與論文

BETTER THESIS, DISSERTATION,
AND RESEARCH PAPER

葉乃嘉／著

五南圖書出版公司 印行

三越乃嘉——我認識的葉乃嘉教授

認識葉乃嘉教授時，他是資訊管理系的助理教授，那一年我們敦請臺灣師範大學新文學翹楚楊昌年教授來明道專題演講，他自稱是楊老師的學生，全程陪同，演講後繼續請教，侃侃而言，讓我印象深刻。後來他轉任通識教育中心，我也在中心工作，最近他到課程所、英語系、中文系任職，都是我所屬的人文學院，屢屢見他提出專案計畫申請，臚列許多論文成就，更讓我驚訝。

我去到他的《個人知識站》，發現他對教育的高見：「學校教育不僅僅是向學生傳播知識，更要引導學生發掘自己腦中的無形資產，增強認識的廣度，讓學生充分發揮自己的想像力，用不同的方式思考。因此，他以身作則，多方涉獵，希望大家能夠相信，只要在本專業以外，多接觸文化、藝術、社會學和大眾科學等方面的知識，學數理的人也能兼通心理，唸科學的人也能夠具有文藝氣息，以人文社會起家的人也能跨足自然理工。」深得我心，所以決定以〈三越乃嘉——我認識的葉乃嘉教授〉的跨界角度來介紹他的人、他的書，他的書正是他生命中穿越、跨越、超越的智慧果實。

在明道的這十多年，他出版了十多本專書，充滿了教育的熱忱，引導學生走上研究的正途：《英文E-mail寫作溝通的第一本書》、《研究寫作的第一本書——如何寫作教育、人文與社會科學的論文》、《個人知識管理的第一本書》、《質性研究寫作的第一本書》等等，都顯現他教育的專業與跨界的能耐。此外，

他還潛入大腦、意識、心靈的研究：《意識、時空與心靈》、《心·靈與意識——新時代的生命教育》，將神祕學與科學做了某種程度的連結，這是深入其中的穿越，出乎其外的跨越，匯聚學術與經驗的智慧結晶，至於「超越」，那就不是文字、書籍所能表述，必須見諸於行事的瀟灑、處事的俐落。

葉老師畢業於國立臺灣師範大學物理學系，留學美國，是美國University of Texas at Dallas環境科學與管理學博士，專攻知識管理、管理資訊系統、教學科技與媒體創作、能源管理、英文學術論文寫作，術業有其專攻之一方，知識又能廣博及於眾方，這正是他所說的「不以一成不變的方式工作，甚至不以一成不變的方式過日子」所達致。他以物理學專業為基礎，擴及於知識管理系統、藝文心靈探索，遊走於科學、管理、資訊、意識之間，令人嘆服。如前幾年國科會計畫——「橢圓曲面式Fresnel透鏡折光模式與其集光區之色光分析」研究成果，榮獲「能源與燃料類」頂級期刊SOLMAT及RSER刊登，受到國際學術界肯定，就不是我所能了解，不是我所能跨越的區塊。但是這種「學習不設限，成就不受限」的學養抱負，卻是我等所要效法學習的。

中文系的課程都在「究天人之際，通古今之變，成一家之言」（司馬遷言），懸著高遠的目標，往往未能度之以金針，授人以舟楫，很少及於方法之學，即使是「治學方法」的課程，往往難能跟上西洋學術倫理與規範，尤其是現代的學術論文，必須引用西方文學理論、美學觀點、知識論、現象論，甚至於引述原文，傳統的研究方法與寫作系統，難以應付這些需求。葉教授這

本書，應用西洋方法學、論文規範，從論文資料管理談起，落實於文字經營，掌握論文的特殊準則，依序討論論文篇前、主體、篇後，甚至於校對、電腦格式，都以實例分析、檢討，中文、英文範例並陳，對於追求國際化的論文寫作，極具示範與引導功能，頗有啓發、拓展作用。

　　對於研究所新生，對於初次嘗試研究計畫寫作與申請的講師、助理教授，應該從這本書踏上研究正途，至於學術專業的充實，其實一樣能從「穿越、跨越、超越」事物現象與本體、葉教授的為學歷程中獲得啓發，若是，這本書就不只是方法論的指引而已。

2016年大暑之日寫於明道大學
明道大學講座教授兼人文學院院長

蕭水順（蕭蕭）

2016/7/22

推薦序

　　論文是表現高等教育及專業研究成果的最具體方式，對博士研究生而言，寫作論文原本就是生涯中不可避免的一部份，而如今，幾乎每一個研究所都要求其碩士學生寫作畢業論文，此外，一些大學科系為了維持較高的水準，以有別於一般泛泛的學位提供者，也開始要求學生做畢業專題研究，寫作小型論文，對這些人來說，畢業論文是一項重大工程，攸關是否能順利取得學位。他們如果能在起步時獲得正確的資訊，當可事半功倍。

　　為讓「研究方法與論文寫作」這類課程能真正幫助有志於學術者減少摸索過程，葉乃嘉教授依據他自己多年的中英論文及研究報告寫作經驗，完成了深受兩岸高教師生肯定與歡迎的《中英論文寫作綱要與體例》和《研究方法的第一本書》這兩本暢銷書。自那以後，來自許多非常不同領域（舉凡資管、企管、工管、材料、教育、環境、中文、農業等背景）的研究生們，常常濟濟一堂，同時選上他的論文寫作課。

　　葉教授完全能夠體會「集天下英才而教之」的樂趣，尤其是所教的學生真正能夠體會他的認真與用心的時候。他指導論文寫作的態度極為熱切，要求也十分嚴格，教學相長之餘，他受到了啟發，比別人更了解不同領域學生寫作論文時的不同需要，如今他精益求精，結合兩書之長，推出這本內容更豐、量級更重、可是卻更加清晰易懂的《中英論文寫作的第一本書》，這本書歸納

了主要的論文寫作原則，選用了數以百計的中英論文體例，其範圍涵蓋了資訊、社會、文學、理工及管理等學門，他把這些實例分別加以評述修訂，又加上腳註一百餘條，真正稱得上是旁徵博引。

《中英論文寫作的第一本書》之所以用「第一本書」為名，就是因為它能為初入門者理清觀念，稱得上是初學論文寫作的人士所必備的第一本工具書，初學者有了它的幫助，必能探得論文寫作的門徑，漸漸進入得心應手的佳境。揆諸市面上有關論文寫作的著作，本書結構之完備、舉例之豐富，是出乎其類的，讓其他論文寫作類書很難超越，它的論文指導效果必然能夠拔乎其萃。

《中英論文寫作的第一本書》雖說是為論文寫作而撰，但難能可貴的，是其第二章「論文的文字經營」中所敘述的文字經營準則，這些準則同時也可以做為一般應用文寫作時的絕佳參考；第三章「論文的特殊規則」中的一些原則，幾乎不見其他同類書籍提及；再則，第七章的論文計畫書撰述及第十章的標點使用法部分，也許不是本書所獨有，但其內容卻是市面書中可見的最完備指南。另外，第十章的電腦輔助論文格式製作更引介了值得任何論文寫作者一學的電腦輔助目錄、註腳、索引的製作方法，這些不但能讓研究生們茅塞頓開，也足以令任何階層的論文寫作人士受益匪淺。

葉老師的寫作風格簡單扼要，白話易懂，讓人讀來沒有什麼

壓力，論文寫作的指引用這種方式來寫，好像有了新的生命，我一向樂於見人閱讀好書，也樂於與人分享人生中美好的事物，葉君囑我為序，我當然樂於為之。

明道大學餐旅觀光學院院長

溫德生　謹識

2015/9/15

自 序

　　教育部呼籲各大學校院廣為開授「研究方法與論文寫作」之類的課程，整合「研究方法」與「論文寫作」這兩項高度相關的科目，期待這門課程在各校得以全面開設之後，發揮功能，有助於大學教學品質的提升。鑑於這種高等教育的需要，加上兩岸都日漸國際化的現實狀況，我乃在2005年初出了《中英論文寫作綱要與體例》這本書，依據自己多年的論文寫作實務經驗，歸納主要的寫作原則，並且舉出很多寫作實例，分別加以評述。該書推出之後，引起了許多迴響，受到許多專家學者及研究生的肯定及歡迎，同時，大陸南京大學也簽了約，於2009年起，在大陸以簡體字版發行。在這期間，持續有公私立大學各系所的演講邀約，以及各地同業們修改英文論文的請求，把我第二生涯的景象漸漸勾勒出來。

　　我在英文寫作上比較得心應手，要歸因於在美國期間的工作性質，我的日常業務與書信和研究報告的寫作都有很密切的關係，至今，我親手寫作與修改的英文書信、報告及論文，遠超過一百萬字，其中一半以上皆已出版，這些成績讓我受到極大的鼓舞。如今，為了讓真正能幫助有志於學術者減少摸索的過程，我再接再厲，整合了這幾年來修改論文所得的經驗、教學時所蒐集的議題、閱讀論文時所碰到的文例、以及授課時為學生解答的問題等，撰述出《中英論文寫作的第一本書》這本很容易閱讀的入門書兼案頭參考書，不論你是初次寫作論文，還是經常需要寫論

文報告，只要願意花幾個鐘頭從頭到尾閱讀一遍，你就能得到很具體的寫作知識，讓你在論文生產過程中少花很多力氣。

　　最後，祝你早日達到目的。

葉乃嘉　謹識

garynyeh@gmail.com

2010/7/5

目　錄

論文資料管理與寫作準則

　　在每個人的工作和學習中，都已經有了資料管理的影子，但這種行而不知的個人資料管理，是無意識的行為，效果不彰，只有透過計畫性的資料管理，才可以讓個人的資料變成更具價值的知識。

本篇大要

第一章
論文資料管理

本章提綱

　　一、論文資料的來源

　　二、論文資料結構的建立

　　三、論文資料的分析

　　四、論文的文字表達

　　五、論文與發表的道德與責任

　　論文資料管理結合了邏輯概念和實際操作的過程，並形成一套為問題求解的技巧，一般而言，此套技巧有七個項目，分別為：資料取得、資料評估、資料整理、資料分析、資料表達、資料保全、資料協作[1]。茲分別說明如下：

1. **資料取得**：提問與回答、練習反覆搜索、利用電子圖書館的資料庫來查尋資料等，對資料的取得都很重要。資料的品質與資料取得的技巧有很大的關聯，附錄 C 提供會更詳盡的資料搜尋技巧介紹。

2. **資料評估**：不僅包括個人對資料品質的判斷能力，也包括判斷這種資料與自己問題的相關度的能力。在這資料多雜的環境下，評估資料的技巧顯得日益重要。

3. **資料整理**：指用不同的工具把各種資料組合起來的能力。在手動的環

1　取材自葉乃嘉《知識管理》，全華科技圖書公司，臺北，2004。

境裡整理資料，用的是文件夾、抽屜和其他的實體方法；在較高科技的環境裡，則是用電子文件夾、相關性資料庫和網頁來整理資料。不管用什麼方法，只要能把資料整理得便於運用，就能算是好方法。

4. **資料分析**：是從資料中找出意義的能力。資料間的關係可以應用量化模型來找出。電子試算表和統計軟體可供分析資料，但是，若要建立各種分析軟體裡面的模型，還是得靠人力。

5. **資料表達**：資料表達的對象乃是聽眾，無論是透過投影片、網站，還是藉文字來表達，都應該把想表達的資料整理得有助於聽眾理解和記憶。

6. **資料保全**：包括應用各種保障資料機密、品質和安全存取的方法。常用到的密碼管理、備份、建檔和加密等，都是保護資料安全的有效方法。

7. **資料協作**：資訊科技提供群組軟體（Groupware）[2]這種工具來支援團隊協同作業，要有效協同作業不僅須會使用這類工具，而且要充分理解協同作業的各種原則，譬如，E-mail 的禮節對團隊的協同作業就很重要。

　　以上的每個論文資料管理技巧，都可視作解決問題的一個環節，也都可以根據需要，交替使用。

　　資料的價值與研究報告或論文的完成大有關係，資料依來源可分為一手資料及二手資料，一手資料是指直接驗證而來的資料，包括觀察、實驗、訪問、調查以及原典文獻，這個部分的論點及解說較具有原創性。二手資料則是經由他人轉述或由分析他人研究而得的結論，包括各

2　群組軟體的主要功能，在使組織成員工作上的溝通及合作更為簡便，它提供多種軟體工具，幫助用戶在相異或相同的時地完成辦公室自動化、資訊存取及各項管理、決策支援、應用發展等任務。

類研究報告、評論、報導等，可以用於研究的參考及驗證。

　　整理資料時宜作成筆記，製作筆記時應將資料就其與研究主題相關的程度予以去蕪存菁，筆記可包含原文的重點和自己的看法，應忠於原文詳實摘錄，筆記中**事件的順序宜合乎邏輯**，重點凌亂的紀錄容易使人迷惑，把事件依重要性從低到高排列出來可以增加其可讀性，也可以讓人比較容易抓住重點。

一、論文資料的來源

　　獲取研究資料的途徑，大致可以分為學習與培訓、人際網路、網際網路、各式交流以及圖書館等：

1. **學習與培訓**：學生日常以上課為務，為的是學習，公司組織的企業內部培訓也是一種學習，這些正規學習的結果，對個人的發展很有價值。除此以外，從事研究者應該利用機會，多方吸收知識（例如多閱讀、多聽演講等）來充實自己，從而增強自己的研究能力。

2. **人際網路**：聊天談話也可以是獲取知識的準備階段。每個人都有人際圈子，在人際交往中，可以獲得其他管道得不到的知識，人際圈又稱人際網路或人脈，人脈是一種無形的網絡，是個人學習知識的重要途徑。不論正規的學習機制如何發達，媒體如何普及，都無法取代在人脈中的學習機會，事實上，有許多情報資料都是透過人脈獲得的，人脈越廣、人脈素質越好，越能學到有用的知識。想要獲得和維持人脈雖然煞費功夫，可是人脈一旦建立，往往是重要知識直接而深入的來源。交往的圈子若大，人脈聯繫方式的管理也就成為很重要的事情。

3. **網際網路**：Internet 是獲取及累積知識的一件重要工具，身為現代的研究者，就必須能夠充分利用豐富網路的資源來學習。上網查詢資料

已經成為學術論文蒐集資料的重要方式，一般學校都有電子閱覽室，這裡能進入各種數位圖書館等專業網站和搜索引擎。只要輸入關鍵字或句子很快能查到與之相關的研究內容。有些文章下載是要付費的，但學校可能已經買了版權。網際網路上的知識多雜，想用它來學習，就必須熟悉搜尋引擎的功能、善用搜尋引擎。又，媒體也是有用的資訊來源。但一般說來，來自網路和媒體的資訊，在質的方面不見得理想，若要真正從中獲益，難免需要費較多的篩選功夫。不論如何，只要有效地建立契合自己學習和研究的網址清單，並熟悉各類相關資源的所在，必然能夠大大提升研究的素質。

4. **各式交流**：在集體的氛圍中激盪思維，不僅能累積知識，更能創造知識，一群人交流知識，每個人的知識都在增長，因此，可以多參加研討會或知識性的座談與交流。又，幾乎每個行業都有相關的專業團體，研究者可以結合研究工作，在相關的專業團體中關注新動向、學習新方法，從而利用專業團體內的專業論壇，來加強個人的知識。

5. **圖書館**：大型的學術機構圖書館資料豐富，書籍多，內容廣，而期刊涉及最新研究以及成果，所以，在圖書館查閱研究導向的資料，應該要結合期刊與書籍。現代的圖書館，早已經不再提供卡片索引這種過時的檢索系統，即使還有些圖書館執意保留卡片系統，也已經不再予以維護及更新，代之而起的，是網路化的電子圖書索引系統，快速準確，不會遺失，而且學習和使用起來都極容易。我們如果還無法利用電腦的輔助來整理資料，研究工作的效率不免大打折扣。

在今天的學界裡，每個人都應該有能力使用電腦蒐集與整理資料，把資料分門別類、註明出處。資料出處應包括書報期刊名稱、作者、出版時地、卷數期別、頁碼等，以作為查證之用。在個人電腦時代來臨前，傳統的資料整理方式是製作資料卡片，但今天的電腦軟硬體提供了

比卡片更方便、更迅速、更完備的資料處理機制，完全可以取代資料卡片的所有用途。

二、論文資料結構的建立

資料量到達一定的程度後，就要妥善管理所得的資料和知識，不然就不可能提高工作效率。因此，論文資料管理的第二步就是建立資料系統架構。

論文資料架構的基礎，就是資料儲存與分類的方法，研究導向的知識分類，要盡量契合自己目前研究工作，同時應該配合電腦的應用，來建立系統化的知識庫和知識架構，以利快速存取手頭的資料，要建立這種架構，先要考慮論文資料的分類。

論文資料的分類不可能一蹴可幾，因此，不妨在實行中找出適合自己需求的最佳分類方法。此外，也要能夠善用數位科技工具，許多蒐集、整理、儲存資料與知識的工具都日益成熟，像知識管理軟體、掃描機、字體辨識軟體（OCR, Optical Character Recognizer）、無線通訊與掌上電腦（PDA, Personal Data Assistant）等，都是個人研究的有用工具。

要管理個人的文件檔案可以用 Windows 檔案總管。幾乎所有的 Windows 工作都必須用到檔案及資料

圖 1-1　視窗檔案總管的樹狀結構

夾。Windows 檔案總管會顯示出電腦上檔案、資料夾及磁碟機的樹狀結構（又稱階層式結構）。

圖 1-1 所示的就是以 Windows 檔案總管把一本論文的結構以標準的樹狀結構表示出來，該結構由學術著作資料夾開始，一層一層列出書中的篇、章、節等層次，清晰而有條理。

三、論文資料的分析

以下是論文資料分析所應該依循的步驟：

1. **仔細閱讀**：分析資料的第一步，就是詳細閱讀該資料，關注於整個案例的細節。為了增加對資料的熟悉度，有時也有必要將之反覆閱讀，藉以發掘更深入的訊息。每個人觀察一個資料的著眼點不同，在相同的資料中也許會發現不同的重點，因此，還有必要和同儕多多交流。

2. **詳細筆記**：要分析資料，除了既定的閱讀材料外，還需要從其他地方取得相關資料，除了在重要的句子下面畫線，或用色筆標出重要的部分外，也必須養成做筆記的習慣，若有電子檔可以使用，那麼要把重點剪貼、重組及潤飾就更方便了。

3. **找出主要問題**：每一個資料裡至少會有一個基本的問題，問題可大可小，小自具體的技術，大至全面的策略，盡量找出主要問題，考慮哪些問題需要優先解決。

4. **識別邏輯觀點**：一個資料可能包含多個邏輯層面，研讀者需要知道其中的邏輯關係，邏輯觀點間有主要、次要之分，有些觀點是獨立的，有些觀點則需要其他觀點的支援，應該盡可能一一尋找出來。同時必須對某些問題做一些假設。

5. **列出可能的解決方案**：一個問題可能有多種解決辦法，列出所有想到

的候選方案，加以比較，從中找出最好的。單靠個人的力量比較不容易順利解決問題，應該利用各種人際的溝通方式，對資料深入探討，有時候，一次不經意的談話就會開出新的思路。

四、論文的文字表達

好的論文有一些放諸四海皆準的原則：

1. **架構清楚**：論文的組織架構宜清晰易懂，各章節的篇幅比例宜分配合宜，各章節要層次分明，標題亦應切合內容的重點。

2. **格式正確**：論文的格式於各學門的規定雖然不一，但紙張、字型、字級、行距、註腳、列舉、標點、頁碼、圖表等，都應循一定的格式與規則，不應自行隨意設定。

3. **內容客觀簡潔**：論文或學術報告的文字應力求簡潔，避免用誇大的或情緒性的用語，且不應刻意將研究導向自己希望的結果，以免有違科學的客觀性。

4. **文獻的探討切合主題**：所蒐集的文獻須加以適當地整合和評論，不要因為捨不得辛苦蒐集的文獻而在論文中塞進許多與研究目的無關的資料。

5. **分析有根據**：論文及學術報告的分析結果不能「想當然爾」，要能有幾分證據說幾分話，除了自己的研究結果之外，也可根據所蒐集的文獻做出適當的解釋。

6. **結論能扼要綜整前文**：論文的結論部分是根據前文做的綜合整理，可對研究限制與建議提出論點，要能前後呼應，前文未提及的事項，不可突然提起，以免無法收尾。

五、論文與發表的道德與責任

在有審稿機制（peer review）的期刊中發表研究結果的能力，已經成為高教界驗證學者、學人及學生研究能力的指標，原因在於有審稿機制的期刊對其作者（author）、主編（editor）、審稿者（reviewer）及出版者（publisher）都有比較嚴格的寫作、評審及出版水準及道德的要求，茲將其中重要者臚列於下：

㈠ 論文作者的責任

作者在論文中應該準確地敘述相關的研究工作，並客觀討論該研究工作的意義。論文中應準確地敘述基本數據，包含足夠的細節及參考資料以利他人複製工作。論文中對他人論文的評述也應準確和客觀，評述若屬作者個人意見，則應明確標示為**「個人意見」**。

作者應該確保論文的原創性，對於自己的研究有確定影響的參考文獻，作者必須明確指出，若有使用他人的成果，則應以適當的方式引用和參照，未經明確書面同意，作者不得在自己的研究中引用：

1. 經由對話、通信，或與第三方討論中獲得的私人信息。
2. 他人在保密協定下的研究成果（如評審意見或研究資金申請書等）。

作者也不得有故意將陳述模糊化及任何形式的剽竊等不道德行為。剽竊有許多種形式，從冒稱他人的文章為自己的文章，未以適當的方式引用和參照即抄襲或意譯他人文字的相當部分，冒稱他人的研究結果為己有等等均屬剽竊行為。

作者應準備提供論文的原始數據以供編輯單位審閱，並應準備向公眾提供這些數據，可行的話，應盡一切可能，在論文出版後一段合理時間保留這些數據。

同時提交相同的論文給不同的期刊構成不道德行為，作者不應在不同的出版物中出版基本上相同的研究描述。一般來說，作者不應將另一個刊物發表過的稿件送審，但若滿足了某些條件，有時在不同的刊物刊出某些種類的文章（例如，臨床指南、翻譯）也屬可行，此時需經相關的作者與期刊編輯同意，此類的出版須反映與原文件相同的數據和解釋，也必須引用原文件為參考文獻。

對研究的構思、設計、執行或結果解釋有重要貢獻者，方得列為共同作者。提供資金或其他參與了部分研究的人，則可列入誌謝中。

通訊作者應確保：

1. 論文中列入所有符合條件的共同作者，
2. 沒有將不符合條件者列為共同作者，
3. 所有的共同作者都認可最後的定稿，
4. 所有的共同作者都同意將該文提交出版。

研究中如果使用到化學藥品、化學程序或化學設備，作者必須清楚在其稿件中表明該化學藥品、化學程序或設備可能造成之任何不尋常災害。研究中如果使用到動物或人，作者必須清楚在其稿件中表明所有的程序均有遵守相關法律和準則，並有經適當的機構批准。研究對象若是人，作者必須清楚在其稿件中表明該研究對象知情並同意該試驗。研究對象之個人隱私權必須始終受到尊重。

任何可能影響到結果解釋之利益或衝突關係，作者均應在其稿件中盡早披露，所應披露之項目包括任何金錢或非金錢之利得（包括專利、聘僱、酬金、股權、補助金、專家證詞費、或其他財務支援）。

作者若發現自己的作品有重大錯誤，則有義務及時通知期刊主編或出版者，並配合收回作品或修正稿件。若主編或出版者由第三方得知已發表的作品有重大錯誤，則作者有義務及時收回和修正該作品，不然就

應向主編提供證據，證實自己的論文正確無誤。

(二) 期刊主編的責任

　　主編者得遵循下列原則：

1. 公平原則：主編者評估稿件內容時，應不考慮作者的種族、性別、性取向、宗教信仰、民族血統、國籍或政治取向。
2. 保密原則：除對通訊作者、審稿者、編輯顧問及出版者之外，主編者和編輯團隊的工作人員不得透露來稿的任何信息給任何人。

　　與相關領域學會協調與合作，依該文論述之有效性及該文對研究界人士和讀者的重要性，全權負責決定論文之刊登與否。主編者得遵循雜誌編委會的規定，並遵循誹謗、侵權和剽竊等相關法律的限制，會同審稿者、學會負責人或其他編輯人員之意見，作出刊登與否之決定。

　　未經作者的明確書面同意，主編者不得在自己的研究中運用作者送審的材料。審閱中的資料或構想必須予以保密，主編者不得將之用於個人利益。主編者不應評審與自己有利益衝突的論文（利益衝突包括來自競爭、合作或其他任何與作者、或機構的關係），而應轉請共同主編、副主編或其他編委會的成員處理。

　　若有相當的證據證明某篇已發表的論文在資料或結論上有誤，主編應立即協同出版者，迅速撤銷該文，或刊出相關的更正與說明。

　　若有人對送審中或已發表的論文有著作道德上的投訴時，主編者應會同出版者或相關學會，採取合理的應對措施。這類措施一般包括**聯繫該文的作者，並對每一項申訴或要求給予應有的重視**，或進一步**通報相關學會和研究團體**。

㈢ 論文審稿者的責任

審稿者得遵循以下原則：

1. **迅速原則**：受委任的評審若自覺無法勝任或及時完成審稿工作，則應迅速告知主編，並退出審閱程序。

2. **保密原則**：任何受審稿件都必須視為機密文件，非經主編授權，不得與他人討論。

3. **客觀原則**：審稿應客觀，不宜對作者做個人的批評，評審應該以相關的論點明確表達自己的評審意見。

審稿者若發現所審稿件與已出刊之論文有重大相似或重複，乃至發現文稿中所引用的陳述、推導、論證或觀察結果未經註明出處者，均應向主編如實指出。

未經作者的明確書面同意，審稿者不得在自己的研究中運用作者送審的材料。審閱中的資料或構想必須予以保密，評審者不得將之用於個人利益。審稿者不應評審與自己有**利益衝突**的論文，利益衝突包括與作者或任何相關機構之競爭、合作或其他任何從屬關係。

㈣ 期刊出版者的責任

出版者應支持主編者、審稿者和作者履行其道德義務。確保廣告、轉載或其他商業收入不致影響到編輯的決定。

第二章
論文的文字經營

本章提綱

　　一、多用主動語態

　　二、減少形容詞和副詞

　　三、少用長句

　　四、注意邏輯並釐清因果

　　五、善用覆述的原則

　　六、多用簡單易懂的字

　　七、小心錯別字及文法、語意上的謬誤

　　八、注意字詞的相對位置

　　合格的論文應該能精確而不偏頗地表達研究的成果。文字的表達能夠讓知識流傳至未來，口頭的表達則能將知識傳達給廣泛的大眾。不論是文字或口頭的表達，都能夠擴大知識的傳播。

　　本章所述的文字經營準則，就是要協助讀者達到這個目的。本章雖說是為論文寫作而立，但也是寫作一般非抒情性的應用文時絕佳的參考。書中所引用的範例，都是摘自論文或其他應用文的實例[1]。

1　其中用來做負面示範者，不便註明其出處，有意者可以自行於網路中搜尋。

一、多用主動語態

在中文裡原本很少用被動語態（passive tense），但由於受到西方文字的影響，中文裡出現被動語態的情形也就增多了。例如：

> 這些皆已清楚的**被**規範在美國心理學會的規章裡。

其實這個句子大可改成：

> 這些皆已清楚規範在**美國心理學會**的規章裡。

被動語態曾經是一種流行的寫作方式，常常出現在老式的英文裡，但經過有識之士幾十年來的宣導，被動語態逐漸失去市場。比較下面兩個同義的句子就可以很明顯地分辨出孰優孰劣：

被動	主動
A decision was made by the committee that all students should meet once a month.	The committee decided that all students should meet once a month.

事實上主動語態能夠更清楚、更直接地表達文意，主動語態較被動語態簡短有力，也是不爭的事實，因此，在任何寫作中如果不是要刻意經營出一種被動的態勢，就應該盡可能避免老舊僵化的被動式。

下面引用的原文，是一篇中文論文的英文摘要，其中有七個句子，每一句都是以被動式「拼湊」而成，作者可能還自認為這樣才算擺脫中

式英文的窠臼，也才更像英文，殊不知整段文字在識者的眼中，十分慘
不忍睹，即使不用看該文的中文原文，也知道原來的中文絕不會寫成這
個樣子：

原文	修訂後
In this paper, a customer relationship management (CRM) platform based on data mining method is constructed to understand customers in detail. An on-line register mechanism is developed. Three web services, data mining, data preprocess, and decision support, are built over Internet to provide data mining service with XML format exchange. The systematic UML analysis and design are used to develop and decompose the entire CRM system. An intelligent data mining algorithm is developed for classification. A simple fuzzy discrimination index (SFDI) and fuzzy entropy are constructed for attribute selection. Finally, the real customer data from a cosmetic company is employed to justify the proposed CRM platform and shows good results. (110 words)	The researcher constructs a data-mining based customer relationship management (CRM) platform with an on-line register mechanism to support detailed customer behavior understanding. This internet platform provides data mining service with XML format exchange. The complete system, as designed via a systematic UML analysis, consists of three web functions (i.e. data mining, data pre-process, and decision support). It uses an intelligent data mining algorithm for data classification. A simple fuzzy discrimination index (SFDI) is built in the system along with fuzzy entropy for the purpose of attribute selection. The proposed CRM platform is validated with the real-life customer data from a cosmetic company. (102 words)

　　碰到這樣的譯文，真正熟悉兩種語文差異的譯者當然知道要怎麼改進，大幅修改的結果，被動句由七個減到了兩個，修訂後的文字顯得更順暢，不像原文那樣一路被動，難以卒讀。

　　下面這段引文就強調了主動語態要比被動語態可取：

　　Our editors find that one of the greatest weaknesses of admissions essays is their frequent use of the passive tense.

　　...Overuse of the passive voice throughout an essay can make your prose seem flat and uninteresting. Sentences in active voice are also more concise than those in passive voice.

—GradSchools.com Information Center[2]

　　當然，被動語句是無法也毋須全面避免的，請看下例：

　　Each dissertation will be listed under the department to which it was submitted, with inter-departmental dissertations listed in each sections.

　　由於本句的行動者不明，很難把它改成合適的主動語態，因此只好保持原狀。

　　而在中文裡無法避免被動語句時，也不用死命抓住「被」字，「經」、「經過」、「受」、「受到」等等都可用來表示被動語態，而且都比「被」更具有本土的味道，需要時不妨交替使用。例如：

2　http://www.gradschools.com/info/cyberedit/lf_verbtense.html, Re-trived on 2007/4/15.

原文	修訂後
1. 該環境評估報告<u>被</u>鑑定後，歸入評估不完整之列。	1. 該環境評估報告<u>經過</u>鑑定後，歸入評估不完整之列。
2. 個案權利仍<u>不被</u>重視。	2. 個案權利仍<u>不受</u>重視。

　　事實上，由於類似這種難以用主動語態取代的句子所占的比例並不高，留用這類句子反而有使文字多樣化的效果。

二、減少形容詞和副詞

　　要寫一篇清楚有力的文章就不要用太多的形容詞或副詞。形容詞是用來修飾名詞或改變名詞意義的；而副詞則是用來修飾或改變動詞、形容詞或其他副詞意義的。用形容詞或副詞來輔助所要說明的事物，意在使讀者更容易了解，所以，除非選用的形容詞或副詞可以增加某些事的重要性，否則不要使用太多，使用太多的結果可能會增加讀者閱讀的負擔，不見得能達到真正的目的。

　　例如下例原文第一行中的副詞 *probably*，就是個贅字，就算沒有了它，這句話也已經包括了 *probably* 的內涵。再看這篇文章第二段最後一句的形容詞 *major* 也是個贅字，就算沒有這個字，該句也已經清楚表達了 *major* 所要表達的目的了。因此在改文章的時候把文中的形容詞和副詞挑出來，如果這些字對原義沒有太明顯的影響就不妨刪去，這樣不但能讓文章更生動，也會幫助讀者更直接地了解文章的中心思想。

原文	修訂後
I would <u>probably</u> have the same feeling that you experienced from our handling of your paper last month. May I assure you that we will do everything in our control to handle this matter in a proper and satisfactory manner? Our major aim is to give you the type of service you want and expect. (55 words)	I would have the same feeling that you experienced from our handling of your paper. We will do everything in our control to handle this matter in a proper manner. Our aim is to give you the type of service you expect. (42 words)

以下是中文的例子，要改善原文，只要刪掉一些不必要的用字和用詞：

原文	修訂後
1. 為提升就業競爭力，在職已婚婦女參與進修成為不可避免[3]的趨勢。 2. 敦煌最早的寫本始於公元三〇五年，最晚的寫於公元一〇二年，前後跨越了七百年左右，歷經了兩晉、南北朝、隋、唐、五代、宋等朝代，全面地[4]反映了	1. 為了提升就業競爭力，在職已婚婦女參與進修成了一種趨勢。 2. 敦煌最早的寫本始於公元三〇五年，最晚的寫於公元一〇二年，前後跨越了七百年左右，歷經了兩晉、南北朝、隋、唐、五代、宋等朝代，反映了這段時期

3　「不可避免」有過度描述之嫌，只是作者順手捻來，並無根據。

4　「全面」實在是過甚其詞，不應妄用在論文之中。只有周延的數學公理可以全面涵蓋，物理定律也還勉強，其他如文學、藝術、管理學、社會學中之學說，涵蓋的範圍再廣，也離全面尚有一大段距離。

原文	修訂後
這段時期中國書法的發展演變情況。	中國書法的發展演變情況。
3. 作者發現助人專業領域中**充斥許多**違反倫理的事件，**嚴重**危害到當事人的福祉與權益。[5]	3. 作者發現助人專業中違反專業倫理的事件，危害到當事人的福祉與權益。

三、少用長句

清晰的思路和方向可以用簡單的語句來表達，長句通常複雜難懂，不但讓人讀到句尾就已經忘了句頭，就連作者也容易迷失其中，失去控制的能力。文章裡長句很多並不表示寫文章的人寫作能力高，反而表示他表達能力有問題，看看以下的例子，便知一二，原文一的句子長達 48 字，很難消化；原文二的句子更長達 62 字，根本無法達意：

原文	修訂後
1. 本研究旨在探討已婚女性在職進修考量之正面激勵因素及負面阻礙因素是如何影響已婚女性在職進修的決定。	1. 本研究探討正負兩面因素如何影響已婚女性在職進修的決定。
2. 探討不同高職美容科學校招生情況在高職美容科專業課程之規劃	2. 探討不同高職美容科之招生情況，還有專業課程規劃與實施、

---

5 「充斥許多」及「嚴重」云云，均係情緒氾濫之詞，沒有客觀價值，為論文所不取。

原文	修訂後
與實施情形、設備之規模與使用情形及高職美容科師資專業知能的差異情形。	設備規模與使用，及師資專業知能差異等對招生情況之影響。

經修訂後，原文一刪去將近二十個贅字贅詞，可讀性大增；原文二改成兩句，其中第二句雖然甚長，但是文中加了兩個頓號，足以減輕讀者的壓力。

請讀完下例原文這長達一段的句子，看你能了解多少，右欄將原文斷成四句後就易懂得多了：

原文	修訂後
As you know, your year's guarantee is one which covers defective workmanship or materials which would reveal itself under normal use conditions within twelve months, likewise, it exempts the company from mechanical failures due to accident, alteration, misuse or abuse, and time also accounts for a certain amount of deterioration which obviously cannot be covered by our guarantee. (58 words)	Your one-year guarantee covers defective workmanship. It also covers materials under normal use conditions within 12 months. The guarantee exempts the company from mechanical failures due to accident, altera-tion, misuse or abuse. Certain amount of deterioration throu-gh time obviously cannot be covered. (42 words)

　　下例原文中的每個句子都長達三四行，讀起來非常困難，不妨運用下述的原則，把長句修短：

1. 大膽斷句
2. 使用音節少的同義字代替長字
3. 刪除贅字

　　在不增加文字長度的情形下，把只有三句的左欄文字斷成六句，把一再重複的長串專有名詞「Aluminum Fin-back Radiation」用它的縮形「AFR」取代，再刪去「convection *type of* heating」和「radiant *type of* heating」中的「type of」，寫成右欄的樣子：

原文	修訂後
One lineal foot of 2" Aluminum Fin-back Radiation is equal to approximately nine lineal feet of 2" bare steel pipe which means a great saving in labor for installation, pipe fittings required and weight of metal and water to heat. Furthermore, Aluminum Fin-back Radiation produces a convection type of heating with rapid circulation of the warmed air (without the aid of fans) while bare steel pipe radiation produces a radiant type of heating which concentrates the heat in small areas and may cause cold spots in the	One lineal foot of 2" Aluminum Fin-back Radiation (AFR) equals to about nine lineal feet of 2" bare steel pipe. This means saving in the labor of installation, the cost of pipe fittings, and the amount of metal and water to heat. Unlike bare steel pipe radiation that uses radiant heating, AFR uses convection. Convection heating rapidly circulates warmed air without the aid of fans, while radiant heating concentrates the heat in small areas and may cause cold spots in the greenhouse. Also, AFR will never rust even

原文	修訂後
greenhouse. Also, Aluminum Fin- back Radiation will never rust even when installed in places with extremely high humidity and thermal conductivity of Aluminum Fin-back is virtually twice that of steel radiation. (117 words)	when installed in places with high humidity. In conclusion, thermal conductivity of AFR is virtually twice that of steel radiation. (108 words)

　　用縮形取代一再重複的冗長專有名詞能增加文章的易讀性，是論文寫作時的習慣做法，可以適時採用。

　　把上面那段文字用條列式的寫法改寫，讀來更是條理分明，因為條列式的寫法可以大量減少修辭的困擾，值得鼓勵以英文為第二語文的英文論文寫作者使用。

Here are some important conclusions about Aluminum Fin-back Radiation (AFR):

1. **One foot of 2"AFR equals to about nine feet of 2" bare steel pipe. This means less pipe to install and heat.**
2. **AFR circulates warmd air without using fans. Bare steel pipe heats by radiation, concentrating the heat in small areas. It may cause cold spots in greenhouse.**
3. **AFR will never rust despite high humidity.**
4. **The thermal conductivity of AFR is virtually twice that of steel radiation.**

條列式的寫法不但寫來比較容易，讀來也比較輕鬆，不論中文英文，都是如此：

本研究之目的如下：

1. 分析高職美容科學校招生情況。
2. 了解高職美容科專業課程之規劃與實施情形。
3. 描述高職美容科設備之規模與使用狀況，及
4. 探討高職美容科師資專業知能。

又，條列式的寫法可以多多使用在結論及建議未來研究方向的章節之中。

大體上，英文句子以不超過二十字為原則，中文因為每個字都是單音節，個句子中的字數可以稍多，但也不宜超出二十五字。不論中英文，過長的句子都容易纏夾繞舌，令人抓不住要點。

當然，較長的句子並不一定就不如簡短的句型，有時候重組一下短句子能把意思變得更清楚，下面的範例中，原文包含了三個句子，簡單易懂，但在修訂後改成兩個較長的句子後，效果也不差。

原文	修訂後
The main ingredient in natural abrasives is crystalline aluminum oxide. Emery was the first natural abrasive found on earth. It is 50% crystalline aluminum oxide.	The main ingredient in natural abrasives is crystalline aluminum oxide. Emery, the first natural abrasive found on earth, is 50% crystalline aluminum oxide.

四、注意邏輯並釐清因果

　　論文的主體應該包含事實、結論和我們所引用的研究和推理的方式，直線性的邏輯是良好論文的基石，紮實的論文主體應該有個線性的組織，完整而邏輯地從引用的事實導出最後的結論，不然，論文會讓人難以捉摸。例如：

原文	修訂後
……本研究在量的研究方面顯示出的最嚴重的問題卻是，大多的受試者誤認為「對個案承諾絕對保密」是助人專業者應有的倫理行為，如本研究顯示有 79.7% 的受試者認為該對個案承諾絕對保密，也有 62.9% 的受試者經常如此做，皆表示助人專業者對這方面最新資訊的不足。事實上，助人專業工作者需告知個案保密的限制（也就是不對個案承諾完全的保密）……	……助人專業工作者不應對個案承諾完全保密，但本研究顯示，有 79.7% 的受試者誤認為「對個案承諾絕對保密」是助人專業者應有的倫理行為，也有 62.9% 的專業者經常承諾「絕對保密」，這表示業者對保密限制方面的資訊不足……

　　原文除了文理不太通順之外，其寫作邏輯也容易讓讀者開始時一頭霧水，不知到底「對個案承諾絕對保密」有何不對？一直要到該段的最後，讀者才會發現，原來行規中早有「不應對個案承諾完全保密」的限制，因此是不宜對個案承諾絕對保密的。

　　那麼為什麼不依照線性的邏輯，先說明原因，再敘述結果呢？重整

了原文的混亂邏輯之後，經過修訂的文字顯得容易了解得多了。

要把論文的組織架設出來，就得先理出論文的要點，一個接一個的，從開始到結束，環環相扣，由前一個要點引入後一個要點，上一個要點引入下一個要點，遵循線性的邏輯，走最直最短的路，直到導出結論為止。寫作論文是一個刺激腦力的工作，清晰的思維才能創造理路清晰的文字。

組織論文較好的方法，是在電腦上把每一個構想大略打下來，把每一個不同的構想記錄在不同的段落上，再把它們分類和編組，哪個構想應該和哪個構想放在一起？哪個應該排在第一？哪個應該跟隨在後？這樣自然有助於思考的過程。

先看一個用前後倒置的不允當立論、責人立論不允當的、有違邏輯的例子[6]：

> 　章太炎、劉申叔把蘇洵說成縱橫家或兵家，以**先秦之流派，套後來之人物，方法錯誤**，立論自難允當。

把韓愈、朱熹等後人說成是儒家並不離譜，反倒是把孟子說成是民主黨、把墨子說成是共產黨才是笑話。

再看看下面這個出自於某心理學教科書的妙語：

> 　由<u>馬斯洛</u>的需求論得知，人有自尊需求的渴望，所以每個人都喜歡得到別人的肯定與讚賞。

---

6 吳孟復、詹並園，〈蘇洵思想新探〉，《安徽大學學報（哲學社會科學版）》，1982 年第 3 期。

　　難道是因為馬斯洛這樣一說，我們才得知「人有自尊需求的渴望」？難道就是因為馬斯洛這樣一「加持」，我們才對「每個人都喜歡得到別人的肯定與讚賞」這句話有把握，才敢把它寫到書裡去嗎？而馬斯洛又是何許人呢？

　　那麼我們是否也要「由告子的『食色，性也』得知，人有吃飯的需要，所以每個人都要滿足食欲」一番呢？

　　因此，除了在導證科學定理或演繹數學方程式這類可以導向固定結果的運算過程之外，絕對不該隨意使用「由……得知」、「由……可知」。

　　尤其是在藝術及社會科學方面，僅只是一家之言，絕對不足以代表真理，所以千萬要慎用這類的語法：

---

1. 根據表 4-5-3 的統計結果可知……
2. 由上可知，在職已婚婦女參與進修時，遭遇最大的學習阻礙層面是……

　　舉例來說：

1. 由本研究之數據可知，學校暴力已經是全面性的問題了。
2. 本研究的數據顯示，學校暴力已經普遍化了。

　　第一句的語意中，有該數據已經證明了「暴力已經全面性」的味道，第二句的語意則比較保守，只有「根據該數據來看，暴力已經有普遍化的趨勢」的意思。請細心想一想，單憑任何人力所及的研究，怎麼可能「全面證明」任何社會議題呢？

　　研究工作像辦案，研究結果就像偵查結果，並不是判決，研究結果只是指出研究者的論點，我們只能說「調查結果顯示某某是嫌犯」，不

能說「由**調查結果可知**某某是真兇」。

　　在此舉一個與論文無關的糊塗邏輯例子：員林街上許多地方可以看到「此處禁止違規停車」的交通警示牌，不知是否因為有別的地方「**准許違規**停車」，員林的交通管理單位方才立下「禁止違規停車」的警示，有別於「禁止停車」，以示鄭重。

五、善用覆述的原則

　　你也許能夠很清楚地把論文或報告的主題表達出來，但是也得考慮讀者能不能吸收得了，要使文章完整清楚，要讓讀者不費力就明白意思，就得了解讀者的立場、揣摩讀者的心意。

　　若要大多數讀者都能更明白你所寫的東西，就應該讓他們有時間先把先前的主題都消化得差不多了，才把下一個主題搬上來，尤其在長篇論文裡，有技巧的作者會把主題用稍為更動過的寫法加以重述，讓讀者有復習的機會。

　　下面有兩個例子是重複重點的代表作，加底線部分的句子主要在加強讀者對其前文的印象，使得原意更加突顯。這種做法的好處在短文裡還不太明顯，但在長文裡就顯出功夫來了，讀者如果在前文中看漏了些東西，還有機會在後文的覆述中再復習一遍，不用回頭費力搜尋。

1. Continued learning is important not only to your health and happiness but to your economic security. Times changes; so do job requirements. Your best guarantee of is your ability to change with them. If you stay flexible-ready, willing and able to learn new things-you have nothing to fear from age or automation.

2. As your head comes above the surface, a slightly stronger push with your

hands will hold it there long enough to inhale slowly through your mouth. Take your time inhaling; don't gulp.

　　下面是幾個適合使用覆述原則的地方：

1. 不夠清楚的地方
2. 需要加強語氣或強調重點的地方
3. 一連串的主題需要加深讀者印象的地方

　　在這些地方可以用不同的覆述技巧像舉例說明、互相比較、或用修改後的句子重新描述一遍等等。

　　用不同的文句來描述所要表達的意思，使句子能更精確、更吸引讀者，如果你沒有做過這些事情，那麼不妨從今天開始，對具有重要性的論文或報告加意斟酌，完成後，請別人幫忙檢查一次，看看別人的意見如何，看看別人能不能輕易的看出你的意思。

　　字句的經營很重要，好好推敲論文中的文句，相似的意思可以用不同的說法來表達，請看下列的例句：

---

1. The seat cover is easily torn. It is made of flimsy material.
2. The seat cover is easily torn, for it is made of flimsy material.
3. The seat cover is easily torn because it is made of flimsy material.
4. The seat cover is made of flimsy material and is easily torn.
5. The seat cover is made of flimsy material which is easily torn.
6. The seat cover, which is made of flimsy material, is easily torn.
7. Being made of flimsy material, the seat cover is easily torn.
8. The seat cover is made of easily torn, flimsy material.
9. The flimsy seat cover is made of easily torn material.
10. The flimsy seat cover is easily torn.

只要覺得任何地方表達得不夠清晰，就不妨想個能讓讀者掌握主題的東西來加以舉例或比較。要加強寫作能力就得付出努力，別無他法。

六、多用簡單易懂的字

簡單易懂的字比較容易取信於人，至少讀者不用擔心自己被艱澀的字所蒙蔽。

有些人誤以為寫重要的論文就該用些重量級的字彙和語詞，像下面這篇就很難解碼，要我了解其中寫了些什麼，簡直可以套用一句英文，那就是 ***It's all Greek to me***.

> 自然語言理解研究本質上應當是獨立於具體的語言的。筆者不太相信脫離自然語言理解研究的全局而能夠單獨或超前取得漢語理解研究的突破。但以漢語為母語的學者又有責任也有優勢以漢語為主要物件對自然語言理解的一般規律進行研究，從而為解決人類共同的科學難題做出貢獻。當研究漢語理解時，首先著力於指稱概念的實詞是理所當然的，但也不能輕視虛詞在漢語句子、談話、篇章中表達意義的作用。本文探討虛詞在漢語理解研究中的價值及其研究方法，倡議建設與北大其他語言知識庫可以有機結合的廣義虛詞知識庫，提出了構建這個知識庫的一些想法。

事實上，越重要的論文越要用簡單、明白、直接的方式來書寫，免得讀者誤解了論文的主旨，因為簡單明白的文字一定比拐彎抹角的更讓人容易接受。明智的人會用讓人容易明瞭的白話口語來寫作，不明智的人才會用非常饒舌的字句去詮釋。

有大量的字彙能力固然是件好事，但是，如果是因為用了太艱澀的字彙而導致溝通障礙，那就不大明智了。例如：

> 一些人**斷斷**於蘇洵與王安石之相互關係……

「斷斷」這個詞現在已近無人使用，連懂得的人也很少，有多少人見了「斷斷」會知道這個詞的意義？它的意思既然是「爭辯的樣子」，為什麼不乾脆使用「爭辯」來達意，比較淺明易懂呢？

思路清晰的人只要用簡單的字彙，就足以明確而不籠統地敘述事實，如果論文中用了許多複雜的字彙，那麼讀者先要搞懂那些字彙都可能有困難，怎麼還有餘力去研究論文內容呢？

充分的詞彙幫助我們了解其他人，也幫助我們傳達自己的想法，但是，使用一般人不太使用的詞彙來溝通是不智的，因為溝通的目的不是令人費解，沒有必要在文章中顯示自己傑出的文學素養，況且我們要考量到其他語系的國家（像是泰國、日本……等）的讀者，那些外國人可能無法立刻了解我們花了功夫醞釀出來的「典雅文字」，即使他們在費了許多時間查字典後，終於知道我們的意思，那文章的傳達力也已經大打折扣。

對於任何沒有把握的字詞都應先查明意義再使用，不然在講求精確的論文裡可能造成讀者的誤判，以表 2-1 為例：

表 2-1　易於混淆的字彙及其代用詞

避免使用	使用	中譯
biannual, semiannual	twice a year	一年兩次
biennial	once every two years	兩年一度

避免使用	使用	中譯
bimonthly	once every other month,	每兩月一次
	twice a month	每月兩次
semimonthly	twice a month	每月兩次

Biannual 與 semiannual 都是一年兩次，biennial 則是兩年一度，bimonthly 有每兩月一次和每月兩次兩種意思，semimonthly 則確定是每月兩次，諸如這類的字可以用最沒有爭議的 twice a year, once every other year, once every other month, twice a month 等來代替。其他如 continuously 是指連續期間沒有中斷（without interruption），continually 則是指斷斷續續（intermittently 或 at frequent intervals）。

諸如此類，不勝枚舉，使用時都應加以釐清。

再看下面這個句子：

作為主體性的最高級形態，類主體性的基本特性是以主體間性（intersubjectivity）核心所形成的整體性。

光是看到就足以使人望之卻步了，遑論將它解讀？

這個句子不是虛構的，是真正寫出來，而且已經發表的文字[7]，其間還夾雜了一些英文單字，以示引論有據。

再看下例：

---

[7] 本段文字可在網路上找到。

原文	修訂後
維繫單字的凝聚力主要來自對立統一的關係。書法作品中點劃的長短粗細，墨色的枯濕濃淡，結體的大小俯仰和疏密虛實，都是一對對具有互補關係的矛盾體，只有挖掘它們之間的內在聯繫，才能使這些沒有筆墨連貫的單字凝聚起來。	而要使字與字之間產生凝聚力，則需注意點劃、墨色、結體之間的內在聯繫，才能使這些沒有筆墨連貫的單字凝聚起來。

　　原文中的「**對立統一的關係**」和「**互補關係的矛盾體**」這兩個打腫臉充胖子的詞，到底能說明些什麼？對文字的內容有何增益？

　　不外是東拉西扯，唬唬外行人罷了。

　　經修訂之後的文字就少了那些引喻失意的爛調。

　　真正言之有物的論述不應盲目地引用別人的陳述，不需要用些東西洋單字來挾洋自重，也不必強套一些莫測高深的名詞來自高。

　　許多研究報告或論文裡的用詞語意纏夾，把文字寫得牽纏難解，這絕不是寫作能力的表現，反而可能是作者思路不清的佐證。在傳達任何事情的時候，首先要考慮的，就是傳達的對象，既然寫的不是法律條文或商業合同，那又為什麼要疊床架屋，重重修飾，以致別人要大費周章，才能明白文中所要表達的意思呢？

　　越白話易懂，越表示寫作者的表達能力高人一等。

　　另外，用否定語引導肯定語會使語意模糊，例如：

> 1. 如果觀察結果與原始假設沒有矛盾或與學理相合……

到底應該解讀成：

> 2. 如果觀察結果與原始假設沒有矛盾，但也沒有與學理相合……

還是應該解讀成：

> 3. 如果觀察結果與原始假設沒有矛盾，且與學理相合……

如果用「肯定敘述」來引導「否定敘述」，寫成：

> 4. 如果觀察結果與學理相合、和原始假設沒有矛盾……

語意就明確得多，要不然就多用個逗號，用第二句或第三句的寫法把句子寫清楚。

　　附錄 B 列有一些長字和它們清晰有力的代用字，值得參考。

七、小心錯別字及文法、語意上的謬誤

　　在文章裡拼錯或用錯了字雖非不可原諒，但總會讓人印象欠佳，請看下面的例子，作者的原意該是糾正（rectify）而非辯解（justify），也許這種失誤會讓明眼人覺得好笑吧：

> We are pleased to send you a copy of our manual, which you re-
> cently requested. If this is not the one you want, just let me know and
> we will *justify* our error.

　　受邀出席的貴賓收到如下的邀請時，其中的有識者大概會哭笑不得，畢竟出席（presence）與禮物（present），兩者截然不同。

> The members of the Country Club will always appreciate your
> *presents* at our meetings.

　　很多人容易誤用形與音相似的字，我們最好只用自己確實認識的字，如果偶爾要用到自己不太確定的字，千萬別怕費事，查個字典。以下面的句子為例：

> 1. The new policy will not be *effected*.
> 2. The new policy will not be *affected*.

　　Effect（生效）和 affect（影響）只有一個字母之差，不會生效與不受影響乃是截然相反的兩回事。

　　中文裡當然也不乏因為字的形音相似而誤用的例子，我自己就曾經因為使用「突顯」，而被編輯人員喧賓奪主地糾正說應該使用「凸顯」才對[8]。

8　「突顯」可以解作「某件事很突出，以致顯出了重要性」，而「凸」字一向僅用於說明「某樣東

　　另外，「券」指的是有**票面值**的文件[9]，例如「票券、獎券、彩券、債券、證券、折價券、優待券、入場券、兌換券」等等，偏偏有人（不乏國文系的學生）會把「獎券、彩券、優待券、憑券兌換」誤寫成「獎卷、彩卷、優待卷、憑卷兌換」，而「卷」指的卻是一般文書、紀錄、檔案類的文件[10]，例如「考卷、書卷、卷宗」等。

　　當然，最氾濫的問題還在「的」、「得」兩字用法的誤區，事實上，只要用心，這兩個字的用法差異不難分別。

　　「的」是形容詞字尾，連接的是**形容詞**與**名詞**：例如：

> **紅色**的**花**、**天大**的**事**、**不得了**的**問題**……等等。

也是所有格的助語詞，連接的是**名詞**、**代名詞**與**名詞**：

> **我**的**家**、**他**的**玩具**、**公司**的**財產**……

　　「得」則是動詞的字尾，連接的是**動詞**與**形容詞**：

> **車開**得**飛快**、**事情做**得**順利**、**感動**得**無以復加**

也是形容詞助語詞，連接的是**形容詞**與**形容詞**：

　　西鼓起來」，除了用來形容形狀上「凹凸不平」、「凸出一塊」之外，幾已不做他用。「凸」字有時可以用「突」字代替，如「突出一塊」，反之，「突」字則不宜代以「凸」字。

9　英文中的 bill, note, token, ticket, coupon, voucher……之類。

10　英文中的 paper, document, statement, manuscript……之類。

窮得要命、傻得可以、聰明得不得了

一旦搞清楚，就不會像有不少人（包括不求甚解的學校老師）一樣，把「**吃得好、睡得著、用得安心、玩得高興、忙得不知如何是好……**」等等，誤寫成「吃的好、睡的著、用的安心、玩的高興、忙的不知如何是好……」了。

下面是個連英美人士都常常搞不清楚的規則，那就是，不論字尾的子音是什麼，所有單數名詞的所有格都要加 s：

誤：Charles' wife
正：Charles's wife

誤：Confucius' theory
正：Confucius's theory

請看下面的範例，每一組有三個句子，分別屬於現在式、過去式和過去完成式，每一個句子都是正確的，我們必須知道它們的正確使用方法，如若不然，請查一下手頭的英文文法書。

1. I sink today; I sank yesterday; I have sunk many times.
2. I swim today; I swam yesterday; I have swum many times.
3. I sing today; I sang yesterday; I have sung many times.
4. I begin today; I began yesterday; I have begun many times.

　　文法上的錯誤出現在論文類的白紙黑字上是很尷尬的，一般未受過嚴格英文訓練的華語系國家作者，寫起英文論文時，難免犯文法上的錯誤，即使避免了文法上的錯誤，也還可能在語意上無法完整表達。當然，這也還情有可原，因為，英文到底不是我們的母國文字。

　　這裡先別說這些人在英文方面的廣泛問題，更不堪的是，有些研究者對自己的母國文字也拿捏不住，會寫出像下例原文中的這種東西來：

原文	修訂後
從文獻中以 Engelmann 所創立的直接教學法模式來教導閱讀困難學生，可以增進其閱讀能力，本文將介紹直接教學法及其實驗成效的探討。	文獻中提到，Engelmann 所創立的直接教學可以增進閱讀困難者的閱讀能力。本文將介紹此教學法及探討其實驗成效。

　　另外，可能是受到英文句型 ***protect... from*** 的污染，像「保護……免受」和「保護……免於」的語意謬誤句型大行其道，例如：

1. **保護**此臺電腦**免於**間諜程式侵擾。
2. 某些蔬菜含有可以**保護**細胞**免於**癌症的化學物質。
3. 防曬油能提供皮膚不同程度的天然**保護，免受**陽光傷害。

　　這幾句略譯成英文，就是：

---

1. Protect this computer from being invaded by spyware.
2. Some vegetables contain chemicals that can protect cells from carcinogens.
3. Sun screen lotions can protect the skin from sunburns.

這種句法在英文中是沒有問題的，但卻不能直接搬到中文來。只要稍加用心，就可以避免這類中西失調的句子：

原文	修訂後
1.要求政府立法保護老師**免於遭受**學生或家長的惡意指控。	1.要求政府立法保護老師，**使其免於**遭受學生或家長的惡意指控。
2.兒童和少年應予**保護免受**經濟和社會的剝削。	2.兒童和少年應予**保護，使其免受**經濟和社會的剝削。
3.周詳的保安策略可以**保護業務免受**攻擊或入侵。	3.周詳的保安策略可以**保護業務，預防**攻擊或入侵。
4.水果、蔬菜和堅果能幫助**保護免受**氣喘和其他過敏症狀。	4.水果、蔬菜和堅果能幫助**預防**氣喘和其他過敏症狀。

處理文字的功力應該在求學生涯的中期（初高中時期）就已經建立起來，要是在大學、研究所階段寫作論文時才發覺不足，解救起來必然相當吃力。可惜的是，這類有心無力的人士普遍存在。

我深能體會這些人士的辛苦，因為，他們讓我想起自己留美早期以英文寫作的苦樂生涯。當時的我戰戰兢兢，把論文底稿交給我那和藹可親的指導教授，他瞄了幾眼，苦笑著對我說：

This work needs a major face lift. I certainly can't do it for you. Why don't you schedule an appointment with a professional editor? Let him or her proofread your work first.

慚愧之餘，我分外努力地彌補自己文字上的缺陷，幾年之間，又經過幾番挫折，終於能夠流利地以英文寫作，成了左手寫英文、右手寫中文的過來人。

如今，我所能給予這些寫作吃力人士的建議，也只是老生常談的「**多讀多寫**」而已。

八、注意字詞的相對位置

相同的字擺在不同的位置上，可以表達不同的意思，像 *only* 所在的位置可以改變句子的全意（見表 2-2）。

表 2-2　字詞的相對位置

原句	意思
1. **Only** I offered to buy the house.	只有我出價買那房子。
2. I **only** offered to buy the house.	我只出價買那房子。
3. I offered **only** to buy the house.	我出價只為了要買那房子。
4. I offered to buy **only** the house.	我只出買那房子的價。
5. I offered to buy the **only** house.	我出價買那唯一的房子。

在英文裡，任何修飾詞（modifier）都得連著該詞所要修飾的對象，例如表 2-2 這些例子中，第一句的 *only* 修飾的是 *I*，第二句的 *only* 修飾的是 *offer*，第三句的 *only* 修飾的是 *offer*，第四句的 *only* 修飾的是

buy，第五句的 *only* 修飾的是 *house*。

　　中文在文字排列的次序方面比較自由，但過於自由的結果，就不免鬆散，看看這個例子：

本文討論二十個學校沒有教的寫作技巧。

　　這個句子翻成英文，可能有兩種相當不同的意思，其中第一種是：

Let's discuss the writing techniques not taught by 40 schools.

　　誰會這麼有心去調查，沒有教某某寫作技巧的，到底是哪四十個學校呢？依直覺判斷達，數詞「二十個」所描述的，應該是「寫作技巧」，而不是「學校」，故上句中文例句比較合理的意思應該是：

Let's discuss the 40 writing techniques not taught in schools.

　　第一個中文例句的表達方式也屬常見，不全算是有錯，它在語意上雖然有點含混，我們還是可以判別其真正的涵義，如果要表達得比較精確些，就應該把上面的句子改寫如下，才比較沒有語意上的困擾：

本文討論學校沒有教的四十個寫作技巧。

　　下面這個例子可能就比較費解了：

以下是五個學生沒有注意的原則。

不知到底說的是「五個學生」呢還是「五個原則」？我們在前後文中雖然可能釐清，但是，為免造成不必要的混淆，文字畢竟是精確些才好。

在英文中沒有同樣的問題，因為英文裡根本就沒有「以下要宣布三個同學沒有注意的原則」這種句法。只有：

1. We will announce the three rules that students did not follow.（以下要宣布同學沒有注意的三個原則。）
2. We will announce the three students who did not follow the rule.（以下要宣布的原則，有三個同學沒有注意。）

第三章
論文的特殊準則

本章提綱

　　一、一律使用第三人稱

　　二、避免不定數詞、量詞及加強詞

　　三、勿隨意使用縮寫及節略字

　　四、減少使用虛主詞

　　五、務必使用西元紀年及絕對指標

　　六、盡量平鋪直敘

　　七、實例分析

　　結構完整的論文應該在緒論或前言裡先說明研究的是什麼，然後在本文裡把要說的一一說清楚，最後在結論節裡告訴讀者本文裡說了些什麼。除了上面這種三段式寫法，論文的文詞還要純樸無華，要用平實的字和標準的寫法，不要用象徵性或隱晦的文學描述手法。論文中涉及其他人的工作或研究成果時，盡量列出他們的名字。

　　又，英文論文中用英式或美式拼法均可，但一經採用，在全篇文章中就須保持一致。

　　另外一些比較重要的準則在下面各節中有擇要的說明。

一、一律使用第三人稱

　　論文所敘述的是研究得來的事實，一種實驗所得的若是真理，則只要是用同一個方法去做相同的實驗，所得的結果都應該相同，因此，不論是撰寫中文或英文的論文或研究報告，都不應該使用「你」、「你們」、「我」、「我們」、「本人」、「**you**」、「**I**」、「**we**」等第一或第二人稱做敘述，而要使用第三人稱的客觀方式：

原文	修正後
I...	The author...
We...	The researchers...
My study (research, paper, etc.)...	This study (research, paper, etc.)... .
Our study (research, paper, etc.)...	

　　再看一些例子：

原文	修正後
In this thesis we propose a formal framework for specifying and validating properties of software system architectures.	This thesis proposes a formal framework for specifying and validating properties of software system architectures.
After defining the model we embed it in the logic of the PVS theoremproving environment and illustrate its utility with a case study.	After defining the model the author embeds the model in the logic of the PVS theoremproving environment and illustrates its utility with a case study.

原文	修正後
Our overall evaluation seeks to prove three hypotheses.	The overall evaluation of this research seeks to prove three hypotheses.
In this section, we outline those assumptions... .	This section outlines those assumptions... .
We believe that the study of courseware can create authenti cated technology	The study of courseware can create authenticated technology

以下是一些中文的例子：

原文	修正後
1. 我們的研究發現我國專科學生對升學科系的選擇會因「原先選定的科系」影響。	1. 本研究發現，臺灣的專科學生選擇升學科系時，會受原先選讀科系的影響。
2. 經調查，本校學生中有 51% 具有投票資格。	2. 經調查，○○大學學生中有 51% 具有投票資格。
3. 吾人無法從論文當中很明確地看出研究者的研究目的，僅或可自摘要及前言部分推測之。	3. 從論文當中無法明確看出研究者的研究目的，僅可由摘要及前言部分推測之。
4. 吾人在進一步由其前人研究內容部分，也比較無法看出文獻回顧的主要成果為何。	4. 由前人研究內容部分，也無法看出其文獻回顧的主要成果為何。

「我國」一詞，屬於第一人稱，在國際討論會中，文中的「我國」

到底是新加坡、臺灣、中國，還是其他使用華文的國家呢？所以，從國際化的眼光來看，應該避免使用「我國」，至於「祖國」、「母校」等亦屬不宜之列，應分別以國名、校名代替。

又，「吾人」這個怪異的第一人稱代名詞，不文不白，早就可以將它自論文中淘汰，也大可將它從任何文章中廢棄。

另外，「筆者」亦有第一人稱的味道，可以代以「作者」。

只有「本研究」、「本論文」乃是直指該文作者所做的該項研究或該篇論文本身，沒有誤會的餘地。

二、避免不定數詞、量詞及加強詞

不定的數詞（**few, a few, many, several** 等）、量詞（**little, a little, much, a great deal** 等）、形容**數**、**量**或**程度**的副詞（**extensive, extreme, pretty, quite, , rather, robust, very** 等）只在寫作非科學作品時加強語氣有用，在論文寫作上應該避免，例如：

原文	修正後
1. Try to do a little better.	1. Try to do better.
2. It is rather important.	2. It is important.
3. On a similar note, after years of robust research into extre me programming, This paper demonstrates the improvement of ＿＿＿. The improvement of scatter/gather I/O would tremendously amplify hierarchical databases.	3. This paper demonstrates the improvement of ＿＿＿. The improvement of scatter/gather I/O would amplify hierarchical databases.

　　三例中的 a little、rather、robust、extreme 及 tremendously 等，可說是贅字而已，刪去不妨。

　　又，論文中應該使用確切的數量代替不定的數量詞：

鬆散	精確
The majority of poll participants agree not to take any action.	Fifty-one percent of the poll participants agree not to take any action.
Slightly decreasing porosity lowers sweep efficiencies drastically.	One percent decrease in po-rosity lowers sweep efficien-cies by as much as 30%.

　　因為任何論文裡講求的都應該是確切的證據及數據，不應該有含糊的敘述，以下舉出一些中文論文中不恰當的例子：

1. 受試者對專業倫理的信念**大致**正確。
2. **大多**受試者在四個主題上倫理觀念不正確，此四主題分別為：⑴過分承諾絕對保密、⑵未善盡預警責任、⑶未避免雙重關係及⑷即未充分尊重及告知個案權利。
3. 有**高比率**之受試者顯示其信念不正確而這些情境也有**高比率**的受試者顯示經常發生不合倫理行為。
4. 有**相當比率**之受試者不知道正確的倫理信念為何。

　　上述例子中斜黑體字所示的量詞，沒有任何一個有可供共同認定的標準，**大致**正確到底是多正確？到底要多少才算**大多**？**高比率**與**相當比率**到底有何差別？

　　任何無法用確切量詞說明的東西在論文裡沒有加值的效果，可以一概刪去。因此，像表 3-1 裡所舉的不定數或不定量詞，不宜出現在論文裡。

表 3-1　論文中所不宜使用之不定數或不定量詞

含糊的用法	正式論文中宜用
a considerable number of（相當多）	
a number of（有些）	
a majority of（大部分）	
a small number of（有一些）	
in almost all instances（幾乎全部）	
a small number of cases（少數情況）	
majority of（大部分）	明確的數或百分比
the great majority of（絕大部分）	
the predominate number of（大部分）	
the vast majority of（大部分）	
a considerable amount of（相當多）	
considerable amount of（相當多）	
quite a large quantity of（相當多）	

三、勿隨意使用縮寫及節略字

　　有些人有動輒使用英文字縮寫（acronyms）的習慣（像是 DIY、DM、CNS 等等），認為只要寫出來就該有人認得，事實上即使是專業

人士對自己專業中使用的專用縮寫也不見得能夠完全清楚，因此，在使用論文專業範圍內所熟悉的縮寫時，也應該在題目、摘要或關鍵詞中至少出現一次全稱。作者雖可以自己擴充縮寫詞，但必須在該縮寫詞第一次出現時用括弧將全稱括在裡面。

原文	修訂後
Retail business in Taiwan has adopted DM as advertisement media. It has been gaining popularity during past twenty years.	Retail business in Taiwan has adopted DM (Distribution Materials) as advertisement media. DM has been gaining its popularity since 1980's.

但已經為大眾所熟悉的節略字，如 radar（雷達）、laser（雷射）、USA（美國）等，則可以直接使用。

中文論文中第一次使用英文名詞縮寫時，不應像下例原文那樣直接在中文譯名後標出縮寫，而務須寫出原文全稱，在原文全稱之後才標出縮寫：

原文	修訂後
直接教學法（DI）是根據行為分析理論而來，以工作分析為架構，用編序的方式來設計教學，並以系統化來呈現教材的一種具高度結構性的教學法；文獻中以 Engel-mann 為主要靈魂人物所創立的直接教學法模式（DISTAR）來教導閱讀	直接教學法（Direct Instruction, DI）是根據行為分析理論而來，DI 以工作分析為架構，用編序的方式來設計教學，並以系統化來呈現教材，是一種具高度結構性的教學法；本研究旨在探討以 Engelmann 為主所創立的直接教學法（Direct

原文	修訂後
困難學生，可以增進其閱讀能力，本文將介紹 DISTAR 及其實驗成效的探討。	Instruction System for Teaching Arithmetic and Reading, DISTAR），及以 DISTAR 教導閱讀困難學生，增進該等學生閱讀能力的成效。

又，論文中應該避免使用各類縮形字（abbreviations），所有的縮型都要完全拼出原字方才合乎要求，例如：

誤：can't, won't, haven't, it'll, it's, etc.

正：cannot, will not, have not, it will, it is, etc.

如表 3-2 所列的一些約定俗成的縮寫，可以不加解釋就使用在圖或表的說明內，但在內文中還是要完整拼出。

表 3-2　可以逕行使用在圖表說明內的節略字

原名	縮寫	意義
Amount	amt.	數量
Approximately	approx.	約……
Average	avg.	平均
Concentration	concn.	濃度
Diameter	diam.	直徑
Experiment	expt.	實驗
Experimental	exptl.	實驗的

原名	縮寫	意義
Height	ht.	高度
Molecular weight	mol. wt.	分子量
Number	No.	數目；數字
Preparation	prepn.	準備
Specific gravity	sp. gr.	比重
Standard deviation	SD	標準差
Standard error	SE	標準誤差
Standard error of the mean	SEM	均值標準誤差
Temperature	temp.	溫度
Versus	vs.	相對於……
Volume	vol.	體積；容積
Week	wk.	星期
Weight	wt.	重量
Year	yr.	年

四、減少使用虛主詞

「虛主詞」就是「it」和「there」，以「it」或「there」開頭，後面接上任何時態的「be」動詞所引導的句子，稱作虛主詞構句（expletive construction）。例如：

1. It is...
2. It can (will, shall, would, should, could) be...
3. There is (are)...
4. There has (have) been...

以虛主詞開頭的句子中若包含子句（It is ... that...或 There are...that...）或不定詞片語（It is ... to + 動詞）時，在絕大部分情況下可以改寫成更精簡有力的句子，例如：

不佳	較佳
1. It is necessary to control atomic energy.	1. To control atomic energy is necessary.
2. It is certain that the scientific method plays a large part in acquiring scientific knowledge.	2. Scientific method certainly plays a large part in acquiring scientific knowledge
3. There are some radioactive isotopes that are produced by bombard ment of nuclei with neutrons.	3. Some radioactive isotopes are produced by bombarding nuclei with neutrons.

順便在此一提，英文寫作時宜多使用具有動作意味的「動狀詞」來代替靜態的「名詞」，在上面最後一個例句中，我們還把「bombardment of」這個名詞片語改成動名詞「bombarding」，就使得句子顯得更有動力。

當然，有時虛主詞構句也有不可替換性，像下面這兩個句子就沒有必要改動：

1. There are nine planets in the solar system.
2. There have been ten accidents this month.

五、務必使用西元紀年及絕對指標

　　論文中的一切非西元的紀年都應該轉換成西元紀年，因為學術研究是國際性的活動，而西元則是公認的國際性紀年方式，正如「大正十七年」對非日本人士缺乏意義，「中華民國八十年」對其他國家人士的意義也不大，同理，我們也不能奢望國人知道光復前三年到底是多久以前，因此不但投稿到國際性的期刊時應該注意這一點，即使是僅在國內流通的各學報，也應要求作者做到這一點。

　　國內論文中若還有用民國紀元者，都該考量到非本國人士引用的可能性而予以標準化，此外，在必須用到歷史朝代紀元的地方，亦應附上其對應的西元年代，不然「漢文帝十五年」與「漢元帝永光元年」到底孰先孰後，一般人從何得知？因此研究者，特別是從事文獻研究的人不要忽略了與下例原文中相類似的缺陷：

原文	修訂後
1.漢靈帝中平五年，日色赤黃，中有黑氣如飛鵲，數月乃銷。	1.漢靈帝中平五年（188），日色赤黃，中有黑氣如飛鵲，數月乃銷。
2.明熹宗天啓四年日赤無光，有黑子二三蕩於旁，漸至百許，凡四日。	2.明熹宗天啓四年（1624）日赤無光，有黑子二三蕩於旁，漸至百許，凡四日。

原文	修訂後
3. 葉乃嘉（民 93）認為知識管理系統平臺的主流有兩類……	3. 葉乃嘉（2004）認為知識管理系統平臺的主流有兩類……

　　我們都期待自己的研究結果長久有意義，希望自己所寫的論文長久存在，因此在論文中提到時間的時候，就該避免使用像「今年初」、「過去十年」、「本世紀」等類的相對性時間敘述，至於像「最近」、「晚近」、「近年來」更是鬆散。例如：

近年來旅遊產業突飛猛進，相關業者紛紛投入……

　　這個「**近年來**」只是作者順手捻來的泛泛之談，完全沒有說明到底是多少年以來，也沒有引用參考文獻來支持此說，是極不負責任的寫法，根本不宜用在論文之中。

　　相對時間會隨時間的不同而改變，比如說，1999 年的「去年」與 2007 年的「去年」就代表不同的時間，1980 年的「本世紀中期」到了 2005 年就失去了原意，1990 年的「未來十年」到了 2000 年便成了「過去十年」，但是「二十世紀」在 1956 年、1999 年甚至到 2038 年都代表了 1901 到 2000 年這段時間，所以，不論是中英文，論文中任何有關時間的描述都應該以絕對時間表示，例如：

原文	修正後
1. during the past five years（過去五年間）	1. during 2000 to 2004（從 2000 年到 2004 年）

原文	修正後
2. in the last century（上世紀）	2. in the 20th century（二十世紀）
3. ten years ago（十年前）	3. since 1995（從 1995 年起）

　　除了避免使用相對時間外，內文敘述還應避免相對性的指標，凡有所指，均應以絕對指標為之，例如：

相對性指標	絕對指標
1. ... as shown in the next figure.	1. ... as shown in figure 2-1.
2. See the figure below.	2. See figure 3-3.
3. The table next page shows ...	3. Table 5-1 shows ...
4. The previous table shows ...	4. Table 6 shows ...
5. The following equation is ...	5. Equation 3-10 is ...
6. ... is defined in the last page	6. ... is defined in page 15
7. 如下圖所示，	7. 如圖 2-1 所示，
8. 上表的數據顯示	8. 表 5-1 的數據顯示
9. 前頁所述之……	9. 第十頁所述之……

　　還有，「國內」、「國外」、「本國」、「本公司」、「本單位」、「本機構」、「本校」等等，均屬相對性指標，因為，在閱讀該文獻的時候，IBM 與臺積電員工立場的「本公司」顯然不同，臺灣大學與清華大學教職員生觀點中的「本校」當然也非同校，故作者在論文中提及所屬國家或單位時，宜使用其所屬國名或單位的名稱。

　　至於「本論文」、「本章」、「本節」乃是直指該文該章該節本身，可以放心使用。

六、盡量平鋪直敘

　　論文是一種研究過程的敘述文體，不同於社論、小說或抒情文，因此要保持冷靜的「樸克面孔」，不要像下例這樣賣弄懸疑：

> 　　本研究有個驚人的重大發現，由於說來話長，我們將在另一篇論文中詳細敘述。

　　像下面這樣的情緒性的抨擊也該避免：

> 　　本研究的發現證明了○○氏的觀點只是**一廂情願**，與事實大相逕庭，令人懷疑其研究動機。

　　另外，也不要使用像下句這種自問自答的疑問句型：

> 　　本研究到底發現了什麼前人所未重視的現象呢？讓我們長話短說，那就是……

　　論文不用高潮迭起，只宜依照規格，按部就班地將事實平鋪直敘，例如上述三個句子就可以改成：

> 　　本研究發現了一個前人所未重視的現象，即……，與○○氏的觀點有所不同。

論文裡也用不上類似下例的應酬性謙詞：

> 本文只是在這些新的成果鼓舞和啓發下，應有關同志之約而**臨時塗寫**的兩則短論。

論文並非娛樂性的文字，作者「臨時塗寫」的東西有何德何能要別人花時間加以重視？

此外，**大言自詡亦為論文所不取**：

> 本論文從學會、機構、政策及教育等方向，提出**寶貴的建**議……

建議的「寶貴」與否，應由受者來判斷，作者自己不宜如此失態。其實，在任何文字中都應該注意禮儀，不宜自大。

還有，火星文、驚嘆句型、悲憫的訴求，口語式的字尾（如：啦、吧、喔、喲、哦……等）均在避免之列。

七、實例分析

本節分析一般人寫作論文時常犯的錯誤（列於左欄），將它們和論文中常見的盲點一一在註腳中詳細解說，並將建議之修訂方式列於右欄，以便互相參照閱讀。

原文	建議修訂
摘要	

原文	建議修訂
~~為了了解現今國中生之父母親所採取的管教方式（民主型、專制型、放任型、不干涉型）、制握信念、學習壓力與學習成就的現況[1]~~；探討國中生之父母親管教方式、制握信念與學習壓力的關係；分析父母親管教方式、制握信念對國中生學習壓力、學習成就的預測力。本研究採問卷調查法，以「父母親管教方式量表」、「制握信念量表」、「學習壓力量表」為研究工具，並以臺北市、臺中縣、彰化縣和臺南縣四個縣市，共五所公私立國中的三年級學生共1484[2]人為研究對象，進而以描述性統計、皮爾森積差相關法及多元迴歸等統計方法分析資料。研究結果如下：~~一、大多數[3]國中生所知覺之父母親管教方式為「民主型」；制握信念[4]人格特質為內控制握信念；學習壓力並不大，但是其中以「考試焦~~	本研究探討國中生父母親之管教方式和制握信念對學生學習壓力和學習成就的的預測力。研究採問卷調查法，使用「父母親管教方式量表」、「制握信念量表」、「學習壓力量表」為工具，以臺北市、臺中縣、彰化縣和臺南縣四個縣市共五所公私立國中的三年級學生共 1,484 人為研究對象，進而以描述性統計、皮爾森積差相關法及多元迴歸等統計方法

1　摘要應該緊密紮實，這類開場白只會讓摘要顯得鬆弛，沒什麼價值，應該刪去。若覺得不捨，這種文字可以移到緒論或引言處。

2　除了年分以外，四位數以上的阿拉伯數字應該加撇節號。

3　論文講求的是確切的證據及數據，不應該有含糊的敘述，如「大多數」、「一小部分」、「少數情況」、「有些」、「相當多」、「大部分」、「絕大部分」、「幾乎全部」等無法用確切量詞說明的東西在論文裡沒有加值的效果，除非可以找到數據明確的數或百分比，不然可以一概刪去。

4　摘要中光是「管教方式」、「制握信念」一詞，就各出現了十一次，修詞方式有改進餘地。

原文	建議修訂
慮」最高；學習成就方面個別差異很大。 二、本研究發現父母親管教方式、制握信念、學習壓力和學習成就有相關存在，採取「專制型」管教方式，則國中生較傾向於「運氣」，學習壓力也比較大；採取「民主型」管教方式，則國中生較不會傾向於「運氣」，而比較會傾向於「努力」和「能力」；採取「放任型」管教方式，則國中生的學習壓力低；採取「不干涉型」管教方式，則國中生的學習成就低；國中生持制握信念的「運氣」傾向者，其強迫學習壓力越大；國中生持制握信念的「命運」傾向者，其「考試焦慮」和「課業壓力」越大；國中生持制握信念的「努力」傾向者，其學習成就越低；國中生的「考試焦慮」越高，學習成就就會越好。[5] 三、本研究發現父母親管教方式、制握信念可以有效預測學習壓力和學習成就。（934字）	分析取得之資料，研究結果發現，父母親的管教方式和制握信念可以有效預測學生之學習壓力和學習成就。（201字）
問題背景	
……根據許福生在 2003 年青少年生活痛苦指數的調查研究中發現，「父母期望」及「學校環境」兩個面向比 2002 年痛苦加深。顯然，	……根據許福生在 2003 年青少年生活痛苦指數的調查研究中發

---

[5] 九百餘字的摘要過於冗長，摘要旨在把研究的主題、研究的方法及所得的結果扼要敘述，不必因為要增加字數而附上不必要的陳述，只要達到所要求的字數下限即可。本文中畫線的文字沒什麼價值，應予刪除。

原文	建議修訂
十年的教改不但無法使青少年快樂的學習，反而增加其功課及學習壓力[6]。因此，有關導致青少年學習壓力的原因為何以及如何減輕青少年的學習壓力，都是我們[7]為人師長和教育有關單位應加以探究並尋求解決方案，以免青少年因學習壓力過大而出現不良的生理、心理反應。 　　青少年因學習壓力過大而產生如：嗑藥、自殺、罹患精神分裂症 (蔡佩芬, 民 86)[8]、憂鬱症（李欣瑩，民 90）、學校適應問題（羅婉麗，民 90）[9]的情況時有所聞。報紙上更是時常[10]看到有關報導，例如：建中資優生疑因課業壓力過大而上吊自殺，他的同班同學兩年前也自縊了；一名文大學生因怕遭受退學而上吊自殺（聯合報，92.4.14）[11]，這些報導讀來真是令人唏噓惋惜，感嘆年輕的生命就這麼消逝了。[12]使研究者不由得生起想要一探究竟的意念，想要	現，「父母期望」及「學校環境」兩個面向比 2002 年痛苦加深。 　　青少年因學習壓力過大而產生如嗑藥、自殺、罹患精神分裂症（蔡佩芬，1997）、憂鬱症（李欣瑩，2001）、學校適應問題（羅婉麗，2001）的情況時有所聞，因此，青少年學習壓力的原因，以及如何減輕青少年的學習壓力，乃是師長和教育有關單位應加以探究和求解的問題。

6　此處立論太弱，任何分析均應有足夠的「對照數據」可供比對，才會顯得較合研究規格，也會較有意義。僅比較連續兩年的數據就斷言十年教改無效，這不是在邏輯判斷上有問題，就是太過方便行事。事實上，研究中可以只提出數據，不加以評論。當然，若有更多的數據可供比較（例如1994 年以來），則有立場說明十年的教改成效彰否。

7　論文或研究報告應使用第三人稱的客觀方式。

8　與國字相連的任何標點符號（包含括號）都應使用全形。

9　見第 3.5 即「務必使用西元紀年及絕對指標」。

10　若無法以具體數字支持，「有時」要比「時常」為中性。

11　報紙之引註應寫出作者及出版日；無作者則呈現篇名及出版日。

12　情緒性的描述，非論文用詞。

原文	建議修訂
了解是什麼因素使得青少年如此輕生，然而青少年周遭的親師友，或者整個社會體系能夠給予怎樣的協助？這是現今社會必須詳加了解並尋求解決辦法之要務。 　　……我國[13]大部分父母望子成龍、望女成鳳的心態，認為子女有較佳的學習成就，將來才能出人頭地，因此為孩子安排各種才藝學習或參加課後補習，以增進子女的才藝技能及課業成績，如此的用心安排，帶給子女是快樂或壓力？是值得關心的議題。	另外，報紙上有時會刊載學生不堪壓力而輕生的報導，這些報導使研究者想要了解是什麼因素使得青少年如此輕生，青少年周遭的親師友，或者整個社會體系能夠給予怎樣的協助。 　　……父母多望子成龍、望女成鳳的心態，認為子女有較佳的學習成就，將來才能出人頭地，因此為孩子安排各種才藝學習或參加課後補習，以增進子女的才藝技能及課業成績，如此用心安排所帶給子女是快樂或壓力，乃是值得關心的議題。

13　「我國」一詞，屬於第一人稱，從國際化的眼光來看，應該避免使用「我國」，而以國家名稱代替。

原文	建議修訂
研究動機	
Chaplain（2000）認為[14]與教師壓力研究相較，有關學生壓力的研究目前仍相當有限。近年來[15]國內[11]雖然有不少探討學生學校生活壓力的研究（王蓁蓁，民89；劉政宏，民92；劉寶，民92），但是以國三學生為對象的學習壓力實證研究至今仍鮮有人探討。因此本研究乃以國中三年級學生為對象加以研究。 　　十多年來[16]倡導教改者都同意讓孩子們紮實學習、快樂長大是教改的共同目標。根據快樂學習教改連線在九十二年六月間的一項民意調查顯示，約八成四的國中小學生在學習時感到快樂；有六成以上的家長認為，孩子的學習是快樂的。但是事實是否真是如此？[17]根據兒童福利聯盟文教基金會在九十三年婦幼節前夕[18]，在臺北市、臺中市和高雄市三區，訪問三百五十名國小五、六年級學生，調查發現小學生負擔很重，四成的小學生放學後還要參加二種以上的才藝班，其中一半學生說是「不得	Chaplain（2000）指出，與教師壓力的研究相較，有關學生壓力的研究仍相當有限。王蓁蓁（2000）、劉政宏（2003）、劉寶（2003）等雖然研究了學生的學校生活壓力，但國三學生的學習壓力仍鮮有人探討，因此本研究乃以國中三年級學生為對象加以研究。 　　讓孩子們紮實學習、快樂長大是教改的共同目標。根據快樂學習教改連線在2003年六月間的一項民意調查顯示，約八成四的國中

---

14 此人之「認為」與任何人之「認為」都同樣「有效」或者「無效」，故引用參考資料時亦應考核原資料之信度。

15 見本章腳註9。

16 見本章腳註9。

17 論文應以平鋪直敘為原則，不用以自問自答的「花俏」方式來變化花樣。

18 如果你不知道明太祖或華盛頓何時誕辰，就要考慮到婦幼節到底是何月何日並非舉世皆知。

原文	建議修訂
已」，並沒有樂在其中的感覺，有七成的孩子放學後最想「回家」，但最常去的地方是「才藝班或安親班」，最期待的親子活動是「買書」和「戶外活動」、但現實卻是「看電視」和「吃飯」（聯合報，93.4.1）[19]。 　　另外根據程振隆立委調查顯示[20]，國中生天天考，有的學校甚至一週考十四科，學習壓力之大可見一斑（自由時報，93.2.20）[15]。在九年一貫課程改中，為了達到教材鬆綁、教學活潑、學習多元，企圖以「多元評量」方式取代過去傳統填鴨式的考試，然而多元評量無法落實，校園內仍充斥著紙筆測驗式的考試與量化測驗，滿天飛的學習單更是壓得學生喘不過氣來。[21]	小學生在學習時感到快樂；有六成以上的家長認為孩子的學習是快樂的。但是根據兒童福利聯盟文教基金會 2004年四月的調查，在臺北市、臺中市和高雄市三區訪問的三百五十名國小五、六年級學生中，發現四成的小學生放學後還要參加二種以上的才藝班，其中一半學生說是「不得已」，並沒有樂在其中的感覺，有七成的孩子放學後最想「回家」，但最常去的地方是「才藝班或安親班」，最期待的親子活動是「買書」和「戶外活動」，但現實卻是

---

[19] 報紙之報導信度不高，凡涉及數字之量化資料宜引用原始文獻。

[20] 立委調查有其問政目的，因而取樣偏頗，其學術意義不明確，在此應改變敘述方式，避免「根據」其「調查」而判斷。

[21] 此段若無法舉證，則不宜提出。不加引證地以誇張的社論方式寫作非論文作者所應為。

原文	建議修訂
	「看電視」和「吃飯」。 　　另外，自由時報（2004/2/20）引述立委程振隆的說法，國中生天天考，有的學校甚至一週考十四科，學習壓力之大可見一斑。
小結	
本研究發現國中生之制握信念「努力」和「能力」層面得分平均高於中間值，而「命運」層面得分平均接近中間值，而「運氣」層面得分平均低於中間值（見下表）[22]。由此可知[23]，目前國中生多認為成功或失敗是由於自己的努力和能力所造成，表示國中生的制握信念人格特質為內在制握信念傾向，這也是我們樂意見到的結果[24]。目前國中生其實並不是如我們想像的較偏向外控者[25]，或許是因為國中生在當今的社會環境中學會了自我掌控的重要性，並且能體認事情的成敗其實是有賴於自己的努力和能力，	本研究發現國中生之制握信念「努力」和「能力」層面得分平均高於中間值，而「命運」層面得分平均接近中間值，而「運氣」層面得分平均低於中間值（見表三），說明了受測者傾向認為成功或失敗是由於自己的努力和能力所造成，表示這些

---

[22] 內文敘述時應避免「見下表」、「如上圖中所示」或「參看下節」等相對性的指標，而應使用像「如表 2-1」、「如圖 3-2 中所示」或「請見第 4.2 節」等的絕對指標。

[23] 類似「由此可知……」或「由……可見……」這類的語法，應該盡量用「……旨在表示……」或「……說明了……」等方式取代。

[24] 研究結果不用為個人喜好服務，故不要以為此種方式能為研究結果加值。

[25] 此句「其實並不是如我們想像的較偏向外控」若無法舉證，不宜提出。

原文	建議修訂
而不是由命運或運氣所決定的。	國中生為內在制握信念傾向。或許是因為國中生在當今的社會環境中學會了自我掌控的重要性，並且能體認事情的成敗其實是有賴於自己的努力和能力，而不是由命運或運氣所決定。

第二篇

論文綱要與體例

期刊或研討會論文和各級學位畢業論文，均屬與研究有關的論述，其中以學位論文（尤其是博士論文）的篇幅最長，而且格式要求最為繁複。各期刊對其所接受的論文以及各學校對其各級學生畢業論文的格式規定均有不同，要了解其中詳情的最好方法，就是直接到各該單位的網站去查詢。

由於學位論文對於組織和格式要求最為繁複，涵蓋了其他各類論文的規定，因此本書採取「取法乎上」的原則，以學位論文為討論中心，藉以闡明所有論文及研究報告的撰寫規範。為了求其完備，本書還涉入了寫作格式和研究方法的介紹。

本 篇 大 要

第四章
論文篇前部分

本章提綱

　　一、論文命名（Title）原則

　　二、摘要（Abstract）的寫法

　　三、關鍵字表（Keywords）

　　四、序文（Preface）

　　五、誌謝辭（Acknowledgement）的寫法

　　六、目錄的格式

　　學位論文的篇前部分包括題目（Title）、摘要（Abstract）、關鍵字表（Keywords）、序文（Preface 或 Foreword）、誌謝辭（Acknowledgement）、目次（Table of Contents）、圖目錄（List of Figures）、表目錄（List of Tables）等，茲一一於下列各小節中予以說明。

一、論文命名（Title）原則

　　好的論文題目可以讓讀者知道該論文所要探討的大概方向，例如：「九二一大地震對中臺灣經濟結構的影響」就比「九二一後的省思」要適合作論文題目。

　　論文的命名力求簡單明瞭，並直接反映論文的主題。英文論文題目

以不超過十五字為原則，中文論文題目可以稍長，但也不宜超出二十字太多為。過長的題目容易纏夾繞舌，令人抓不住要點。

　　以下幾個題目都簡明易懂，是合適的論文題目：

1. Multi-dimensional Interval Routing Schemes
2. Pulse Flow Enhancement in Two-Phase Media
3. Shortest Path Queries in Very Large Spatial Databases
4. Static Conflict Analysis of Transaction Programs
5. Topic-Oriented Collaborative Web Crawling
6. Inappropriate Interpretation of Teaching Material and Its Disadvantage to the Cultivation of Creative Thinking
7. Differentiating the Art of Teaching and the Pitfall of Promoting Fake Science
8. 從校園善念實驗論有礙於科學教育的教學藝術
9. 從僵化的教材解讀方式論無益於創意思考的教學活動
10. 從創造力白皮書探究國民小學學校教育之創新經營策略
11. 以後設認知技能探討創新與捷思力啓發
12. 成人學習者的智慧與創造力關係的探討

　　下面這兩個題目遊戲意味過濃，不宜於作為論文題目：

1. 神奇的稻米
2. 奇形怪狀玩創意

像：

超級變變變——遊戲式創意肢體律動對幼兒創造力之探討

就不如改為：

從遊戲式創意肢體律動探討幼兒之創造力

論文英文題目起首處不用加上「The」、「And」、「An」和「A」等冠詞，其他如「Studies on」、「Investiga-tion on」、「Observations on」等類的字樣，徒然增加題目的長度，因此並無必要，請看下面幾個例子：

原命名	修改後
Studies of a Framework for Machine-Assisted Software Architecture Validation	Framework for Machine Assisted Software Architecture Validation
The Statistical Assessment of a Process to Evaluate the Commercial Success of Inventions	Statistical Assessment of a Process to Evaluate the Commercial Success of Inventions.
A Probabilistic Approach to Image Feature Extraction, Segmentation and Interpretation	Probabilistic Approach to Image Feature Extraction, Segmentation, and Interpretation

至於論文的中文題目，在不損及原題所欲代表的意義時為了避免題目過長，有時候類似「**之研究**」的字樣也可以刪去，例如：

原命名	修正後
九二一大地震對中臺灣經濟結構的影響之研究	九二一大地震對中臺灣經濟結構的影響
兩岸政局互動對臺灣經濟結構的影響之研究	兩岸政局互動對臺灣經濟結構的影響

題目中盡量少用縮寫詞，必用時亦需在括弧中註明全稱，題目中少用或盡量不用數學符號和希臘字母等特殊字元。

若一般長度的題目不足以完全表達論文的主題，但又想要避免題目太長、太繞舌，就可以在原有題目之後附上一個副題，如下例，在冒號後面的部分就是副題：

Distinguishing successful from unsuccessful venture capital investments in technology-based new ventures: How investment decision criteria relate to deal performance

整體上，上面的題目仍然有點不太達意，有改進餘地。下面這個改進後的題目用字比較簡約，顯得清爽易懂了一些。

Success and failure of venture capital investments in technology-based new ventures: How investment decision criteria affect venture performance

又，在論文的封面，大標題要打在中央，全部用大寫字母，小標題可以打在中央，也可以齊頭打，除下述三種情形外，小標題中每個英文字的第一個字母都要大寫：

1. 冠詞（a, an, the）
2. 不超過四個字母的介詞或前置詞（with, for, at, in, on 等）
3. 連接詞（and, or, but 等）

因此，把上面的題目打在封面就應該像這樣：

SUCCESS AND FAILURE OF

VENTURE CAPITAL INVESTMENTS IN

TECHNOLOGY-BASED NEW VENTURES:

How Investment Decision Criteria

Affect Venture Performance

副題的功用，在於補足原命題敘述不夠完備之處，以下幾個題目及其副題都搭配得恰到好處：

1. 中英論文寫作綱要與體例：研究報告與英文書信規範
2. 中英雙向翻譯新視野——英文讀、寫、譯實務與體例
3. 知識管理——實務、專題與案例
4. 英文書信與履歷的藝術：E-mail 時代的英文寫作溝通
5. 心靈與意識：新時代的生命教育
6. 中英論文寫作綱要與體例：研究報告與英文書信規範

　　上面各個主題由於言猶未盡，因此分別加上適當的副題，以求更為貼切地代表作品的內涵。

　　副題要能夠像上列各例那樣增益原題，不應該反過來壓抑原題或為原題設限，說到這裡，就不能不提起社會科學類論文中流行的一種「以⋯⋯為例」的風氣[1]，例如：

> ## 臺灣高鐵交通運輸網絡之研究──以彰化地區為例

就是副題反過來壓抑原題或為原題設限的例子，依筆者之見，此類題目可以改成：

> ## 臺灣高鐵彰化地區交通運輸網絡之研究

　　因為，僅僅研究了區域性的「臺灣高鐵在彰化地區的交通運輸網絡」的數據，卻以全稱性的「臺灣高鐵交通運輸網絡之研究」來命名，實在太過「巧取豪奪」，而在題目後面補上「以彰化地區為例」，又有如遮羞，實在並不可取。

　　其他例子之多，可以信手拈來，當然也可以一一修正：

原命名	修改後
1.區域及鄉土地理電腦輔助教學之研究──以雲林地區為例	1.雲林地區區域及鄉土地理電腦輔助教學之研究

---

[1] 此風不知起自何時，尤以教育類及管理類之主題為然。

原命名	修改後
2. 國民小學推動知識管理現況與期望之研究——以臺中地區為例	2. 臺中地區國小推動知識管理現況與期望之研究
3. 創造力融入教學之理論與實務——以「自然與生活科技領域」課程為例	3. 以「自然與生活科技領域」課程探討創造力融入教學之理論與實務
4. 問題解決教學策略與成效研究——以綜合高中程式語言單元為例	4. 從高中程式語言單元探討問題解決之教學策略與成效

另外還有類似以上「以……為例」的命題：

> 1. 教師地位與權利義務——以臺灣中小學教師為中心
> 2. 晚清中國的政治轉型：以清末憲政改革為中心

　　這些「以……為中心」的命題法同樣不可取，為什麼不老老實實改成：

> 1. 以臺灣中小學教師為中心探討教師地位與權利義務
> 2. 以清末憲政改革為中心考察晚清中國的政治轉型

或：

> 1. 臺灣中小學教師的地位與權利義務
> 2. 從清末憲政改革論晚清中國的政治轉型

　　還有，下面這個命題中，副題的用字與本題幾乎相同，並沒有多餘的意義，可謂多此一舉：

　　藝術治療研究法：以藝術為基礎的研究法

倒不如將之改為：

　　以藝術為基礎的藝術治療研究法

　　市面上有一本書以這樣的方式命名：

　　如何撰寫學術論文：以「政治學方法論」為考察中心

該書在封面上將本題「如何撰寫學術論文」用絕大的字標出，而副題<以政治學方法論為考察中心>則聊備一格地埋在本題之間，心急的讀者可能買回去一讀，才知道買錯了書，這種命名方式難脫「別有用心」之嫌。
　　有識之士實在不應盲從這些謬誤的命題方式。

二、摘要（Abstract）的寫法

　　摘要是整篇報告的精華，影響所有讀者對該篇論文的第一印象，寫得好的摘要有「促銷」的效果，因此作者應該盡可能用最簡潔的白話寫出來，使閱讀者可以很快對此報告有所掌握。正式的學術論文中皆附有論文摘要，摘要是論文的先鋒，是全文中最廣受閱讀的部分，它提供了

整篇論文的資料內容，並揭示該篇論文所包含的主要概念和討論的主要問題，幫助讀者抉擇這篇文獻對自己的工作是否有用。摘要裡大致宜包括研究目的，資料來源，研究方法、過程、步驟及結果等，若有特別重要的貢獻或發現，亦應加入摘要內。

摘要寫作的第一要素是簡潔，除少數例外情況，一般期刊多會規定論文摘要長度的上下限，常見的下限是五十至一百字，上限則是二百至四百字，視原始文獻而定。至於長篇如博、碩士論文者，其摘要也不宜太冗長，應以五百字為限。

摘要雖然列在論文結構之首，但在寫作的順序上應是最後完成的，作者應該在整篇論文完成後自己閱讀一遍，把論文的重點依以下三部分用一段完整的文字敘述出來：

1. **目的**：說明此論文的目的或主要想解決的問題。
2. **過程及方法**：說明主要工作過程及所用的方法，使用的主要設備和儀器等。
3. **結果**：說明此研究過程最後得出的結果和結論，如有可能，可以提出該結論和結果的應用範圍和情況。

一般寫作摘要最常犯的毛病，就是像左欄的原文一樣，在開頭處來一段與研究毫不相干的開場白，奉勸有此錯誤習慣的人士，你的摘要字數若是足夠，就完全沒有必要加上這種畫蛇添足式的描述，而摘要字數若是不足，加上這種無用的填料只會曝露你論文的薄弱，不論哪種情形，泛泛之詞式的開場白都無助於你的論文，因此請不要在這上面浪費筆墨。

請參考右欄中改寫後的摘要：

原文	改寫後
近十幾年來，國內休閒農場如雨後春筍般蓬勃發展，除了帶動農業的成長外，也讓民眾在從事休閒活動上有更多的選擇機會。但在這契機的背後，因國內休閒農場經營者缺乏管理技能，追求短期利潤，使農場資源被經營者所忽略，等到休閒農場正式營運時，許多問題便接踵而來，此時無形資源才突顯出其重要性，因此，休閒農場如何運用資源特性，達到消費者預期效益、滿足消費者偏好將是本研究所要探討之重點。本研究參考 B. Joseph Pine II 與 James H Gilmore（2003）對經濟型態產物所作分類，運用在休閒農場上，將農場分成農作生產休閒農場、農物販售加工休閒農場、客製服務休閒農場及主題體驗休閒農場。並先行前往所選定休閒農場與負責人進行深度訪談與田野調查，了解農場資源內涵，進而做現地觀察記錄，蒐集各農場資源項目、分布、使用方式、狀態等第一手資料。訪談之結果將	本論文之目的在於探討各類型休閒農場資源應用現況，比較各類型休閒農場之消費者偏好之差異及分析休閒農場資源應用與消費者偏好之關聯。研究者把文獻中對經濟型態所作的分類應用在休閒農場上，將農場分成農作生產休閒農場、農物販售加工休閒農場、客製服務休閒農場，及主題體驗休閒農場，往訪所選定之休閒農場，與負責人深度訪談，並進行田野調查以了解農場資源內涵，進而做現地觀察記錄，蒐集各農場資源項目、分布、狀態、使用方式等，並歸納分析訪談結果，設計問卷。以擁有評估、決策權之成年遊客為問卷調查對象，共回收有效問卷 320 份，採用因素分析、卡方檢定、變異數分析及皮爾森積差相關分析等統計方法進行分析探討，又透過因素分析將消費者偏好歸類為實質環境、活動導覽、餐飲品質、交通環境、服務品質、商品特色等六個構面後。結果發現：1)人口變項與消費者偏

原文	改寫後
進行歸納分析，以作為問卷設計參考依據。歸納研究目的如下： 1. 探討各類型休閒農場資源應用現況。 2. 比較各類型休閒農場之消費者偏好之差異。 3. 探討休閒農場資源應用與消費者偏好之關聯。 　依照研究發現，提出供經營者在休閒農場資源規劃經營上之參考。（448字）	好在不同經營型態休閒農場有顯著差異。2)人口變項與重遊意願及推薦意願，有部分顯著相關。3)資源應用與消費者偏好顯著相關。（409字）

　　寫英文摘要時要用單一時態，最好使用現在式。摘要第一句應避免與題目（Title）重複。通常一個既方便又合宜的方法，是用一個簡單的句子直接切入主題：

1. This research shows....
2. This study investigates....
3. This paper compares insurance premium principles with current financial risk.
1. 本研究旨在……
2. 本論文的目的在於……
3. 本研究旨在探討提升學生問題解決能力之教學策略，期能作為教師在課程調整、規劃時之參考。

然後引出整篇論文的要點。例如：

英文範例

　　The author uses distorted probabilities, a recent development in premium principle literature, to synthesize the current models for financial risk measures in banking and insurance. This work attempts to broaden the definition of value-at-risk beyond the percentile measures. The author uses examples to show how the percentile measure fails to give consistent results, and how the failure can be manipulated. This paper also investigated a new class of consistent risk measures.

中文範例

　　研究者藉由文獻探討建立理論基礎，建構問題解決之教學、評量策略，並選取＿＿＿高中商業學群學生，進行準實驗設計之教學實驗。實驗組樣本為＿＿＿名，運用問題導向之教學策略；控制組樣本為＿＿＿名，採用傳統教師講授之教學法。實驗科目為計算機之程式語言單元，依本研究所擬的教學系統模式，分別進行為期＿＿＿週之實驗教學。本論文所使用之研究工具包括「問題解決態度量表」、「學習感受量表」及研究者自編之「單元學習成就試題」。

　　要在短短的一段文字內把整篇論文的內涵都包括進去是不可能的，因此，摘要旨在把研究的主題、研究的方法及所得的結果扼要敘述，不必因為要增加字數而附上不必要的陳述，只要達到所要求的字數下限即可。

　　在摘要中應適當地簡化單位以及一些通用詞，也該盡量避免不必要

的字句，例如下文左欄中的開場白就沒什麼價值，應該取消，把文中不必要的字句刪除，把「人工智慧歸納學習法」簡化為 AIM，並將文字去蕪存菁後，整篇摘要顯得清晰易讀得多了。

原摘要	修改後
~~「早期發現、早期治療」是預防疾病的不二法門，如何建立技術，有效發現疾病癥兆以採取先機先制是職業病預防研究者之最終目的。~~本研究應用「人工智慧歸納學習法」進行職業病預測技術的開發，使用此資訊技術所建立決策樹之研究方式，有別於以往預測職業病發生的各種動物體實驗，及假設過於嚴謹，分析時間冗長的流行病學研究方法。本研究發現「人工智慧歸納學習法」是一種經濟又有效率的研究方法，能將業界豐富的健檢資料化減為簡單的決策樹（decision tree method），決策樹建立後，可轉變成許多條律成為知識庫（knowledge bases），便於讓職業病醫生預防研究者作為職業病診斷及監控的輔助工具。本研究以鉛蓄電池廠鉛暴露為例，將勞工健康檢查資料輸入利用「人工智慧歸納學習法」，找尋十七個生理與人事資料變數與血中鉛濃度的關係，相互影響越緊密，就會藉由決策樹出現在分割點中。預測結果血中鉛偏高和人體	本研究應用資訊技術——人工智慧歸納學習法（AIM）——開發職業病預測技術，使用 AIM 建立決策樹的方式有別於以往預測職業病發生的動物體實驗，也不同於假設過於嚴謹、分析時間冗長的流行病學研究方法。本研究發現 AIM 經濟有效，能將健檢資料簡化為簡單的決策樹，進而轉成一些知識庫條例，讓醫生作為職業病診斷及監控的輔助工具。本研究以鉛蓄電池廠鉛暴露為例，將勞工健康檢查資料輸入，利用 AIM 找尋生理與人事資料變數與血中鉛濃度的關係。預測結果，血中鉛偏高和人

原摘要	修改後
出現貧血、高血壓等臨床表徵有明顯的相關性，都與過去文獻結果呈現一致的現象。（395字）	體出現貧血、高血壓等臨床表徵有明顯的相關性，與過去文獻結果一致。（241字）

其他縮短摘要的方法有：

1. 避免介紹論文中的圖、表、方程式和參考文獻；
2. 取消或減少背景資料（Background Information）；
3. 只表示新情況、新內容，過去的研究細節可以取消；
4. 避免納入文獻中所談及的未來計畫。

以下這段文字以論文摘要的標準而言，稍嫌太長，而且其中所提到的只是泛泛的說法，並未明確指出哪一個部分與其研究有關，因此完全不適合作為論文摘要，乃是個失敗的例子：

當人類的壽命不斷的延長，心理學者開始對智慧產生研究的興趣；智慧指的是處理人類生活所面臨到的困難問題，一種較高層的知識、判斷，並給予勸告，因而可以以平衡的態度去處理特定的問題，擁有智慧的成人較能認知到生命中的不確定性，知悉生命的有限以及文化的角色會影響人們的生活與性格；但若單純的把智慧和年齡畫上等號，其實並不妥當，唯有隨著生命的歷程和環境的不斷的互動與運思，智慧才會隨著年齡的增加而增長；一個不與環境產生互動的個體，即使生物年齡不斷的增加，智慧也不會增長，甚至會停滯或退化。

　　此外，在自然科學中一直隱藏著一種廣泛的偏見，就是年齡較大的人比較沒有能力，去做創造性的工作；創造力所指就是透過擴散性思考，可以使人們藉由打破先前所建立的思考方式，來產生新觀念；而透過對數學家、科學家所做的研究，顯現出這些學者的生產量是呈現穩定模式，所以雖然研究發現創造力的高低和年齡是有關係的，但不同的領域，其專業的創造力會有不同階段的高峰期。

　　最後，關於智慧與創造力的關係有其相同點包括：一、都會受到性別及歷史的背景的影響。二、兩者都會利用他們的認知和情感的應變能力來處理，生命中的難以理解的事。三、兩者都和智力有重疊處。所以智慧有助於創造力的產生，智慧能將個人與社群的最大利益加以融合，並提出一個平衡的決定與政策；要成為有智慧的人，除了必須要有足夠的真實的知識外，還須具備有思考的能力，透過思考的訓練，可以內化成自己的能力，當面對問題時，就不同的角度或價值觀去思考。

　　下例的原英文摘要太鬆散，尤其是第一句，充其量只不過是個填料，沒有存在的必要，原摘要可以加以精簡如右欄，改善後的摘要刪去了一些離題的陳述，精簡了幾個長句，比原文短了近三分之一，文章顯得更流暢：

原摘要	修改後
Humankind's ability to ensure sustainability of the biosphere depends upon the integratedand concerted efforts of all peoples	This study examines achievement of sustainability in urban centers and evaluates

原摘要	修改後
in all places. This study examines the critical need to focus on the achievement of sustain-ability in urban centers and evaluates the po-tential for city core neighbor-hoods to contrib-ute to the accom-plishment of this goal. 　　Four criteria are presented as nece-ssary for the realization of urban sustaina-bility, two of which, livability and equity of access (identified as the 'social' criteria) become the focus of this inquiry. Community involvement at the neighborhood level is also identified as necessary to the process by which sustainabil-ity will be achieved. The synergy of livability and equity to create a sense of community and attendant community involvement is explored. 　　_____ serves as a case study to in-form future efforts to ensure livability, equity, and the resulting community involvement neces-sary to achieve urban sustainability, and points to subtle but important les-sons regarding the dynamism of various conditions within a neighborhood that can contribute to this po-tential. (168 words)	the city core neighborhoods' poten-tial in achieving this goal. Livability, equity of ac-cess, community involvement, and equity to create a sense of community are four criteria necessary for ur-ban sustain-ability. Among the four, liv-ability and equity of access are identified as the "social" criteria and become the focus of this paper. _____ serves as a case study to identify livability, equity, and the resulting com-munity involvement necessary to achieve urban sustainability. This case study points to subtle but important lessons regarding the dynamism of various con-ditions within a neighborhood that can contribute to urban sustain-ability potential. (107 words)

　　下例的原中文摘要第一段也是應予刪除的填料，改善後的摘要刪去了一些累贅的陳述，比原文短了逾五分之二，文章顯得更清楚：

原摘要	修改後
二十一世紀人類面臨第三次產業革命，一個以「腦力」決勝負的「知識經濟時代」來臨。創新、批判思考、解決問題的能力，不但成為世界公民的重要基礎能力，亦是學校教育所要培育的首要能力；又學校教育環境面對少子化的衝擊、校園衝突以及組織異見……等，愈形弔詭的組織氛圍，學校教育工作團隊，更須以全新的思維模組，透過創造思考、創新與創新經營之前瞻做法，建立學校的品牌形象，不斷創造親師生的高峰經驗，方能持續屹立於競爭激烈的時代洪流中。本文之撰寫，首先從教育部創造力白皮書論起，兼探創造思考、創新、創新經營等概念及其相關研究；繼之探討學校創新經營的條件因素，並對國民小學學校教育創新經營的具體做法，提出：一、採行情境企劃，架構學校創新經營願景；二、溝通觀念，凝聚創新經營共識；三、成立推動小組，縝密計畫與執行；四、採擇適當的領導方式，引領親師生達成創意經營目標；五、建構學習型組織，塑造學習型組織文化；六、精緻	本研究自教育部創造力白皮書論起，探創造思考、創新、創新經營等概念及其相關研究；繼之探討學校創新經營的條件因素，並對國民小學學校教育創新經營的具體做法，提出：一、採行情境企劃，架構學校創新經營願景；二、溝通觀念，凝聚創新經營共識；三、成立推動小組，縝密計畫與執行；四、採擇適當領導方式，引領親師生達成創意經營目標；五、建構學習型組織，塑造學習型組織文化；六、鼓勵精緻的多元活動，延伸創新經營成效；七、實施知識管理，實踐知識經濟理想；八、落實學校本位管理，

原摘要	修改後
的多元活動，延伸創新經營成效；七、實施知識管理，實踐知識經濟理想；八、落實學校本位管理，實現創新經營新境；九、善用「梅迪奇效應」，激發創意思維與做法；十、貫徹考核與研究，創新研究與發展等十項解決策略；最後，透過實務案例之分享，印證學校創新經營的具體、可行作為。　　筆者依據理論與實務之經驗，將主題做如此之布局與組織，盼能對逐漸式微的學校創造思考教育及創意創新作為，提供參酌與助益。（582 字）	實現創新經營新境；九、善用「梅迪奇效應」，激發創意思維與作法；十、貫徹考核與研究，創新研究與發展等十項解決策略；最後，透過實務案例之分析，印證學校創新經營的具體可行作為，期為學校創造思考教育及創意創新作為提供參酌與助益。（335 字）

下例中的原摘要過於簡化，遺漏了某些重點，改善後的例子中補足了研究方法的敘述，但並未加入任何贅詞。

原摘要	修改後
Using high-tech com-puter applications, an environmental monitoring and emergency response systems with real-time data acquisition and analysis capability have become a reality. Sys-	This paper describes the implementation of a real-time data acquisition strategy that can transform the onetime assessment of hazards into a continuous monitoring of potential risks in an industrial community. While a snapshot hazard assessment is not sufficient to provide true safety in a rapidly changing environment, micro-processors have stimulated the construction of

原摘要	修改後
tems that embody block diagram pro-gramming, geographical information system, graphical user interface, and real-time data acquisition device achieve sustainable development and foster environmental protection. (45 words)	a completely new inventory of data acquisition schema. To foster environmental protection, the researcher uses high-tech computer applications (Block Diagram Programming), combines user-friendly software (Graphical User Interface) with easyto-install hardware, and adopts realtime data acquisition systems to form an Emergency Response Systems with real-time data capturing and analysis capability. (103 words)

　　由於國際化的需要，大多數論文都會被要求加上英文摘要，作為中文摘要的對照。英文摘要可以自成一體，只要能順暢達意，事實上並不需要是逐句中英對照的翻譯。以下兩個例子中，不論是中文摘要或其對應的英文摘要，都明確指出研究目的及方法，是論文摘要的合格範例：

摘要一	**Abstract A**
探討人的意念對事物影響的校園善念實驗，廣泛流傳於網際網路上，那些實驗以不當的誘導方式，指出煮熟的米飯和饅頭能感受人的意念。本論文旨在探討此類實驗的正面及負面教育意義，指出其雖然在公民教育上有正向的貢獻，	Via pointing out the deficiencies of some science projects that have been conducted in the primary school campuses, this paper intends to identify the pitfall of fake science residing within the art of teaching. The author uses some widely spread examples on the Internet to discuss the misleading aspects of the experiments that are claimed

摘要一	Abstract A
但在科學教育上確有可議之處，甚至可認定是誤用了教學藝術，使得對於真正科學方法缺乏認知的孩童與成人誤解了正確的科學方法，並無意間為偽科學作了有效的背書。本論文並具體提出增進實驗步驟之方向及改善實驗結果解釋之方式，以為結論。	to have proved human emotions (such as love, hatred, and jealousy) do affect the behavior of living and non-living objects. To those primary school teachers who intend to direct similar projects in their classroom, this paper provides advices to improve the experiment procedure as well as the result interpretation skills.

摘要二	Abstract B
本論文指出，傳統教材及流傳於網際網路上諸多跟風式的校園善念實驗，受到教條式或部分學校教師僵化的解讀方法所影響，衍生出不利於創意思考的教學活動，藉此探討此類教材及實驗對於培養學生創造思考、批判思考，及解決問題知能所造成之阻礙。研究者舉出案例，就其中可能障礙創意與批判思考以及問題解決能力的因素，向有意在課堂上應用類似教材及指導類似實驗	Via pointing out the inappropriate way some school teachers have been using to interpret certain teaching materials and the deficiencies some science projects that have been conducted in the primary school campuses, the researcher intends to identify the hurdles that may hinder students from obtaining creative thinking and problem solving capabilities. This paper discusses the downside aspects regarding some popular interpretation of a few conventional teaching materials and an experiment that has been widely spread on the Internet. To those

摘要二	Abstract B
的學校教師提出具體改善的芻議，論文最後並提出非傳統的教材解讀方式與更嚴謹的實驗方法，供案例中人開拓創意思路。	school teachers who intend to use similar materials in their classroom, this paper provides unconventional alternative to enhance their interpretation skills.

　　前面幾篇文字可以代表一般期刊論文的摘要，其特點在把所有重點集中在一段文字內敘述完畢，下面這篇探討《哈利波特》內涵、屬於文學類的摘要，取自一篇碩士論文，篇幅較長，摘要中把各章的要點都分別臚列出來，值得撰寫博士或碩士論文者取法：

　　This research examines the ideology or value system implicit in Joanne Rowling's Harry Potter series. Many of the images in the series, despite being fantastic or empirically unprecedented, are minor transformations of popular books and of common physical and cultural reality. However, these imaginative transformations of mundane reality actually imitate, reiterate, and conserve common and contemporary secular values. On a third level the thesis shows that this conservation of contemporary secular values is undermined by a cynical and subtle transformative element of satire, parody, and criticism.

　　Depending on the theme explored by the particular chapter, a different level of meaning might be evident. Chapter One discusses Rowling's parody of popular secular values. Chapter Two focuses on her parody of Christianity. Chapter Three focuses on Rowling's representations of nature and technology and on her cynical reversal of their traditional representation in similar literature. Chapter Four discusses how Rowling has made a critical appropriation of popular culture reliance on thought-less and instant solutions, and discusses how she has made a mockery of her own hero, Harry Potter.

The conclusion discusses the value of literary devices that trans-form literal meanings and verbal images into new meanings and images, and concludes that Harry Potter should be read cautiously. A second conclusion is that the author claim the series is incomplete is a hoax. This argument is defended with a demonstration that the existing four Harry Potter books form a complete unit, and with a reminder that an element of hoax pervades Rowling's entire series.

三、關鍵字表（Keywords）

關鍵字表旨在提供索引以利圖書書目系統編碼，供日後有興趣的人士按字索取論文，電腦化的索引系統建立後，研究者更可以依關鍵字找到資料庫內所有與該字有關的文章，關鍵字表應列出在論文中一再出現的、與研究內容有重要關係的字彙。

說到與研究內容有關，某生在名為「日月潭數位導覽系統之分析與製作」的專題報告中，把「日月潭」列入關鍵字之中，他的理由是日月潭是他專題的重心，將之列入關鍵字表中，當然合情合理，但是，依我之見，「日月潭數位導覽系統之分析與製作」也者，其重心乃是「數位導覽系統」，並非日月潭，若強將日月潭收列為關鍵字，對日後研究者

在檢索資料時沒有多大好處，因為，用日月潭作關鍵字來搜索時，所得到的條目可能包括「日月潭的霧」、「日月潭的香魚」、「日月潭的神話」、「日月潭的遊艇時刻表」等等，千奇百怪，「日月潭數位導覽系統」會掩埋在超過百萬的「日月潭」條目裡，無法突顯。而以「數位導覽系統」為關鍵字則很有針對性，只出現數百個個「數位導覽系統」條目，尚屬人力可以處理的範圍，其中有許多條目，對日後想製作類似系統的人士而言都具有參考價值。

關鍵字表中的西文字彙應**依字母次序**，中文字彙則應依筆畫數目排列，表中較長的字詞若在後文有用縮寫字代替的情況，可以在各該字詞之後附上該縮寫字。

關鍵字表的寫法變化不大，關鍵字的數目宜以五個為上限，過多關鍵字易於造成索引時失去焦點，最好是三到五個，請看下面的中英文關鍵字表例子：

Keywords: Block Diagram Programming (BDP), Environmental Monitoring System, Geographical Information System (GIS), Graphical User Interface (GUI), Real-time Data Acquisition.

Keywords: human emotion, fake science

Keywords: creative thinking, problem solving, teaching material

關鍵字：人因工程、人為疏失、行為失效、潛在性失效

關鍵字：善念實驗、教學藝術、科學方法

關鍵字：創意思考、教學方法

四、序文（Preface）

　　一般而言，「序文」或「序言」可有可無，通常只出現在長篇論文裡，「序」可分「自序」與「他序」。「自序」可用以敘述研究的過程及價值，有些也簡單介紹報告的編排程序、資料取捨的依據、所用術語符號及不常見的名詞說明等，不過這類自序的內容可以植入本文內之「緒論」中，「他序」則多請師長或專家學者執筆，有推介之意。

五、誌謝辭（Acknowledgement）的寫法

　　一篇論文可能是在許多人的協助與鼓勵下才得以完成，有些作者會在論文內加入誌謝辭，向所有對其研究提供協助的單位或個人表示感謝，學術論文的致謝用詞宜含蓄、簡樸，應避免濫情和流於俗套的溢美之詞。

　　誌謝辭格式與內文相同，只是應盡量控制在兩百字以內。一般期刊論文內的誌謝辭比較簡短，若要文字**格式一致**，不妨使用第三人稱的方式寫作，這類的誌謝辭可以用如下的句子起頭：

1. The author wishes to thank ＿＿ for funding this research.
2. ＿＿ has supported this research.
3. ＿＿ has supported a part of this work.
4. Thanks to ＿＿'s support... .
5. The success of this research... .

　　下面是兩篇值得參考的期刊論文誌謝辭範例，其一使用第三人稱的寫作方式：

> The author acknowledges the guidance, support and direction of Dr. ____ who oversees this research. In addition, the author acknowledges the helpful comments and suggestions on this thesis from Mr. ____, Ms. ____, and Dr. ____.

　　由於誌謝辭是論文中比較具有人情味的部分，因此英文誌謝辭用較人性化的「**I**」、「**we**」、「**me**」、「**us**」等第一人稱並不違例：

> This work was supported by ____ research grants No. ____. We thank ____ for helpful discussions and suggestions and ____ for excellent technical assistance. We also gratefully acknowledge the technical support of ____ for providing the ____ device for the project.

　　至於博士或碩士論文的誌謝辭可能篇幅較長，不容易一路用第三人稱的方式寫作，不妨採用較人性化的寫法，唯字數以一頁以內為宜，請看下面的例子：
　　其一：

> Thanks to ____ and ____ for their kind words, and for being helpful and insightful discussions.
> Thanks to ____ for his enthusiastic demand to be on my committee and his insights into the academic life.
> Thanks to ____ for support and friendship through the long, "Yes, I'm going to finish this sometime", years.

A huge "thank you", to _____ for helping me turn a collection of papers and ideas into a thesis, and for always being cheerful when I pointed out that something might well be impossible.

Special thanks to my long-time collaborator, _____, for dragging me into the world of software reliability in the first place, challenging my blithe assertions, and helping me explore smoked-salmon around the world.

Thanks to _____ for helping me understand statistics and calculus I never thought I'd have to know.

Thanks to all my family and friends (especially the faculty, staff and graduate students at the University of _____) for their support over the years, and especially to my parents for waiting all these years, with only occasional hints, for there to be a Doctor in the family.

And last, but not least, thank you, _____, for being there for me and providing the love and support to help me get through it all!

其二：

Special thanks must go to my supervisor Dr. _____. His insights and criticisms proved to be invaluable, and his patience was infinite.

I must also thank Dr. Naichia Yeh for he is truly an inspiring person and capable of great things.

Thanks to the members of the Programming Languages Group, who provided not only intellectual moments, but also many needed distractions.

This work has been made possible through generous funding by the National Sciences and Engineering Research.

最後舉個中文的誌謝辭例子：

> 本論文承蒙國家科學委員會基金資助，特致殷切謝意。
> 衷心感謝指導老師＿＿教授和論文評審教授們的精心指導，這些教導是本篇論文得以完成的重要因素。
> 感謝＿＿電腦中心主任＿＿教授以及中心全體老師和同學的熱情協助和支持！
> 感謝家人和同窗的關心和支持！
> 感謝所有付出心力幫助過我的人們！

適切的誌謝辭除了讓人知道作者是知書達禮的人之外，還會讓受感謝者覺得自己的熱心沒有被遺忘，受到感激的人進而會樂意繼續幫助有需要的人，從而引導出一股正向的學界、甚至人際的互助風，因此，誌謝辭值得好好經營。

六、目錄的格式

篇幅較長的論文一般以「章」來構成，每章又由數節構成，各節中又可分小節，目錄把這些章節的層次臚列出來，使閱讀者能對論文的大綱一目了然。

㈠ 內容目錄（Table of Contents）

一般論文目錄的內容含括序言、緒論、論文各篇、章、節之標題、參考文獻以及附錄，加上各項目的頁碼。階層以阿拉伯數字表示。第一章第一節以 1.1 表示，第一章第一節第一小節以 1.1.1 表示，依此類推。

圖 4-1 是一個結構完整的論文目錄範例：

TABLE OF CONTENTS

圖 4-1　長篇論文目錄示意

　　期刊論文及一般專題或報告的頁數不多，其目錄格式也較簡單，只要直接在章節標題前加數字編號即可。

　　圖 4-2 是一般期刊論文、專題或讀書報告目錄表的範例：

TABLE OF CONTENTES

ABSTRACT

KEYWORDS

1.　INTRODUCTION

2.　SYSTEM OVERVIEW

　2.1 The Front End

　2.2 System Communication

3.　SYSTEM ELEMENTS

　3.1 Application Hardware

　　3.1.1 Data Acquisition And Control Hardware

　　3.1.2 Communication Hardware

　3.2 Application Software

　　3.2.1 Data Acquisition System

　　3.2.2 Communication And Control System

4.　SYSTEM AT WORK

REFERENCES

圖 4-2　短篇論文或報告目錄示意

　　仔細檢視上兩圖例，可以看出一些規則，即：

1. 每章的開頭均在新的奇數頁。
2. 篇前部分的目次頁數以羅馬數字（I、II、III）標示，但封面、標題頁、簽名頁不用列入。
3. 論文本文章節部分的頁數以阿拉伯數字標示。
4. 標題到頁數之間通常以「…」符號連接，頁數則放置在版面最右端。
5. 論文章節的標題，第一階層不縮格，爾後每一階層均需縮格，如階層超過三層，第三層以後可視情況決定是否放入目次內。
6. 篇前及篇後的標題均不需縮格，與本文的第一階層同階。

　　另外，本書的目錄極為詳盡，完全依照上述的規則，可以用來做論文目錄的參考。

　　現在一切都有電腦代勞，以人工的方式製作目錄就變得落伍了，MS-Word 及 Openoffice[2] 中製作目錄的功能簡單易學，目錄製作完成後，即使論文的內容或頁數有所變更，有了電腦之助，重製目錄或為目錄重新編頁只是按幾下鍵盤之勞，圖目錄和表目錄亦同，實在是不可不學。

㈡ 圖形及表格目錄（List of Figures and Tables）

　　論文中的圖與表目錄應分開標示，**圖目錄**標出論文中所有圖形的標題與起始頁數，而**表目錄**則標出論文中所有表格的標題與起始頁數，圖目錄與表目錄的格式與內容目錄相同，標題如超過一行，第二行應縮格。

---

[2]　OpenOffice 與 Microsoft Office 相容，使用介面和功能也很近似，而且能在 Windows 以及其他多種作業系統上執行，是一個完全**免費**的辦公套件。本書光碟中附有完整的一套 OpenOffice.org 2.0 版，供讀者安裝使用。

圖 4-3 及 4-4 分別是圖目錄與表目錄格式的範例：

圖 4-3　圖目錄示意

LIST OF TABLES

TABLE PAGE

圖 4-4 表目錄示意

第五章
論文主體（Body）部分

本章提綱

一、緒論（Introduction）

二、本文（Main Text）

三、結論（Conclusion）

　　論文主體部分包括緒論、本文及結論，要論文有創見，作者就要有自己的見解，對於研究所得要能提出明確的證述，對於主題中研究未及之處應能指出困境與難題，進而提供可能之對策，並提出可供後續探究之方向或建議。

　　每篇論文最好專攻一個主題，如果某個主題過於龐大，不妨把它分成幾個子題，分別提出論文。

　　論文的文字敘述應力求客觀，注意連貫性，避免過度褒貶或情緒性的敘述。組織要合乎邏輯，由原因至結果，或以對照比較方式陳述，文中的論點要一一敘述清楚，寫完一個再接下一個，用讀者最容易吸收的方式由簡而繁依序排列，要想**論點有組織**，最好在寫作前把論點一一列出，作為參考。寫作時若有必要，不妨重組字、句及段落的順序，一切以合乎邏輯為要，把一個個論點當作磚頭，一塊塊往上疊，不要交叉混淆。又，各部分都可因應需要而加以分項或插入註腳。

一、緒論（Introduction）

　　論文的第一部分應該是緒論或導論，在這一部分裡應該簡單介紹該論文所要研究的方向，必要時把前人所做的類似研究作一個歸納，緒論旨在指出研究主題及其相關背景，敘述研究的過程、方法、範疇、動機與目的等，有時也可描述自己所要進行的工作與前人所做的異同，把整個論文的內容作一概略說明，如果緒論或導論的篇幅很短，可改為「前言」。

　　以下就是個精簡緒論的良好範例：

> 　　凸透鏡具有集光效果，如果要聚集大面積的光於一小點上，就需加大凸透鏡的面積，這樣一來，透鏡中間也就需要加厚，增加的厚度不但會造成透鏡的重量加大，而且透光率也會減低，在太陽能的應用上，追蹤日照方向的耗能也就增加，連日光能集光系統的結構也需要加強方能負荷，因此，若以凸透鏡來集中陽光做太陽能的應用，並不理想。
>
> 　　Fresnel 透鏡為 1822 年法國科學家 Fresnel 所發明的一種集光透鏡，真正折射光線的，並不是透鏡的厚度，而是透鏡的曲度，因此，Fresnel 的想法是，如果把凸透鏡中央的材料移除，使得透鏡只剩下薄薄的一層必然仍有集光效果，結果他的想法正確，依他的構想所發明的透鏡，便稱為 Fresnel 透鏡。
>
> 　　……
>
> 　　太陽能研究界在 1975 年前後開始對 Fresnel 透鏡的集光性質投入許多心力去研究，初期的研究專注在平面型的 Fresnel 透鏡上。

可是，對於平面型的 Fresnel 透鏡，其入射面的日光入射角是 0 度，並沒有折光效果……

　　由於幾何光學已經發展得極為完備，純粹用數學的方式已經可以精確描述光的折射行為，因此採用幾何光學來進行光線追跡（Ray tracing），可以正確分析出 Fresnel 透鏡的光學行為。

　　……計算 Fresnel 透鏡上各個稜鏡所折光角度之公式，都集中在數值近似法上，稜鏡折光之類似推導分析雖見於 W. J. Smith（1990）之作，但至今尚未有任何概括性的幾何光學公式，可以完備描述 Fresnel 集光系統的集光特性，本研究的主旨就在導出此一概括性的光學公式。

二、本文（Main Text）

　　本文是論文和研究報告的主要部分及核心所在，是詳細說明理論基礎、研究的程序和方法、使用的材料和設備之處，這些說明能夠幫助其他有意進行類似工作者重設本論文的實驗或觀察，從而取得相同的結果。

　　在實驗數據或觀察結果的解釋方面，數字類的資料可以使用統計的方式分析其相關性，亦可以用其他數學方法把它們的規則導證出來，並且應該善用圖、表、照片來增益文字的說明。

　　非數字類的資料則應該用簡潔的邏輯加以分析，拿來驗證自己的假設，如果觀察結果與學理相合或與原始假設沒有矛盾，就該用最不複雜的方式把它描述出來。其間可以穿插圖、表、公式等使論文的說明更易讓讀者了解，最後則應提供研究的結果並予以足夠的討論。

如果發現某些問題或方法會造成錯誤的結果，也應該把它們列舉出來，以免後來的人重蹈覆轍。

凡是引用他人見解或是不適合在正文中詳加說明者，皆須依序加註標號，予以註釋。

㈠ 文獻蒐集與研討（Literature Review）

學術研究是承先啟後的事業，因此，除了確定所發表的是個空前的創見以外，在我們的論文裡都應該從文獻蒐集來進入本文，作者應該在訂定研究方向後開始蒐集相關文獻，作為論文的起點。

文獻研討的目的，在於確定：

1. 前人沒有做過自己想要做的研究，或
2. 前人做過但並沒有值得一提的成果，或
3. 前人雖然研究出一些成果，但自己的研究方式能提供更具體更精確的結果。

因此文獻的蒐集的數量沒有固定的標準，但應該具有廣泛度。對於一些冷僻的學門，由於參考文獻不易取得，文獻蒐集的數量可以少一點。至於一些較熱門的學門，文獻較豐富，也就必要蒐集較可觀的數量，總之是多多益善。

下文是文獻蒐集與研討部分的一個範例：

在 1970 中期至 1980 前期，出現許多 Fresnel 透鏡的研究（Cosby 1975; Hasting et. al., 1976; 1977; Collares-Pereira 1979;

Kritchman et al., 1979; Lorenzo et. al., 1981），其中 Cosby 和 Hasting 發現，有曲度的 Fresnel 透鏡比平面型者效果為佳。

下文中蒐集了數十種參考文獻，並標出各該文獻在參考資料節裡出現的次序：

The definition of distributed-system management is the dynamic observation of a distributed computation and the use of information gained by that observation to dynamically control the computation [9]. Distributed-system observation consists of collecting runtime data from executing computations and then presenting that data in a queryable form for computation-control purposes. The purpose of the control varies and includes debugging [8, 21, 25, 35], testing [2, 17, 29, 76], computation visualization [37, 49, 51, 67, 71, 73, 89], computation steering [11, 15, 38, 58, 59, 60, 81], program understanding [72, 93, 94], fault management [57, 79], and dependable distributed com- puting [19, 69].

文獻研究的部分完成後，開始討論前人研究中有所不及的地方，從而歸納出自己要進一步探討的部分。下文是接續上文把文路轉折到自己所要研究主題的一個範例：

With various researchers' views of what constitutes a distributed system, the author arrives at a general consensus that the distributed computation is composed of multiple processes communicating via message passing. The distributed computation processes are physically distributed [97], their number may vary over time [131] and they are sequential. The requirement for sequentiality is somewhat problematic at this stage because of the prevalence of multi-threading. A multi-threading model is fundamentally a shared-memory model, which is very different from a message-passing model. This paper will concentrate in the discussion of such multi-threading model.

要把文路轉折到自己所要進行的研究工作上，可以試用下面這些類型的例句：

1. Although other research papers have reached ＿＿＿＿ conclusion, yet they have not covered ＿＿＿＿ aspects.
2. While some work has started to address this issue, the author wishes to explore two serious limitations in current methodology and define the approach to reduce the in- fluence of such limitations.
3. 這些研究者在＿＿＿＿的研究上，都採用＿＿＿＿的方式，至於 ＿＿＿＿，則至今尚未見在期刊上發表過。

為了擴充篇幅而必須增加論文字數時，一種比較技巧性的寫法，就是在文獻探討部分，將與自己論文有關的前人研究一一簡述。一旦決定如此做之後，最簡單的方法，就是取來各該文獻的摘要，將之濃縮改寫，然後一一植入文獻探討的章節裡，這樣一來，不但可以相當大幅地增加論文的篇幅，也可以省去讀者一些自行查閱的功夫，可謂一舉兩

得。

　　下例**原始文獻摘要**欄中所引述的是某論文的原始摘要，而**改寫後**欄中所列的，則是濃縮精簡後的文字，字數少於原文的一半，但並不減損原意，且不致流於抄襲。原文以過去式為主軸，然而，現在式及現在完成式在論文中是廣為接受的時態，因此，作者將原文中以過去式為主的寫法全部以現在式及現在完成式來取代，以中文為主要語文的研究者對這種寫法較易上手。

原始文獻摘要[1]	改寫後引入文獻探討章節之中
Light-emitting diodes (LEDs) are a potential irradiation source for intensive plant culture systems and photobiological research. They have small size, low mass, a long functional life, and narrow spectral output. In this study, we measured the growth and dry matter partitioning of 'Hungarian Wax' pepper (Capsicum annuum L.) plants grown under red LEDs compared with similar plants grown under red LEDs with supplemental blue or far-red radiation or under broad spectrum metal halide (MH) lamps. Additionally, we describe the thermal and spectral characteristics of	Brown et. al. have measured the growth and dry matter partitioning of 'Hungarian Wax' pepper (Capsicum annuum L.) plants grown under red LEDs compared with similar plants grown under red LEDs with supplemental blue or far-red radiation. Pepper biomass reduces when grown un-

---

[1] Brown, C. S., A. C. Schuerger and J. C. Sager. Growth and pho-tomorphogenesis of pepper plants under red light-emitting diodes with supplemental blue or far-red lighting. J. Amer. Soc. Hort. Sci. 1995; 120:808-813.

原始文獻摘要	改寫後引入文獻探討章節之中
these sources. The LEDs used in this study had a narrow bandwidth at half peak height (25 nm) and a focused maximum spectral output at 660 nm for the red and 735 nm for the far-red. Near infrared radiation (800 to 3000 nm) was below detection and thermal infrared radiation (3000 to 50,000 nm) was lower in the LEDs compared to the MH source. Although the red to far-red ratio varied considerably, the calculated phytochrome photostationary state (phi) was only slightly different between the radiation sources. Plant biomass was reduced when peppers were grown under red LEDs in the absence of blue wavelengths compared to plants grown under supplemental blue fluorescent lamps or MH lamps. The addition of far-red radiation resulted in taller plants with greater stem mass than red LEDs alone. There were fewer leaves under red or red plus far-red radiation than with lamps producing blue wavelengths. These results indicate that red LEDs may be suitable, in proper combination with other wavelengths of light, for the culture of plants in tightly controlled environments such as space-based plant culture systems. (265 words)	der red LEDs without blue wavelengths compared to plants grown under supplemental blue fluorescent lamps. The addition of far-red radiation results in taller plants with greater stem mass than red LEDs alone. Fewer leaves developed under red or red plus far-red radiation than with lamps producing blue wavelengths. The results of their research indicate that with proper combination of other wavelengths, red LEDs may be suitable for the culture of plants in tightly controlled environments. (118 words)

請注意，論文的主線時態必須全篇一致，免得前後失調。

以下再舉一例，示範如何適切地改寫文字，使之更為清爽易懂，藉以增益自己的作品。

原始文獻摘要[2]	改寫後引入文獻探討章節之中
Red light-emitting diodes (LEDs) are a potential light source for growing plants in spaceflight systems because of their safety, small mass and volume, wavelength specificity, and longevity. Despite these attractive features, red LEDs must satisfy requirements for plant photosynthesis and photomorphogenesis for successful growth and seed yield. To determine the influence of gallium aluminium arsenide (GaAIAs) red LEDs on wheat photomorphogenesis, photosynthesis, and seed yield, wheat (Triticum aestivum L., cv. 'USU-Super Dwarf') plants were grown under red LEDs and compared to plants grown under daylight fluorescent (white) lamps and red LEDs supplemented with either 1% or 10% blue light from blue fluorescent (BF) lamps. Compared to white light-grown	Goins et al. grow wheat under red LEDs and compare them to the wheat grown under 1) white fluorescent lamps and 2) red LEDs supplemented with blue light from blue fluo-rescent lamps. The results show that wheat grown under red LEDs alone displayed fewer subtillers and a lower seed yield compared to those grown under white light. Wheat grown under red LEDs+10% BF light

---

2 Goins G. D., N.C. Yorio, M.M. Sanwo and C.S. Brown. Photo-morphogenesis, photosynthesis, and seed yield of wheat plants grown under red light-emitting diodes (LEDs) with and without supplemental blue lighting. J. Exp. Botany 1997; v48:1407-1413.

原始文獻摘要	改寫後引入文獻探討章節之中
plants, wheat grown under red LEDs alone demonstrated less main culm development during vegetative growth through preanthesis, while showing a longer flag leaf at 40 DAP and greater main culm length at final harvest (70 DAP). As supplemental BF light was increased with red LEDs, shoot dry matter and net leaf photosynthesis rate increased. At final harvest, wheat grown under red LEDs alone displayed fewer subtillers and a lower seed yield compared to plants grown under white light. Wheat grown under red LEDs+10% BF light had comparable shoot dry matter accumulation and seed yield relative to wheat grown under white light. These results indicate that wheat can complete its life cycle under red LEDs alone, but larger plants and greater amounts of seed are produced in the presence of red LEDs supplemented with a quantity of blue light. (246 words)	had comparable shoot dry matter accumulation and seed yield relative to those grown under white light. These results indicate that wheat can complete its life cycle under red LEDs alone, but larger plants and greater amounts of seed are produced in the presence of red LEDs supplemented with a quantity of blue light. (118 words)

　　事實上，有些 SCI[3] 期刊主要是刊登文獻回顧式的論文，投稿於這類期刊時，這兩個例子所介紹的方式不失為事半功倍的寫作方法。

　　寫作文獻回顧式論文的訣竅，不外乎在文意轉折的橋段之間拿捏住

3　Science Citation Index，詳細說明請見附錄 C-1「知名的國際文獻檢索系統」。

接軌的技巧，將這些來自多方的片段文字用合乎邏輯、易於閱讀的方式組合起來。這類期刊中的論文，其主要貢獻在於幫助研究者節省論文檢索及閱讀的時間和精力，因此也有固定的讀者群，其 impact factor[4] 也不算低。以 Renewable and Sustainable Energ Reviews 為例，截至 2010 年其五年平均點數為 4.123，在能源與燃料類期刊中的排名高居第二。

㈡ 數據分析和解釋（Data Analysis）

數值性的資料如量度的結果、統計的數據等定量的資料，宜以圖或表的方式提出，數據資料的分析，可以包括座標曲線和圖表，也可以用統計學的方法找出數字間的關係。如果所得的數據支持自己的假設或證實了研究的理論，就應該把這些證據組織起來，用最清晰的邏輯方式臚列出來。

分析和解釋與數字無關的觀察資料時，要以待證的假說為基礎，觀察性資料（如型態或習性）等定性的資料應該以簡單又合乎邏輯的方式報告出來。例如，下面的報告把考察項目的性能與運作狀況簡明地列出來，沒有不相關的資料出現在報告裡，讀者不用花費不必要的時間就能掌握重點。

The only equipment in first-class condition was three ABS ball-mills with drives, feeders, etc. The mills are driven through herringbone gears by direct-connected, slow-speed electric motors. The ball-mills are 6'x 6', 5'x 5', and 5'x 6' in size. The 6'x 6' mill was in the best condition, and was located in a position where removal from the plant would not

---

4　詳細說明請見附錄 C-2「Impact Factor（影響點數）」。

be difficult.

The ITI Company, liquidators, has reduced the price on the 6'x 6' mill complete with motor, starters, apron feeder, and miscellaneous spare parts from $16,000 to $9,000.

1.圖形（**Figures**）

論文中常見的圖形包括曲線圖、示意圖、流程圖、圓形圖、長條圖等，圖中標註的符號和縮寫詞必須與正文內的一致。圖形應向中央對齊，圖形編號應使用阿拉伯數字，按各圖形在整篇論文中出現的順序編以序號：

Figure 1, Figure 2..., Figure 10, etc.

Or: Fig. 1, Fig. 2 ..., Fig. 10, etc.

或：圖 1、圖 2......、圖 10 等。

圖形也可以按其在各章出現的順序分章編號，如此一來，若在不預期的狀況下要更動論文中的圖形，只要改變該章內的圖形編號即可，避免了前述編號法中需要變動該圖後所有圖形編號的麻煩，例如：

Figure 1-1, Figure 1-2, Figure 2-4, etc.

Or: Fig. 1-1, Fig. 1-2, Fig. 2-4, etc.

或：圖 1-1、圖 1-2、圖 2-4 等。

論文篇幅較長時，甚至可以依各圖形在各節出現的順序，依各節的

序數予以編號，例如：

Figure 1.1-1, Figure 2.2-2, Figure 6.2-4, etc.

Or: Fig. 1.1-1, Fig. 2.2-2, Fig. 6.2-4, etc.

或：圖 1.1-1、圖 2.2-2、圖 6.2-4 等。

　　每一圖應有簡短貼切的圖名或標題，連同圖序號置於圖的正下方中央處，與內文之間應空一行行距。標題文字大小與內文相同，如須強調可加粗或改變字體，圖形若屬引用，須在下方註明資料來源。原則上，圖形應置於內文所提及的同一頁下方，或次頁的上方。實例如下：

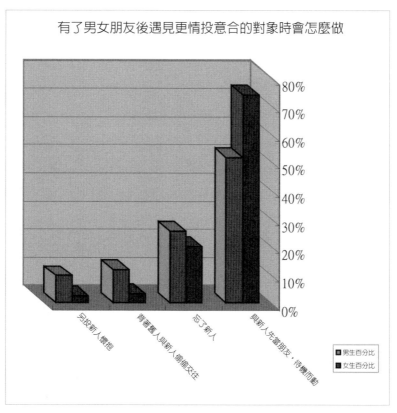

有了男女朋友後遇見更情投意合的對象時會怎麼做

資料來源：葉乃嘉，《愛情這東西你怎麼說》，紅葉出版社，2004/12。

圖 5-1　兩性愛情性向分布

　　圖形超過半頁時，可以單獨自成一頁。圖形寬度如超過頁寬，可逆時針轉九十度編排，圖形如超過一頁，可分為數個部分，並在圖形第一頁右下角註明「續下頁」（continues...）下頁的標題改為「圖 3-3（續）」、[Figure 3-3（continued）]。

2.表格（**Tables**）

　　一般的表格包括欄位和資料，欄位由左至右分類，資料從上到下依序排列。欄位標題中必須標明符號或單位，資料格內容一律填寫具體的數位元或文字，不宜出現「同上」、「同左」等詞。表格應向中央對齊，編號應使用阿拉伯數字，按各表格在整篇論文中出現的先後編以序號，例如：

Table 1, Table 2..., Table 10, etc.

Or: Tab. 1, Tab. 2..., Tab. 10, etc.

或：表 1、表 2……、表 10 等。

　　表格也可以按其在各章出現的順序分章編號，如此一來，若在不預期的狀況下要變動論文中的表格，只要改變該章內的表格編號即可，避免了前述編號法中需要變動該表格後所有表格編號的麻煩，例如：

Table 1-1, Table 1-2, Table 2-4, etc.

Or: Tab. 1-1, Tab. 1-2, Tab. 2-4, etc.

或：表 1-1、表 1-2、表 2-4 等。

　　論文篇幅較長時，甚至可依各表格在各節出現的先後，依各節的序數編號，例如：

> Table 1.1-1, Table 2.2-2, Table 6.2-4, etc.
>
> Or: Tab. 1.1-1, Tab. 2.2-2, Tab. 6.2-4, etc.
>
> 或：表 1.1-1、表 2.2-2、表 6.2-4 等。

　　每一表應有簡短貼切的標題或表格名稱，連同表序號置於表的正上方中央處，與內文之間應空一行行距。標題文字大小與內文相同，如須強調可加粗或改變字體，而表格中的文字可略小。表的欄位名稱應置中對齊，表內的數字應以個位數對齊，文字則應向左對齊。表格若引用他人資料，需在表格下方註明資料來源。原則上，表格置於內文所提及的同一頁下方，或次頁的上方。實例如下：

Table 1. Some common types of LEDs

Peak Wavelength (nm)	Color	Material and structure of LEDs	Substrate
730	far red	GaAs	GaP
700	red	GaP:Zn-O	GaP
660	red	$GaAl_{0.35}As$	GaAs
650	red	$GaAs_{0.6}P$	GaAs
630	orange-red	$GaAs_{0.35}P_{0.65}$:N	GaP
610	orange	$GaAs_{0.25}P_{0.75}$:N	GaP
590	yellow	$GaAs_{0.15}P_{0.85}$:N	GaP

Peak Wavelength (nm)	Color	Material and structure of LEDs	Substrate
585	yellow	$GaAs_{0.14}P_{0.86}:N$	GaAs
565	green	$GaP:N$	GaP
450	blue	GaN	SiC

　　表格超過半頁時可單獨自成一頁。表格寬度如超過頁寬，可逆時針轉九十度編排。表格如超過一頁，可分為數個部分，並在表格第一頁右下角註明「續下頁」（continue...）下頁的標題改如「表 2-4（續）」、[Table 2-4（continued）]。

3.計量單位與公式（Units and Equations）

　　正文中的公式、算式、方程式等，必須用阿拉伯數字編排序號，可以按各式在整篇報告出現的先後編以序號，例如：

> Equation 1, Equation 2..., Equation 10, etc.
> Or: Eq. 1, Eq. 2..., Eq. 10, etc.
> 或：式（1）、式（2）……、式（10）等。

也可以按各式在各章出現的順序分章編號，如此一來，若在不預期的狀況下要變動論文中的公式，只要改變該章內的公式編號即可，避免了前述編號法中需要變動該式之後所有公式編號的麻煩，例如：

Equation 1-1, Equation 1-2, Equation 2-4, etc.

Or: Eq. 1-1, Eq. 1-2, Eq. 2-4, etc.

或：式（1-1）、式（1-2）、式（2-4）等。

論文篇幅較長時，甚至可依各式在各節出現的先後，依各節的序數編號，例如：

Equation 1.1-1, Equation 2.2-2, Equation 6.2-4, etc.

Or: Eq. 1.1-1, Eq. 2.2-2, Eq. 6.2-4, etc.

或：式（1.1-1）、式（2.2-2）、式（6.2-4）等。

其他在書寫公式、算式、方程式時，應該注意的事項有：

千位以上的數字一律使用三位撇節號（,）。

誤：1345　　254000

正：1,345　　2,546,000

小於一的數，在小數點之前應置 0。

誤：.15　　.369

正：0.15　　0.369

長度超過一行的公式只可在運算符號處（如：+、-、*、/、<、>及 =等）換行，公式序號應標注於該式最末行的最右邊，且連續性的公式在

等號（＝）處切齊，見圖 5-2。

$$Sin2X/2nCosX= \cancel{2SinXCosX}/ \cancel{2nCosX}$$
$$= SinX/n$$
$$= Six$$
$$= 6 \qquad (Eq.\ 6.2\text{-}1)$$

圖 5-2　公式寫作格式示意圖[5]

注意：公式中單位名稱和符號的書寫方式一律採用國際通用符號。

㈢ 列舉（Listing）

內容可以分成數點來陳述時，就要使用列舉。

列舉可直接嵌在論文段落中，此稱內文列舉，也可以分段為之，此稱陳列列舉。又，以英文列舉事物的時候，可用：

> **first, second, third, last...**

也可以用：

> **firstly, secondly, thirdly, lastly....**

一旦開頭用了 firstly，為了文字的一致性，後面接的就必須是 secondly, thirdly, lastly，切不可以接用 second, third, last。而若開頭時用了 first，

5　此扭曲之公式純為幽默示意之用，勿追究其正確性。

後面接的就必須是 second, third, last，千萬不要接用 secondly, thirdly, lastly。

1. **內文列舉**：如果有數個點要在內文段落中陳述，則可以阿拉伯數字置於括號內來分隔各點，每一點若是句子，則以分號分隔，各點若非句子，則以逗號分隔，例如：

> 　　美國 Harvard Business Review 歸納出知識管理實施成功的六項法則：⑴有高層的全力支持，加上聰明的執行團隊；⑵各層級員工對知識管理的理解和支援；⑶採用正確的知識管理實施順序；⑷知識進入知識庫前由專家審核過；⑸創建評估的文化；⑹選用適當的軟硬體及適當的資訊部門人員。

2. **陳列列舉**：如果所陳述的每一點都自成段落，則各點可以用段落方式分列，並在每一段落前使用數字或符號標示，每一小點可設標題，標題可加粗，若為多階層列舉，每層應有適當的縮格，使各層能明顯區分。例如：

> 　　知識工作者有必要對自己的知識結構有所認識，對自己的知識進行分析是認識自己知識結構的方法之一，這種分析可以從知識累積及知識應用兩方面進行：
>
> 　1. 在知識累積方面，需要分析自己專業知識深度與廣度的平衡，還有自己知識及社會需求契合個人興趣的程度；在了解個人需求後，可以根據實際情況選擇資料管理的軟體平臺，一般有三種選擇：

　　⑴自建知識檔案夾以收藏資料

　　⑵使用企業知識管理系統的個性化平臺

　　⑶使用市售的知識管理平臺

2.在知識應用方面，需要分析自己對問題的解決方法，到底是能夠綜合應用不同領域的廣泛知識來求解，還是只會朝單一方向找答案。

　　陳列列舉的段落次序並不重要時，可在列舉各點前用符號（圓點或方點）代替數字，如下例：

　　知識管理不但是一個計畫，也是一個長期的持續改善的過程，缺乏長期的支持和持續的改善必然導致計畫的失敗，其他導致知識管理失敗的原因還有：

1.沒有將知識管理與企業的組織、策略和業務流程結合起來；

2.沒有形成良好的知識共享的企業文化；

3.沒有顧及用戶的需求，又缺乏技能的培訓；

4.沒有顧及管理面。

　　上例中值得注意的是，列舉的各點都以否定的「沒有」開頭，用這種一致的格式寫作，可以大大增加文字的表達強度和可讀性。

㈣ 文獻引用與註腳（Citations and Footnotes）

　　凡敘述一項事情或援引其他作者的見解時，皆須註明來源及作者姓名，引用他人的文獻──尤其是一字不漏地引用──時，不但要註明出

處，還要符合引文的格式規定。引用的句子如果不長，中文引文可直接使用引號表示他人的說法，例如：

> 「只有人類在知識創新中占據主要的地位，電腦只是一種擁有較強的資訊處理能力的工具。」
>
> ─野中郁次郎，1999

引文中的引文以雙引號『』標示，並依序交互使用單引號與雙引號。引文末之句號、驚嘆號若屬於引文的一部分，放在後引號之前；否則放在後引號之後，引文末之逗號（，）則放在後引號之後。[6]

引用他人整段或數段的文句，稱為「陳列引文」，引文段落的上下方各多空一行，並使用小一號字體，整段引文前要縮格四個字元（兩個中文字），且第一段不再縮格，引文也不用再加引號，例如：

> 知識管理結合資訊管理和學習組織的管理，旨在加強組織內部的知識運用和促進組織的整體利益，以下是兩位專家的見解：
>
> 知識管理是企業面臨不斷變化的環境時，針對組織的適應、生存和競爭力所採取的一種迎合措施，這種措施力求將科技中的資訊與資料處理能力和人的生產與創新能力結合起來。
>
> ─Yogesh Malhotra, 1998

---

[6] 西文引文之標點符號請參照第 9.2.3 節「雙引號、單引號」及第 9.2.5 節「標點間的相對位置與關係」。

> 　　知識管理是將各種來源的資訊轉化為知識，並將知識與人聯繫
> 起來的過程。知識管理是對知識進行正式的管理，以便於知識的產
> 生、獲取和重新利用。
>
> 　　　　　　　　　　　　　　　　　　　　—Daniel E. O'Leary, 1999

　　為使讀者知道一些重要項目的根據，就要註明那些項目的出處，並用一個簡明的語句予以說明。所附帶的解說若不適宜直接插入本文，就應該放在註腳裡，註腳的註標應該用阿拉伯數字，緊跟在需要註解的文字之右上方，並以全篇作一計算單位，使用同一順序，註釋則置於該頁下方。

　　註解單詞，則標註於該詞之後，註解整句，則標註於句末標點符號之前，唯註解獨立引文時放在標點後。每個直接引語一定要在註腳中說明來源，若一些事實或數種見解在同一段文章中出現，而又來自同一出處，則在該段文章下用一個註腳即可。如原文中某一項目，所提及資料來源不只一處，亦可用一項註腳寫出幾個出處。例如：

　　葉乃嘉氏曾經敘述：「管理上一般比較具體有效的激勵方式有三類：即金錢、成就感與升遷[1]。」

　　野中氏認為，一個公司真正有用的知識庫是植基於非正式的工作知識[2]，例如顧客祕書的姓名，以及與頑固的供應商打交道的方法等看似瑣碎的東西。

1　知識管理，2004。
2　野中郁次郎，1999；參看第六章「超越知識管理：日本的經驗」一節。

㈤ 再次徵引

再次徵引時可隨文註，例如：

　　許多研究者往複雜的數值模型中鑽研，卻忽略了「尺有所短，寸有所長」的單純事實，精確設計的旋轉燈組讓光照區的植物有均等機會暴露在燈組上各位置的光源之下，乃是比電腦試誤法更為簡單有效的實驗設置（見註 18）。本研究擬回歸基本面，將適切排列 LED 燈組周而復始、持續旋轉，以此方式從事植物胚性細胞形態發生的研究，因此，本提案中之迴轉燈組照具確實有不宜忽視的研究價值，不應驟然以「已有套裝軟體之模擬機制」而予以否定。

或可使用下列方式處理，例如：

1. 王叔岷：〈論校詩之難〉，《臺大中文學報》第 13 期（1979 年 12 月），頁 123。
2. 同註 1。
3. 同註 1，頁 133。
　　……
5. 那波魯堂：《學問源流》（大阪：崇高堂，寬政十一年〔1733〕刊本），頁 22 上。
6. 同註 5，頁 28 上。
7. 王叔岷：〈論校詩之難〉，頁 125。

若為西文，則用下列方式表示：

1. Patrick Hanan, "The Nature of Ling Meng-Ch'u's Fiction," in Andrew H. Plaks, ed., Chinese Narrative: Critical and Theoretical Essays (Princeton: Princeton University Press, 1977), p.89.
2. Hanan, pp. 90-110.
3. Patrick Hanan, "The Missionary Novels of Nineteenth Century China," Harvard Journal of Asiatic Studies 60/2 (December 2000): 413-443.
4. Hanan, "The Nature of Ling Meng-chu's Fiction," pp. 91-92.

採用他人的意見或解釋時，即使該項意見或解釋與我們自己想出來的完全相同，也一定要在註腳中寫明來源，其格式[7]應包括引述之著作者姓名、篇名或書名、出版地、出版者、出版年月日、卷期、及起訖頁數等，古書版本可緊標示於出版者之後。註釋中有引文時，亦應註明所引注文之出版項。

敘述每一項不屬普通常識範圍的事實，都應在註腳寫出根據，而普通常識性的事實陳述則無需在正文中引註，也不必另作註腳，例如下面的幾個陳述若出現在論文裡，作者就不必費心去尋找出處：

1. The World War II, which ended in 1945, lasted for eight years.
2. The first man landed on the Moon in 1969.
3. Ostrich is the biggest bird on earth.
4. Scientist are paying more attention at the greenhouse effect.

---

[7] 請參考第 6.1 節「參考文獻表」。

原則上，出現在內文或腳註中的參考文獻都應登錄在參考資料或書目中（Reference 或 Bibliography）[8]，以示對該資料著作者及著作權的尊重。

三、結論（Conclusion）

在論文最後一節需要附上一個簡要的結論，把研究結果簡單歸納一遍，扼要敘述研究報告的重點，闡明研究的價值所在，說明作者有什麼具體的發現，對更進一步了解現有的學說有什麼具體的貢獻，還可提出研究期間所發現的問題、遭遇的困難及解決的方法，或提出此次研究之不足。結論中也宜提出未來在相關研究上可繼續進行的工作，供自己或後來者在進一步探索類似主題時思考或參考，因為研究事業本來就是一種承先啟後的事業，為自己或他人點出未來的研究方向，不但有利於學術研究的傳承，也是任何研究工作中很重要的一環。

身為作者要能設身處地想一想，讀者閱讀後能否清楚這篇論文在講些什麼，而明確的結論能再次點出論文要傳達的意思，因此，在文末加個清楚的結論能增加論文的清晰度，結論的重要性不言可喻。**總結要明確**，別讓讀者想半天才明白全文的涵義，用一個明確的收場白來提供讀者讀後思考的方向，提醒讀者可以採取的行動。

又，切莫把不相關的東西引進來，例如：不必引述「**因九二一大地震，本研究中斷了三個月**」這種事件。

結論與摘要類似，可以使用如下的開頭：

8　見 6.1 節「參考文獻表」的寫法。

1. The principal findings of this study are...
2. The conclusion of this research shows...

然後將發現或貢獻一一列出。下面是一篇值得參考的結論範例：

This thesis provides a framework for the use of reliability composition for software component-based systems. There are five contributions of this work:

1. The use of fault blocks as the basic element of paths and the continuity of the related program domains;
2. The addition of sound sampling to the set of approaches to classifying the probabilistic correctness of domains;
3. The algorithm to generate an ongoing sequence of the domains in decreasing relevance to the program's probabilistic correctness for a given profile;
4. The application of PDFs to program analysis;
5. A description of how a component economy could be structured to utilize these techniques to make probabilistic correctness a first-class property of components.

下面這篇結論包括了對未來研究方向的建議，雖然比較長，但在篇幅較不受限的期刊論文及博士或碩士論文裡仍屬恰當：

This study show that pressure pulsing as an enhanced oil recovery technique would increase oil recovery rate by 10%. The two-fluid laboratory results as concluded in this research are as follows:

1. Pulsed tests has maximum flow rates, 2.5-3 times higher oil recovery rates, and final sweep efficiencies that were more than 10% greater than non-pulsed tests.

2. Decreasing the porosity lowers the sweep efficiencies.

3. Longer pulsed tests (reservoir-depletion tests) suffers from a limitation of the Consistent Pulsing Source (CPS). They were periodically stopped to refill the water reservoir, resulting in reservoir depressurization and lower flow rates.

4. The pulse shape changed slightly as water was removed from the reservoir.

5. The pulse pressure and period studies were limited by early tests, which did not have the necessary time duration. Both increasing pulse pressure and decreasing pulse period increase the final sweep efficiency.

6. An emulsion appears after water breakthrough when using the CPS on light oils (mineral oil). This may be the result of sharp pulses that tear apart isolated oil ganglia for earlier studies that used hammer pulsing, where the pulse was not as strong or sharp, did not cause emulsion.

The followings are the author's recommendations for future work:

7. To eliminate both the reservoir depressurization problem and the

shift in pulse shape, an improvement in current CPS design is necessary in order to accommodate water level changes within the reservoir.

8. More experiments are necessary for the pulse period and pulse pressure studies. This is an important topic that the current study has only touched on.

9. It is possible that variations in pulse shape have an effect on the oil emulsification. More studies are necessary to find what causes the emulsification of light oils.

論文不需要華麗的形容詞，也不需要不具科學意義的修飾性文字，只要抓住重點，在結論裡要一一檢視論文中所提出的假設，檢出不正確的假設而加以揚棄，證明為有價值的假設可以暫時接受，以待更進一步研究，同時，也要適當解釋各該假設之取捨如何影響以前所討論的理論。以下是幾個合適的中英範例。其一：

The results of this research lead to a number of areas for future research.

Research into the changing risk and return profile of the venture capital industry as a result of the shift to Internetrelated investments can provide insight into changes in the structure and profitability of the venture capital industry. Extending the study to include more investments in different economic periods can help to confirm or refute the findings of the study. In particular, further research into the importance of technology- related considerations in the investment decision and the related impact on investment performance is warranted.

In addition, further research into developing valid and reliable tools for assessing the technologies and technological capabilities of new ventures may benefit venture capitalists.

These tools can also benefit entrepreneurs seeking venture capital.

其二：

The findings of this study suggest a number of areas for future research:

1. The changing risk and return profile of the venture capital industry as a result of the shift to Internet-related investments can provide insight into changes in the structure and profitability of the venture capital industry.

2. Extending the study to include more investments in different economic periods can help to confirm or refute the findings of the study.

3. Further research into developing valid and reliable tools for assessing the technologies of new ventures may benefit venture capitalists. These tools could also benefit entrepreneurs seeking venture capital.

其三：

　　本研究所設計之模式，其模擬結果較數值模式所模擬的結果更為貼近實測值，其中模擬所得的集光峰值僅為實測峰值之 1.23 倍，就入射至集光區之輻射總量而言，模擬值與實測值之差異小於 5%，顯示本論文中此項以幾何光學為核心所設計之模式較諸數值模式更為精確。

　　揆諸理論值高於實測值之原因，主要在於本模式中未計入稜鏡材料中之缺陷，至於是否應加入其他參數以調低峰值，研究者認為，實驗中若採用不同之稜鏡，個別稜鏡之缺陷亦皆不同，實屬個別案例中無法控制之因素，並無一統一參數可以一應解決。

　　另外，模擬值之集光程度較實測值為均勻而集中的原因有下列數端：

1. 模式中之透鏡對應於光學中軸完全對稱，而由實際製程所壓製成形之透鏡則無法達到如此理想之對稱；
2. 模式中假設太陽表面發射來的輻射極為均勻，而實際上太陽表面有黑子等因素造成輻射之不均勻；
3. 模式未計入擾動氣流所造成的光散射效應；及
4. 模式中未計稜鏡材料熱脹冷縮所造成的光偏折效應。
5. 其中氣流、雲量、太陽光源之非均勻狀況及其他天候等因素，實驗所難以控制之變項，也是理論值恆優於實測值之基本原因。

　　此外，Cosby（1977）提出，通常 Fresnel 透鏡的集光峰值會隨其曲度而增加，集光的靶區也會隨著減小，在下一步研究中，本模式當然也可以用來探討此兩項議題。

第六章
論文篇後部分

本章提綱

　　一、參考文獻表（References or Bibliography）

　　二、附錄（Appendix）及索引（Index）

　　三、作者簡介（Author）的寫法

　　一般論文的篇後部分包括參考文獻表、附錄和索引，也可以在論文後面加上作者簡介。以下各節會將這幾個項目依次探討。

一、參考文獻表（References or Bibliography）

　　參考文獻表裡所列的是所有在論文中引述的著作，它提供了引用文獻的依據，也表示對被引用文獻作者的尊重，並且為讀者深入探討相關問題提供了文獻搜尋的線索。

參考文獻常用縮寫字

　　在參考資料或參考書目中有許多常用的縮寫字，這些縮寫字有英文字也有**拉丁字**，我們寫論文或報告時雖然未必用得上所有的常用縮寫字，但在閱讀別人論文時多少可能會碰到，所以我們把這些常用的縮寫字臚列於表 6-1（斜體者為**拉丁字**），以供參考。

表 6-1　參考文獻表中常用的縮寫字

anon.	作者佚名
bk. 或 *bks.*	*book(s)* 書
c. (circa)	某個日期（指大約某個日期）
cf. (confer)	比較（或用英文 *see*）
ch. 或 *chaps.*	*chapter(s)* 章
col. 或 *cols.*	*column(s)* 欄
ed.	*edit/edition* 編輯或版本
e.g.	例如（或用英文 *for example*）
enl.	擴展
et al. (et alii)	其他（數作者中可用第一作者姓名加 *et al.*）
f. 或 *ff.*	下文一頁或數頁，即所指之頁碼後數頁
Ibid. (ibidem)	在同一作品中（指上項附註已註明的作品）
id. (idem)	同上
i.e.	即（同英文 *that is*）
il. 或 *illus.*	*illustration(s)* 插圖
infra	以下（指下文所討論的）
Intro.	*introduction* 引論
l. 或 *ll*	*line(s)* 行
loc. cit. (loco citato)	前已註釋（前文已述明參考資料來源）
MS.	manuscript 手稿
n. 或 nn.	Note 註腳
n.d.	no publishing date 無法確定出版日期

n.p.	no publishing location 無法確定出版地
no publ.	no publisher 無法確定出版者
op. cit. (opera citato)	前已引用之作品（加上作者姓名表示資料來源前面已註過）
p. 或 pp.	Page(s) 頁
par. 或 pars.	Paragraph(s) 段
passim	在不同處（參考之項目在同作品中已提過數次）
pref.	preface 前言
pseud.	pseudonym 假名
pt.	part 部
q.v. (quod vide)	參看（同英文 see）
rev.	revised 已訂正
See	參看
Seq. (sequentes)	下文（同英文 f. 或 ff.）
supra.	以上（該項目上文已討論過）
tr. 或 trans.	translator/translation 譯者或譯文
vide.	參看（同英文 see）
Vol. 或 vols.	volume(s) 卷或冊數

　　無論用英文或拉丁字縮寫，在同一論文的參考資料或參考書目中定要前後一致，即，若已在前文中用了「**see**」就應一路用到底，不應在後文中改用「***cf.***」、「***confer***」或其他同義字。

參考文獻排序方式

　　英文參考文獻可按照兩種方式列出，其一是以資料在論文中出現的先後次序排列，此時資料應予編號，以利在內文中引用。

1. Cortada, James W. & Woods, J. A., "The Knowledge Management Yearbook," 1999-2000, Butterworth- Heinemann, 1999.
2. Davenport T., D. De Long, and M. Beer, "Successful Knowledge Management Projects," Sloan Management Review, Winter, pp. 43-57, 1998.
3. Broadbent, Marianne, "The Phenomenon of Knowledge Management: what does it mean to the information pro- fession," Information Outlook, Vol. 5, 1998, pp. 23-36.

　　參考文獻若以在論文中出現的先後次序排列，在內文中引用時只要標出編號即可：

　　The distributed computation processes are physically distributed [9], their number may vary over time [13].

　　其二是以作者姓氏（若無作者則以書名）為準，按字母順序排列：

　　Broadbent, Marianne, "The Phenomenon of Knowledge Management: what does it mean to the information profession," Information Outlook, Vol. 5, 1998, pp. 23-36.

Cortada, James W. & Woods, John A., "The Knowledge Management Yearbook," 1999-2000, Butterworth-Heinemann, 1999.

Davenport T., D. De Long, and M. Beer, "Successful Knowledge Management Projects," Sloan Management Review, Winter, pp. 43-57, 1998.

參考文獻若以作者姓氏字母順序排列，在內文中引用時應標出第一作者之姓氏及該資料之出版年分：

Davenport (1998) indicates....

另一種常用的格式是把文獻的出版年分接在作者之後，這種排序方式多見於理工科期刊。

Cosby, R., 1977, "The Linear Fresnel Lens: solar Optical Analysis of Error Effects," ISES-America Sec. Proceedings, Orlando, FL.

Cosby, R., 1975, "Performance, Manufacture, and Protection of Large Cylindrical Fresnel Lenses for Solar Collection, Final Report," Ball State University, Marshall Space Flight Center, NCA8-00103, Mod. No. 2.

這種格式的好處，在於當某作者有不同年分的論文同時出現在參考文獻表時，可以將之依年份次序做第二級排序，注意，文獻排序應以年

代較近者排年代較遠者在之前。

　　中文參考資料的排列方式，則是以資料在論文中出現的先後次序排列，例如：

---

1. 李開偉、許耀文，《新竹科學園區從業人員肌肉骨骼系統傷害症狀分布調查》，勞工安全衛生季刊第六期第四卷，1998，頁1-19。
2. 林桂碧，《事業單位推行員工協助方案之績效評估》，行政院勞工安全衛生委員會，臺北，2000。
3. 蔡永銘「現代安全管理」，揚智文化事業公司，臺北，1993，頁7。

　　還有，應將參考資料的出版年換算成西元：

誤：行政院勞委會勞工安全衛生研究所「半導體製造業重複性工作傷害之現場評估與改善」，IOSH85-H326，民國八十五年。

正：行政院勞委會勞工安全衛生研究所，《半導體製造業重複性工作傷害之現場評估與改善》，IOSH85-H326，1996。

參考文獻格式通則

　　參考文獻應將中、英文分開，並以筆畫及英文字母排序。參考資料的來源包括書本、期刊（分學術期刊及非學術之雜誌或報紙等），本來各有各的寫作格式，幸運的是，經過長年的演化，各類來源的寫作格式有類化的趨勢。以中文參考文獻習用之標點符號為例：

1. 書名、刊名、報紙、劇本應為《》；論文篇名、詩篇名則為〈〉，例
   如：

   ⑴《史記》
   ⑵《詩經》
   ⑶〈項羽本紀〉
   ⑷〈豳風・七月〉

2. 單指一書中某篇文章時，篇名可併入書名並用，例如：

   ⑴《史記・項羽本紀》
   ⑵《詩經・豳風・七月》

3. 篇名中之書名以「」標示，例如：

   ⑴〈論「史記・項羽本紀」〉
   ⑵〈釋「詩經・豳風・七月」〉等

4. 篇名中之篇名以『』標示，例如：

   ⑴〈評牟宗三之『心體與性體』〉
   ⑵〈評『豳風・七月』〉

5. 如篇名中的篇名還含有其他書名、篇名，則只在篇名中的篇名使用
   「」以示區別，例如：

   ⑴〈評李○○之「論史記項羽本紀」〉
   ⑵〈對張○○「評牟宗三之心體與性體」之回應〉

　　無論中西文獻來源怎麼不同，總以作者的姓名先行（姓先名後），其後依次是論文的題目、期刊（或書或其他出版品）的名稱、出版地及出版者（西文以出版者先於出版者，中文反之），然後是出版日期（西文以月先年後，中文反之），資料出現的章節及頁數列在最後。出版地、出版者以及出版日期若有不可考者，可以酌情從缺。

　　參考文獻若太多而不利閱讀或查閱，可再依其性質分類，如書籍、期刊、論文等等。各學門的參考文獻寫法可能不同，有些細部的規則非常瑣碎，有順序、字體、符號、是否加底線等等的差異，但是同一篇論文中，只可擇用一種方式，從一而終，切忌各種格式混用。

　　本書不去探討各類參考文獻的寫作格式，而僅介紹現今最廣為大家所接受的格式舉例。參考文獻格式也適用於註腳[1]，所以在撰寫論文的各章節內文時，遇到註腳處，可以參考以下的格式。

㈠專書（Books）資料

　　資料若出自書本，應該在參考資料處依照下面的方式註明：作者的姓名，其後依次是書名、出版地及出版者以及出版日期，引用書本上的資料應註明章節及頁數，例如：

1.單一作者

⑴Johnson, Gary W., "LabVIEW Graphical Programming: Practical Applications in Instrumentation and Control," New York, McGraw-Hill, 1997.

---

[1]　參照第 5.2.4 節「文獻引用與註腳」。

⑵葉乃嘉：《中英雙向翻譯新視野》，臺北：五南圖書出版公司，2007/3。

⑶葉乃嘉：《個人知識管理的第一本書》，臺北：松崗圖書公司，2007/7，頁 121-130。

2.兩位作者

⑴Wells, Lisa K. and Jeffrey Travis, "LabVIEW for Everyone, Graphical Programming Made Even Easier," New York, Prentice Hall, 1996.

⑵夏志清著，劉紹銘譯：《中國現代小說史》，香港：友聯出版社，1985，頁 21-30。

3.超過兩位作者

　　所引用的文章若有兩位以上的作者，可以把所有的作者姓名都列出來，也可以只註明第一作者的姓名，然後加 *et al.*，這種作者列名原則在資料出自任何來源時都適用，例如：

⑴Heywood, D. Ian, et al., "An Introduction to Geographical Information Systems," New York, Prentice Hall, 2000, pp. 345-348.

⑵西村天囚等：〈宋學傳來者〉，《日本宋學史》，東京：梁江堂書店，1909，上編（三），頁 22。

㈡ 論文（Paper, Thesis, and Dissertation）資料

　　論文資料有來自期刊、學術會議、論文集以及學位論文者，茲分別敘述其資料來源格式寫法如下：

1. 期刊（**Journals**）資料

　　一般期刊都要求詳細列出參考資料來源，依引用的次序排列，列出的每一項著作應包括：作者姓名、著作名稱（如篇名或書名等）、期刊名稱、版次或卷期數、出版地、出版者以及出版年月、頁碼等，因此，資料若出自期刊論文，應在參考資料處依照上面的方式註明，例如：

⑴Zwerling, C., et al., "The Efficacy of Pre-employment Drug Screening for Marijuana and Cocaine in Predicting Employ-ment Outcome," Journal of the American Medical Association, Nov. 1990, pp. 2639-2643.

⑵Logan, B. K., and Schwilke, E.W., "Drug and Alcohol Use in Fatally Injured Drinking Problems," Journal of Forensic Science, May 1996, pp. 505-510.

⑶陳漱渝：〈柏楊談魯迅〉，《國文天地》，第 7 卷第 4 期，1991，頁 26-28。

⑷子安宣邦：〈朱子「神鬼論」言說的構成──儒家的言說比較研究序論〉，《思想》792 號，東京：岩波書店，1990，頁 133。

2.學術會議論文（**Conference Papers**）資料

　　資料若出自學術會議論文，應該在參考資料處依照下面的方式註明：作者的姓名，其後依次是論文的題目、學術會議的名稱、會議地點以及會議日期等，參考資料的頁碼列在最後，例如：

　　已經出版：

⑴Kaiser, G. D., "Development of Guidance for EPA Hazard Assessments of Toxic Substances," Int'l Conf. on Modeling the Consequence of Accidental Release of HazMat, CA, USA, 1999, pp. 123-128.

　　未經（或尚未）出版：

⑵Zugman, Ruth, et al., "Classification Methodology for New Industrial Facilities Handling Hazardous Materials," presented at Int'l Conf. and Workshop on Modeling the Consequence of Accidental Release of Hazardous Materials, San Francisco, CA, USA, 1999.

3.論文集論文（**Conference Papers**）資料

　　資料若出自論文集論文，應該在參考資料處依照下面的方式註明：作者的姓名，其後依次是論文的題目、論文集的名稱、出版地及出版者、出版年月，最後是參考資料出現的頁碼，例如：

⑴Weinstein,Stanley, "Imperial Patronage in the Formation of T'ang Buddhism," in Arthur F. Wright and Denis Twitchett, eds., Perspectives on the T'ang, New Haven, Conn.: Yale University Press, 1973,

> pp. 265-306.
> ⑵郭秋勳：〈師資培訓制度的變革與展望〉，《轉型與發展：創造師範教育新風範學術研討會論文集》，彰化：彰化師範大學，2005，頁 21-36。
> ⑶伊藤漱平：〈日本『紅樓夢』之流行──幕末現代書誌的素描〉，收入古田敬一編：《中國文學──比較文學的研究》，東京：汲古書院，1986，頁 474-475。

4. 學位論文（**Thesis and Dissertation**）資料

　　資料若出自學位論文，應該在參考資料處依照下面的方式註明：作者的姓名，其後依次是論文的題目、學校及學位的名稱、出版地、出版年月及參考處之頁碼，例如：

> ⑴Zeuschner, Robert, "Analysis of the Philosophical Criticisms of northern Ch'an Buddhism," Ph.D. dissertation, University of Hawaii, 1977. pp. 165-166.
> ⑵吳宏一：《清代詩學研究》，臺北：臺灣大學中文研究所博士論文，1973，頁 20。
> ⑶藤井省三：《魯迅文學形成日中露三國近代化》，東京：東京大學中國文學研究所博士論文，1991，頁 62。

㈢技術報告（Technical Reports）資料

　　資料若出自技術性報告，應該在參考資料處註明作者的姓名、報告的題目、出版者、出版地、出版品的名稱和編號以及出版日期，章節及

頁數就列在最後，例如：

1. Yeh, Naichia, "The Site, a Decision Support System for Hazardous Waste Management," AEPCO, Inc., Rockville, MD, Tech. Rep. TR-0202, May 1990, p. 16.
2. Yeh, Naichia, "An Integrated Graphical and Textual HW Site Clean-up Management Information System," Dynamac Corp., Rockville, MD, Inside Dynamac, Vol. 6, No. 1, Winter, 1989, p. 8.

四 古籍（Antient Literature）資料

資料若出自古籍，會有下列情形：

1. 原書只有卷數，無篇章名，註明全書之版本項，例如：

(1) 〔宋〕司馬光：《資治通鑑》，〔南宋〕鄂州覆〔北宋〕刊龍爪本，約西元 12 世紀，卷 2，頁 2 上。

(2) 〔明〕郝敬：《尚書辨解》，臺北：藝文印書館，1969 年《百部叢書集成》影印《湖北叢書》本，卷 3，頁 2 上。

(3) 〔清〕曹雪芹：《紅樓夢》第一回，見俞平伯校訂，王惜時參校：《紅樓夢八十回校本》，北京：人民文學出版社，1958 年，頁 1-5。

2. 原書有篇章名者，應註明篇章名及全書之版本項，例如：

(1) 〔宋〕蘇軾：〈祭張子野文〉，《蘇軾文集》，北京：中華書局，1986 年，卷 63，頁 1943。

(2) 〔梁〕劉勰：〈神思〉，見周振甫著：《文心雕龍今譯》，北京：中華書局，1998 年，頁 248。

(3) 王業浩：〈鴛鴦塚序〉，見孟稱舜撰，陳洪綬評點：《節義鴛鴦塚嬌紅記》，收入林佰蒔主編：《全明傳奇》，臺北：天一出版社影印，出版年不詳，王序頁 3a。

3. 原書有後人作注者，例如：

(1) 〔晉〕王弼著，樓宇烈校釋：《老子周易王弼注校釋》（臺北：華正書局，1983 年），上編，頁 45。

(2) 〔唐〕李白著，瞿蛻園、朱金城校注：〈贈孟浩然〉，《李白集校注》（上），上海：上海古籍出版社，1998 年，卷 9，頁 593。

㈤ 報紙（Newspaper）資料

資料若出自報紙，應該在參考資料處註明作者的姓名、文章的題目、報紙名稱、版面以及出版日期（包括年、月、日，中西文各依其原寫作格式），例如：

1. 余國藩著，李奭學譯：〈先知・君父・纏足——狄百瑞著《儒家的問題》商榷〉，《中國時報》第 39 版〈人間副刊〉，1993 年 5 月 20-21 日。

2. Michael A. Lev, "Nativity Signals Deep Roots for Christianity in China,"Chicago Tribune [Chicago] 18 March 2001, Sec. 1, p.4.

3. 藤井省三：〈文學賞　中國系　高行健氏：言語盜逃亡極北作家〉，《朝日新聞》第 3 版，2000 年 10 月 13 日。

㈥ 網路（Internet Publications）資料

自從 1990 中期之後，Internet 席捲全球資訊網，電子媒體無可避免地成為重要的資料來源，網路上的資訊面臨隨時更新的狀態，這一次在此網站取得的資料，不知在下一次到同一網址時還是否存在，因此取材自這類媒體的資料，其參考資料的註明應加上取得日期，其他部分則與前述各節的格式雷同，以作者的姓名先行（姓先名後），其後依次是論文題目、出版者、出版日期（西文以月先年後，中文反之），並要列明網址，例如：

1. Erickson, Janet, "An SGML/HTML Electronic Thesis and Dissertation Library," draft,
   http://www.umich.edu/janete/teietd.htm, retrived 2004/2/3.
2. Fox, Edward A. et al., "Networked Digital Library of Theses and Dissertations: An International Effort Unlocking University Resources," *D-Lib Magazine* Sept. 1997. Sept. 1996 version, http://www.dlib.org/dlib/sept96/09fox.html, retrieved 2003/12/3.
3. Frappaolo, Carl, "What's Your Knowledge IQ?" The Delphi Group, http://www.delphi.com/case_stud/knowledge.htm, retrieved 2004/6/14.
4. Kipp, Neil A., "User's Guide to Electronic Theses and Dissertation Markup Language,"
   http://etd.vt.edu/ETD/ml/userguid.htm, retrived 2004/1/23.

二、附錄（Appendix）及索引（Index）

　　附錄及索引是論文中比較少受到重視的部分，尤其附錄常被視為可有可無，但是，在論文篇幅顯得薄弱的時候，附錄頗可以加厚論文的外觀。至於索引，則確實有助於檢索論文內容，在閱讀大部頭的著作時大有幫助。

㈠ 附錄的內容

　　附錄是論文主體的補充，舉凡內容冗長、不便記載於正文中，但卻與研究相關的重要資料，均可納入附錄，供讀者查閱。附錄一般包括下列內容：

1. 冗長的電腦程式；
2. 冗長的公式推導或計算過程；
3. 歷史性的文物、問卷調查內容、訪談內容原本；
4. 為閱讀方便所需之輔助性數學工作或重複性的圖表資料；
5. 任何對同專業者有參考價值的資料、對照表等。

　　附錄若超過一個，則按附錄 A、附錄 B、附錄 C……編號，附錄的格式並沒有特別的限制，可以依本書附錄的格式為之。

㈡ 索引格式

　　有些學術論著附有索引供讀者查閱，索引用於列出文件中的名詞、主題及其出現的頁碼。中文索引以筆畫少者在前，並於每一筆畫前，標示該筆畫；英文索引則依字母順序為之。索引多以兩欄的方式編排，其格式可參見本書索引。

　　在電腦工具不發達時，以人工的方式製作索引是極為費神的工作，

因此在論文中加入索引的情形不多，也無法強求。但是現在一切都有電腦代勞，MS-Word 及 OpenOffice 中製作索引的功能簡單易學，索引製作完成後，不管論文的內容或頁數怎麼變更，藉電腦之助，只要按幾下滑鼠和鍵盤，就可以為索引重新編頁，實在值得一學。

　　長篇的論文中若不加入索引，就顯得作者不夠用心，在此建議大家在論文中加入索引項目，引導風氣。

三、作者簡介（Author）的寫法

　　作者簡介部分只要介紹作者與本論文有關的學經歷，而不需要加入其他不相關的資訊，如出生年日、婚姻狀況及社會地位等，像左欄這個作者簡介的例子，就不宜出現在期刊論文上，可將之簡化如右欄：

作者簡介（原文）	作者簡介（修訂後）
Dr. ＿＿ was born on Oct. ＿, ＿＿ in ＿, Taiwan, Republic of China. He is married with three children. He received the B.S. degree from the Department of Computer Engineering in ＿＿, the M.S. degree from the Institute of Computer Engineering in ＿, and the Ph.D. degree from the Institute of Computer Science and Information Engineering in ＿, all from ＿＿ University, ＿, Taiwan.　　In ＿, he joined the ＿＿ Division	Dr. ＿＿ has a BS degree and an MS degree in Computer Engineering, and the Ph.D. degree in Computer Science and Information Engineering, all from ＿＿ University.　　Dr. ＿＿ has managed an images and graphics technology development project and participated in other projects that include software engineering

作者簡介（原文）	作者簡介（修訂後）
of the Institute for Information Industry, Taipei, Taiwan. He has joined many projects, including the research and development of software engineering environments, study of a man-machine interface, development of a desktop publishing system, and development of Chinese MS-Windows. He was a project manager for the research and development of an images and graphics technology project.　　He is now an Associate Professor at the ＿＿. His current research interests include image processing, pattern recognition, neural networks, and optical character recognition. (151 Words)	environments R&D, man-machine interface study, desktop publishing system development, and Chinese MS-Windows development.　　As an associate professor in ＿＿ University, Dr. ＿＿'s research interests include image processing, pattern recognition, neural networks, and optical character recognition. (82 word)

　　學歷方面只要介紹作者大學及學士以後的學歷，經歷方面除了現職，其他的經歷一概可免，與論文無關的頭銜和兼職也不宜納入。如果篇幅許可，可以加入自己的研究興趣，但也應以一至二項為原則。

　　像左欄這個無休無止的例子就非常過當。簡介中提到許多看似重要的頭銜，頗有炫耀的意思，既然是簡介，就應簡單扼要，不用把半生經歷都端出來，尤其是身為第二作者，若在簡介上有意無意地壓倒第一作者，其僭越程度雖不如以非主要作者而妄居第一作者之位，但還是非常不當的，大可把它改成右欄的樣子：

原簡介	修訂後
Dr. ____ was born in ____ on ____ . He received the B.S. degree from ____ University, Taipei, Taiwan, Republic of China in ____ , the M.S. degree from ____ University, U.S.A. in 19 ___ , and his Ph.D. degree from ____ University, U.S.A. in 19 ___ , all in electrical engineering. Since 19 ___ , he has been on the faculty of the Institute of ____ at National ____ University, ____ , Taiwan. From 19 ___ to 19 ___ , he was an Assistant Director and later an Associate Director of the ____ Center at ____ University. He joined the Department of ____ at ____ University in 19 ___ , acted as the Head of the Department from 19 ___ to 19 ___ , and is currently a Professor there. He serves as a consultant to several research institutes and industrial companies. His current research interests include ____ , ____ , ____ , and ____ . Dr. ____ is an Associate Editor of ____ , the International Journal of ____ , the Journal of ____ , and the ____ Journal, and was an Associate Editor of ____ Journal. He was elected as an Outstanding Talent of Information Science of the Republic of China in 19 ___ . He was the winner of the ___ th Annual Best Paper Award of the ____ of U.S.A. He obtained the ____ Outstanding Research Award and the ____ ____ , ____ Distinguished Research Awards of the ____ , Council of the ____ . He also obtained the 19 ___ Distinguished Teaching Award of the ____ . He was the winner	Dr. ____ has a BS, an MS, and a Ph.D. degree in ____ . He is a professor at ____ University and serves as a consultant to several research institutes and industries. His research interests include ___ , ____ , and ____ . As a winner of many awards in teaching and research, Dr. ____ has published over ____ papers in well-known international journals. He is a senior member of the IEEE. (68 words)

原簡介	修訂後
of the 19__ and 19__ Long Term Award for Outstanding Ph.D. and Master Thesis Supervision, the ____ Award for Ph.D. Dissertation Study Supervision, and the ____ Foundation Award for Science Research. He was also the winner of 19__ Outstanding Paper Award of the ____ Society of the ____. Dr. ____ has published more than ____ papers in well-known international journals. Dr. ____ is a senior member of the IEEE, and a member of the ____ Society, the Computing Linguistics Society of the ____, and the Medical Engineering Society of the ____. (323 words)	

下面是一篇值得參考的作者簡介範例：

> The author, Dr. ____, is an assistant professor in ____University. He holds a Ph.D. degree in Environmental Sciences. Specializing in environmental information management, Dr. ____ has managed several large-scale environmental information systems design and implementation projects for the U.S. Military and the Republic of China Environmental Protection Administration.

第七章
論文校閱與計畫書撰述

本章提綱

　一、論文的校閱

　二、論文計畫書綱要與體例

　　論文類的著述應考慮讀者的觀點、閱歷，要簡明扼要，使用普遍詞彙，用自然體例寫作，不要任意使用行話或專用術語，也不要拖泥帶水。論文除了格式正確、架構完整外，文字應力求精確、通順和流暢，寫成的文字要能就思想條理和組織仔細修正，刪去重複及累贅，避免前後矛盾。

一、論文的校閱

　　有些簡單易行的原則可以幫我們在撰寫論文或報告時，不致在文字上進退失據。這些原則是：

1. 相關資料應該經過仔細核對，務使準確無誤。

2. 研討部分是論文的主體，應該占論文或報告的主要部分。

3. 標點符號宜恰當，文章轉折宜清楚，文意必須通順且符合文法。

4. 涵蓋的項目都應該與研究的宗旨有關，一切無關的資料均應剔除，也不要光只是堆疊一些摘要或引用語。

5. 摘要、引用文字（citations）、註腳（footnotes）、參考書目及資料

的格式必須正確而且前後一致。

6. 應該提出自己對該研究主題的貢獻、分析自己見解與其他研究的異同，並舉出實證支持自己的論點。

7. 應該敘述研究過程的全貌，並對該研究所要解決的問題提出明確的結論或建議，且結論應該簡潔有力，並正確表達研究成果。

8. 若論文是對前人研究的討論或闡述，則討論中應該增添新的證據，或對現有證據的新安排方式確實比前人的舊方法更清楚。

校稿時一定要紮實審閱，遣詞用字可以依下面幾個要點多加修飾，以期更具可讀性：

不要咬文嚼字：有些人喜歡賣弄才情，在論文中偶然會引用一些成語，加些流行或其意不明的用詞，乃至放進一些自己引以為傲的「優美」文句，自信能增加文章的文藝氣質，但事實上這類文字的實用性有限，不宜出現在像論文、報告等的應用文上，因此在改寫或刪除之列。例如：

原文	修訂後
1. 國內學術界在此領域的發展亦不遑多讓[1]，成果亦多已提供國內企業於導入品質成本制時作為參考。 2. ……強調企業在提升品質的同時亦可降低成本，一改傳統高品質即高成本的迷思[2]。	1. 台灣學術界在此領域的發展成果亦多已提供台灣企業於導入品質成本制時作為參考。 2. ……強調企業在提升品質的同時，亦可降低成本，一改傳統高品質即高成本的想法。

1　「不遑多讓」在此只是沒有根據的泛論，與學術論文並不協調。

2　迷思只是 myth 的流行中譯法，「高品質即高成本」的說法不見得是一種迷思。

　　不要驟然轉變話題：就像開車急轉彎可能把乘客拋離座位，談話間突然改變話題常會讓人摸不著頭緒，論文裡的議題轉得太快也同樣讓人難以捉摸，因此在準備移開話題的時候，最好給個新的標題好讓讀者跟得上來。

　　刪除不相關的陳述：許多人寫論文的時候會來一段開場白，開場白通常只是要為論文起個頭，不見得會直接觸及論文的主題，這類的開場白在演講的時候有暖場的效果，但是在講求簡潔的論文裡就不太有必要，因此不妨把這類不相關的文字給刪掉。例如：

原文	修訂後
無線射頻辨識系統（Radio Frequency Identification, RFID）應用日漸普及。而 RFID 在導入圖書館的應用方面，目前只有使用在借還書以及書籍盤點。圖書館每學年配置預算添購書籍、雜誌給讀者閱讀，但是管理者對書籍、雜誌在館內的取閱率次數和閱讀時間仍無從得知……	無線射頻辨識系統（Radio Frequency Identification, RFID）目前在圖書館的應用上，只限於借還書及書籍盤點方面，以致管理者仍然無從得知館內書籍、雜誌的取閱率次數和閱讀時間……

　　刪除障礙性的陳述：把完成的論文朗誦一遍，如果在朗誦的過程中碰到唸起來不是很通順的文句，就該刪去或重寫，至於一些突兀而和上下文意不太相容的文句，當然可以大刀闊斧地除掉，這樣可以使整篇論文的文路更暢通，使意思表達得更平順。例如：

原文	修訂後
……使用 RFID 無線識別偵測的特性，來對圖書館的書籍、雜誌取閱次數和閱讀時間做研究和探討。未來進一步知悉讀者們的喜好，作為添購新書籍、雜誌的參考。	……使用 RFID 的特性來探討圖書館書籍、雜誌的取閱次數和閱讀時間，可以知悉讀者們的喜好，並進一步作為添購的參考。
因此進修的時間點在婚前或婚後，是否會造成已婚女性的參與在職進修的學習阻礙，值得進一步查證。	因此，在職婦女於婚前就開始進修或於婚後才開始進修，對其進修的影響有否不同，值得進一步查證。

　　此外，文章分段是一種迎合讀者心理的技術，分段良好的文章在外觀上較易吸引讀者，尤其對於比較生硬的論文式文字，更不要吝惜段落間的空行。文章分段的準則有二：

1. 在文意轉折時應該分段，
2. 要吸引讀者的注意時可以分段。

　　論文的最後需要附上一個簡要的結論，把研究結果簡單歸納一遍，扼要敘述研究報告的重點，闡明研究的價值所在，說明作者有什麼具體的發現，對更進一步了解現有的學說有什麼具體的貢獻，還可提出研究期間所發現的問題、遭遇的困難及解決的方法，或提出此次研究之不足。

　　身為作者要能設身處地想一想，讀者閱讀後能否清楚這篇論文在講些什麼，而明確的結論能再次點出論文要傳達的意思，因此，在文末加個清楚的結論能增加論文的清晰度，結論的重要性不言可喻。**總結要明確**，別讓讀者想半天才明白全文的涵義，用明確的收場白來提供讀者讀後思考的方向。

　　結論中也宜提出未來在相關研究上可繼續進行的工作，提醒讀者可以採取的行動，也供自己在進一步探索類似主題時思考或參考，因為研究事業本來就是一種承先啟後的事業，為自己或他人點出未來的研究方向，不但有利於學術研究的傳承，也是任何研究工作中很重要的一環。一旦論文具備了大綱及草稿，所有引用語都插入文中，所引用的事實與見解（無論是直接引用或摘要）亦已一一在註腳中說明，也有了一份參考書目列出了曾經參考過的文獻，這時就可以仔細就格式、文字和內容部分來檢查是否有需要修改的地方。

　　寫作者不時會有「想當然爾」的盲點，會不切實際地認為讀者要明白他們所寫的東西應該沒有問題。對於讀者的困難點，熟悉自己題材的作者有時不容易察覺，就像寫字潦草的人不見得知道別人看不懂他的筆跡，這時，就有必要請第三者來讀讀自己的文章，請他們把看不懂的部分挑出來，還要虛心接受他們的意見。

　　有兩類人士可以在校閱論文上對我們有所幫助，一是**對我們所研究的範圍有相當認識的人士**，他們能夠在內容方面提出專業的建言；二是**在經營文字上有能力的人士**，他們則能夠在文字和修辭上提供意見。

　　不論校閱者是不是該領域的專才，只要有相當的閱讀能力，任何人都可能有助於改進我們文章的品質，因為第三者不太會像作者一樣，把許多應該說明清楚的事情「想當然爾」，反而可能輕易看出作者習慣性地忽略的地方，甚至能一舉發現作者讀了好幾次也沒發覺的錯別字或文

法失誤。因此，虛心受教也是增進品質的大好方法。

㈠ 格式及文字方面的審閱要點

　　對下述文字及格式等問題的答案若是「否」，就應依照來需要修正。

---

　1. 研討部分是否占的主要部分？

　2. 文章轉折是否清楚？

　3. 不相干的資料是否已經清除？

　4. 是否文意通順、符合文法？

　5. 標點符號是否恰當？

　6. 摘要、引用文字（citations）、註腳（footnotes）、參考書目及
　　　資料的格式是否正確且前後一致？

㈡ 內容方面的審閱要點

　　檢查論文時不要同時兼顧很多問題，審閱時一次只追究一個問題才可收到最佳效果。對下述文字及內容等任何問題的答案若是「否」，就應該著手修改論文。

---

　1. 主題範圍是否確定與清楚？

　2. 主題陳述是否明白透徹？

　3. 是否切合研究大綱？

　4. 緒論是否明確？

---

5. 組織是否完備[3]？

6. 材料是否分配均衡？

7. 結論是否簡潔有力並且正確表達了研究成果？

8. 是否言之有物而不僅是引用語或摘要的彙編？

9. 有否舉出自己對該研究主題的貢獻？

10. 有否舉出實證支持自己的論點？

11. 有否舉出自己見解與其他研究的異同？

12. 若論文是對前人研究的討論或闡述，則討論中是否增添了新的實據？或對已有實據的新安排確比前人的舊方法更清楚？

　　研究的成果若能夠發表，那不但是研究成果和論文寫作能力得到肯定，同時，在往後的職業或學業方面，也可以有或多或少的幫助。

　　研究論文能否被採用發表，除了取決於論文的品質之外，作者的職稱、工作和學術水準等，雖然不是決定性的因素，但編輯審稿時還是不免會受這些因素影響。當然，投稿的藝術也占有一席之地。

　　論文投稿應該注意下面一些因素：

1. 論文稿的圖表文字是否清晰？

2. 文中體例是否統一？

3. 格式是否符合刊物的要求？

4. 稿件是否列印工整勻稱、易於閱讀？

　　在同樣條件下，編輯首先選用的，就是可以省去很多修改、排版編輯時間、而可以順利排印的文稿。

　　有的論文雖然品質高，但是不符合目標期刊的特點也不行，因此要

3　見第一篇「論文資料管理與寫作準則」。

注意，看論文的研究方向、特點和風格是否符合期刊的要求？

　　要選擇適宜自己論文的對象，就應該經常閱讀相關刊物，了解其宗旨、讀者群和主要刊登文章的類型，看它們

　1. 是理論還是應用？

　2. 是科普文章還是研究報告？

　3. 是綜述性的還是評論性的？

然後選定投稿的對象，根據其刊登文章的傾向，讓自己的稿件符合其選用範圍。

二、論文計畫書綱要與體例

　　一般研究所規定，學生在修業滿了一定的時間[4]之後，必須提出**論文計畫書**（thesis proposal）以為撰寫正式論文之雛形，而大多數機構團體在正式提撥研究經費之前，也會要求申請人提出**研究計畫書**（research plan），以為審核之依據。

　　計畫書依詳盡的程度，大致可分為兩類，一類是在正式進行研究前，或是在修業早期就提出的、具體而微的「**基本型**」，一般的研究計畫書多屬此類；另一類是在修業末期才提出的、萬事具備只欠東風的「**完備型**」，完備型的計畫書與正式畢業論文或是研究論文的寫作綱要大同小異，只是前者還缺了正式研究數據分析和結果的討論，且深度與困難度不如後者之高而已。

　　撰寫論文或研究計畫書時，首先得決定主題或範圍，沒有把主題訂好，不容易寫出清楚的論文來，因此，作者應把要探討的主題清晰地定

4　碩士生多應於擬畢業口試日六個月前，提出論文計畫書。博士生則多應於取得博士候選人資格後及提出論文口試申請前提出。

義出來，說明該研究工作的重點，最好還要說明該主題與學說學理的關係。主題應切合實際，避免空泛，同時要考慮資料蒐集的難易，並**抓住中心思想**，另外應該注意的是，我們對自己所選擇的題目要有基本的興趣及認識。

主題選定之後，就要建立論文大綱，大綱標出論文的研究方向，是論文的主軸，可以引導論文使其內容有一貫性和聯繫性，大綱旨在讓論文聚焦，在研究過程中，可以隨時斟酌損益、補充修正，視蒐集資料內容而調整。

成功的論文應該有個能凝聚論文重點的中心主旨，論文中所有其他的條件都必須為它服務，中心主旨就像是一塊磁鐵，論文的內容應該繞著它去組織，所有與主旨無關的枝節則不妨刪除。如果主旨不只一個，最好分成幾篇來寫，不然論文容易主題散亂、宗旨不明。

有些人花功夫寫好一篇論文計畫，回頭細讀時，卻發覺沒有完全表達到自己所想表達的意思，這時就要回頭探討這篇論文的目的何在，把思路理清，用一個簡單的句子把論文的主旨寫出來，然後直達重心，避免不必要的閒岔，用最短、最直接的方式達到目的。

論文計畫書的寫作有一般的模式可循，其籌備、組織等等事宜，就是本章要演繹的部分。

計畫書的內容都不外乎敘述研究題目之定義與基本假設、研究動機、背景說明與文獻綜覽、研究方法及步驟、所須設備材料、預期結果、時程安排及參考資料等等。

本撰寫綱要適用的範圍除論文計畫書外，還包括研究計畫書，甚至還觸及了正式研究的**結案報告**（Final Report），擴而充之，亦可以當作正式論文（Research Paper, Thesis, and Dissertation）的寫作架構來參考。

　　計畫書格式與內容大致應該包含以下各要項：

1. 題目（Title）
2. 摘要（Abstract）
3. 研究目的（Purpose）
4. 文獻探討（Literature Review）
5. 研究內容描述（Description）
6. 結果分析與討論（Results and Discussion）
7. 結論（Conclusion）

　　只要能清楚介紹研究的詳細內容，以上這些要項的標題可以增刪、修改或合併，其順序亦可調整。

　　建議讀者廣尋期刊或研討會論文集，以不同類型與不同研究主題之研究報告做例子，參考其寫法。為了讓讀者評量自己所選用的範本有無參考價值，以下自數個不同的來源舉了一系列的例子[5]，作為參照的依據。

　　利用本章所述的寫作**論文計畫書**的方式，將經過整理和分類的資料融會貫通，依序放入綱目內，就可以理出論文的初形。

(一) 題目（Title）

　　論文的命名力求簡單明瞭，並直接反應論文的主題。英文論文題目以不超過十五字為原則，中文論文題目可以稍長，但也應以二十字為限，在論文題目起首處不用加上「The」、「And」、「An」和「A」等冠詞，其他如「Studies on」、「Investigation on」、「Observations on」等類的字樣，徒然增加題目的長度，因此並無必要，過長的題目容易纏

---

[5] 這些例子較偏向於自然科學方面，人文科學方面可酌參第四章「實例分析」中「建議修訂」欄內的例子。

夾繞舌，令人抓不住要點。如果一般長度的題目不足以完全表達論文的主題，又為了避免題目太長太繞舌，可以在原有題目外，加上一個副題。

㈡ 摘要與關鍵詞（Abstract and Keywords）

摘要宜簡潔，一般論文計畫的摘要下限可以訂在五十至一百字，上限則訂在二百至四百字，至於長篇如博、碩士論文者，其摘要也不宜太冗長，應以五百字為限，把計畫的重點依研究的**目的**[6]、**方法**[7]、**結果**[8]三部分用一段完整的文字敘述出來。

以下是摘要的寫作例子：

寫作項目	寫作範例
點出研究目的	本論文旨在： 1. 探討各類型休閒農場資源應用現況。 2. 比較各類型休閒農場之消費者偏好之差異。 3. 探討休閒農場資源應用與消費者偏好之關聯。 4. 依照研究發現，提出供經營者在休閒農場資源規劃經營上之參考。
敘述研究方法	研究者擬將 B. Joseph Pine II 與 James H Gilmore (2003) 對經濟型態所作的分類應用在休閒農場上，將農場分成農作生產休閒農場、農物販售加工休閒農場、客製服務休閒農場及主題體驗休閒農場，研究者將往訪選定

6　說明此論文的目的或主要想解決的問題。
7　說明主要工作過程及所用的方法，所需使用的主要設備和工具等。
8　說明此研究過程的預期結果，如有可能，可以提出該結果的應用範圍和情況。

寫作項目	寫作範例
	之休閒農場與負責人，進行田野調查與深度訪談，以了解農場資源內涵，進而做現地觀察記錄，蒐集各農場資源項目、分布、狀態、使用方式等第一手資料。並將訪談結果歸納分析，以作為問卷設計參考之依據。
說明預期結果	本研究預期證明： 1.農場資源的完善與否，會是吸引消費者之主因。 2.消費者前往休閒農場後，結果若不如預期，會降低重遊意願。 　　研究結果將可供消費者參考，裨其能依個人偏好，選擇適合農場從事休閒。

　　寫作英文摘要[9]的要領與中文摘要寫作相同：

寫作項目	寫作範例
點出研究目的	The purpose of this research is to: 1. Discuss how different types of leisure farms use their resources differently 2. Compare the preferences of the customers who visit each type of farms 3. Study the relationship between the way a leisure farm uses its resource and the preferences of its customers. 4. Provide the result of this research to the farm management as a reference for better business planning.

9　由於計畫書係於正式寫作論文或執行研究計畫之前所作，故以英文寫作時應採用未來式。

寫作項目	寫作範例
敘述研究方法	This study **will apply** the economic conditions classified by B. Joseph Pine II and James H Gilmore (2003) to categorize the leisure farms as 1) Agricultural Production Farms, 2) Agricultural Processing and Vending Farms, 3) Customer Service Oriented Farms, and 4) Theme Park Farms. The researcher **will visit** the chosen farms and their management for field investigation and indepth interview so as to explore the insight of each farm's resource planning. Further, the researcher will gather the first hand information by recording onsite observations, collecting resource items as well as their distributions and utilizations in each farm. The findings **will be** concluded and analyzed to serve as the guidelines for questionair design.
說明預期結果	The research should be able to prove that: 1. A well planned resource shall be the farms' major attraction to the leisure farm goers 2. A customer's desire to revisit a farms will reduce when the farms fails his/her expectation. 　The result of this research **will be** suitable for the leisure farm goers as a reference for better vocation planning.

　　至於關鍵詞，其寫法變化不大，只要選擇計畫書中三至五個重要字詞，按英文字母或中文筆畫順序列出即可：

1. Keywords: Block Diagram Programming (BDP), Geographical Information

System (GIS), Graphical User Interface (GUI), and Real-time Data Acquisition.

2. 關鍵字：人因工程、人為疏失、行為失效。

㈢ 研究目的（Motivation and Purpose）

在此節應標出所要解決的問題（what）及要解決該問題的原因（why），詳細敘述（不見得須要依照下述的順序）：

1. 題目的重要性，

2. 選定這個題目的原因，

3. 要做些什麼，

4. 預計如何做，及

5. 希望達到的成效等等。

寫作項目	寫作範例
問題的重要性	傳統計算 Fresnel 透鏡中每一稜鏡所折射之光線角度的公式，多集中在個別稜鏡的數值近似法上（numerical approximation），稜鏡折光之類似推導分析雖見於 W. J. Smith（1990）之作，但迄今尚未見以概括性幾何光學公式來完備描述 Fresnel 透鏡集光特性之工作。因此，導證出一 **Fresnel 透鏡折光模式**，使其能接受任何不違背光學原理的設計參數，並依之計算該種透鏡之上個別稜鏡之稜鏡角及折光角度，用以探討各色光在該種透鏡下的分布情形，有其重要性。
選上此研究方向的原因或背景	由於幾何光學已經發展得極為完備，純粹用數學的方式已經可以精確描述光的折射行為，因此採用幾何光

寫作項目	寫作範例
	學來進行光線追跡（ray tracing），確實可以把 Fresnel 透鏡的光學行為正確分析出來。而且電腦工具已經發展得極為成熟且價廉，在此大力提倡太陽能源利用的資訊時代，自然宜於進行此類研究。
要做些什麼	本研究預計執行下列工作： 1. 導證出一 **Fresnel** 透鏡折光模式，使其能接受任何不違背光學原理的設計參數， 2. 並依該模式計算該種透鏡之上個別稜鏡之稜鏡角及折光角度，用以探討日光在該種透鏡下的分布情形。 3. 藉現階段已發表在國際期刊、具有信度的 Fresnel 透鏡實驗結果歸納出模擬調整參數， 4. 以經過實驗數據驗證後之電腦模式，來分析 Fresnel 透鏡下的日光分布態式。
預計如何做	本研究以幾何光學和數學的模式，結合大氣層內外太陽光譜分布和壓克力材料光透射率，將光譜切割成 22 光段，計算每一個光段透射每一個稜鏡的折射在目標區的位置和光帶寬度，其中計入了透鏡材料的透射及折射損耗，將每個光段透過每個稜鏡而折射到目標區的光帶能量加總之後，就得出了目標區的能量分布曲線。 　　另外並預計將導證出來的模式寫入電腦模擬程式，藉以分析 Fresnel 透鏡下的日光光譜分布情形，以變換透鏡曲度、稜溝大小、透鏡焦距等參數的方式，控制聚焦面上的太陽光譜分布態式，找出適合不同色光應用的最佳集光設計。

寫作項目	寫作範例
希望達到的成效	希望藉由此研究達成以下成效： 1. 把現有的應用整理並回歸到理論，同時計算出橢圓曲面式 Fresnel 透鏡上每一個稜鏡的理想角度，使 Fresnel 透鏡之製作不用再倚靠「試誤」的方式來調整稜鏡角度。 2. 發表一篇論文於相關期刊，並將成果轉移業界，作為生產精密 Fresnel 透鏡的種子，為太陽能源之利用提供一個值得發展的方向。

㈣ 相關文獻探討（Literature Review）

本節介紹別人做過的相關研究，旨在點明前人做了些什麼，也可以提出那些研究的優缺點，然後引導出自己要做的主題目，合格的研究主題可以是：

1. 別人沒做過的，
2. 為改進別人研究的缺點而作，或
3. 應用相同的方法來解決不同領域的問題。

以下引用的範例強調該研究沒有別人做過：

寫作項目	寫作範例
引言	The first Fresnel lenses are flat lenses. The design freedom of the flat lenses is more limited than that of a curved

---

10 即使只是計畫書，也要把所參考的文獻一一按需要的格式標明與列出。

寫作項目	寫作範例
	base lens because the first face incident angle in a flat lens is always zero and refraction does not occur there. The entire refraction burden for a Fresnel lens is shifted to the second face.
介紹別人做過的相關研究	During late 1970's and early 1980's, Fresnel lenses has received more attention in the field of solar energy application [1, 2, 3, 4, 5][10]. A more recent work [6] also discusses, in some details, the function and design of dome Fresnel lenses. Hasting, Cosby and their coworkers [7, 8, 9] found that the optical performance of the Fresnel lens improves when its smooth base surface is curved rather than flat.
表明前人未做過類似的研究	While the problem of arriving at an equation such that each facet making up the lens focuses in the designated absorber has previously only been solved by numerical approximation, this research will take a new approach to investigate and present the formulation of the curve based Fresnel lens system with optical geometry and ray tracing.

　　本節內容若不足以自成一節，可併入前「研究目的」節。

㈤ 研究內容描述

　　本節是全篇的重頭戲，份量較多，可以拆成幾個小節，各給予適當的標題，描述研究的假設、進行的方法及大概的研究程序與步驟，詳細介紹要做的內容

1.研究程序與步驟

　　在正式論文報告內，在這部分要詳細介紹論文所涉及的內容（如系統架構、採用的方法或模型、實驗設計、程序與步驟、雛形系統發展等）。而在計畫書階段，如果詳細的方法尚未成形，可以只寫出大概的方法，但仍以清楚明白為上。

　　在此節應詳盡描述所要做的東西，必要時可輔以圖表，可能的話也不妨介紹相關的專業知識（如：圖形識別、資料探勘、IC 製程等），以引導審閱者進入該研究領域的知識內。

　　接著要詳細介紹研究的或解決問題的方法，例如：

　(1)要發展一個系統，就要畫出其系統架構圖；

　(2)要發展程式來解決問題，就要寫下詳細的步驟或程序；

　(3)要做問卷調查，就要詳細說明問卷設計與抽樣方法；

　(4)要做實驗，就要詳細介紹實驗的條件與步驟等。

　　由於此部分所占分量極大，限於篇幅，某些內容只能以大綱的方式來舉例如下：

寫作項目	寫作範例
系統介紹	SYSTEM OVERVIEW 　1 The Front End 　2 System Communication 　3 The User Interface

寫作項目	寫作範例
系統架構圖	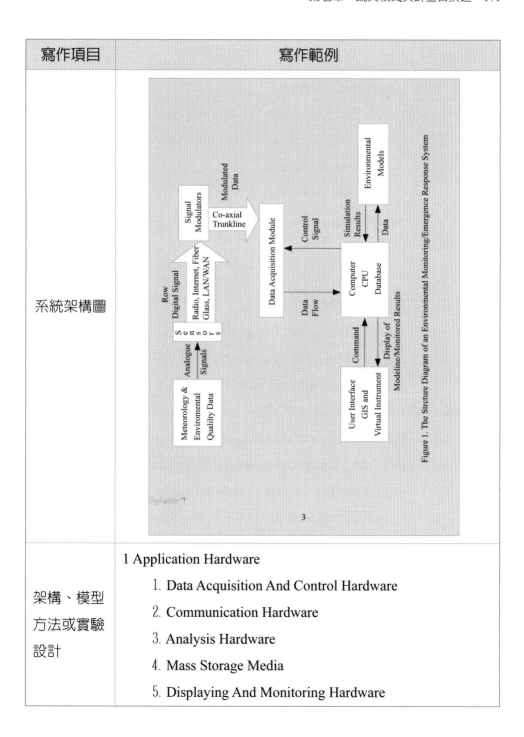
架構、模型方法或實驗設計	1 Application Hardware 　　1. Data Acquisition And Control Hardware 　　2. Communication Hardware 　　3. Analysis Hardware 　　4. Mass Storage Media 　　5. Displaying And Monitoring Hardware

寫作項目	寫作範例
	2 Application Software 　　1. Data Acquisition System. 　　2. Communication And Control System 　　3. Analysis System 　　4. Presentation System
雛形系統說明	An Environmental Monitoring/Emergence Response System (as shown in figure 1) **will consist** a system front end, a communication system, and a user interface, as described in the following overview.
系統功能說明	The system **will use** an array of sensors to collect environmental quality data. The collected data **will then be** transmitted to a node collector via radio frequency, telephone line, cable, and/or, most economically, Internet. The collector in turn **will transmit** the data via telecommunication trunkline to a node processing station. This station will organize and clean up erroneous data. The validated data **will then be** sent via trunkline to a regional computer network for compilation, display, analysis, and storage. 　　Finally, the computer network **will transmit** the compiled data to the central computer network within an environmental control center (this network simultaneously monitors the community for environmental quality). The data **will be** compiled at each regional network before transmission to the main network to avoid re-analysis of the raw data and to cut down on the volume of data sent to the central network.

此外，在本節中，研究範圍與限制的說明也不可免：

寫作項目	寫作範例
導入研究領域	The design equations of Fresnel lens **will be** incorporated with solar radiation spectrum and the refractive indices of lens materials and written into a computerized model that calculates the magnitude of each facet angle on lens to facilitate the lens production. The basic design parameters such as facet density (i.e. number of facets per unit length), lens aperture, and focal ratio can be varied systematically and the performance of each design evaluated.
研究的範圍	This research **will extend** the work of Yeh [6] and integrate ray tracing technique to formulate a complete elliptical-based Fresnel lens solar concentrating system with the intention to identify the curvature of maximum light transmission for lens performance evaluation.
限制與假設	To avoid unnecessary complication in lens design, the model **will assume** the following simplifications: 1. The height of a lens serration is negligible compared to the distance between lens top and the absorber plane. 2. The deflection of the system due to the wind loads and the thermal expansion/contraction effect is negligible. 3. All points on the solar disc have equal energy emission rate. The solar flux refracted by each single facet is uniformly distributed over the beam spread.

2. 具體工作項目與預期成果

　　具體工作項目與預期成果部分是計畫書不同於論文或其他報告的一節，在這一節中應該：

　(1)詳細列出要做的工作項目，

　(2)強調成果以突顯研究的價值，以及

　(3)說明對什麼有幫助？有什麼幫助？

寫作項目	寫作範例
預期完成之工作	本計畫以植物工廠最佳化光源參數為主要目標，著重 LED 光組設計與模擬植物最佳化光源，因此預期完成之工作項目有： (1)準備植物工廠指標作物之材料。 (2)各植物最佳紅、藍、遠紅 LED 組合光源試驗。 (3)各植物間最低光周效應時間試驗。 (4)探討各植物間最佳化紅、藍、遠紅各光度比例試驗。 (5)探討間歇閃爍照明對植物之影響。
預期成果	預期研究完成後的工作成果包括： (1)發表一篇論文於相關領域的國際期刊。 (2)參加一個數位典藏相關領域的研討會。
預期效益或貢獻	研究完成後預期獲得以下的效益： (1)設計與製造出新式 LED 燈組提供組織培養之最佳光源環境。 (2)申請一項專利，並 (3)轉移技術給相關產業。

必要時可以用甘特圖呈現計畫的時程：

時間（月） 工作項目	1	2	3	4	5	6	7	8	9	10	11	12	13	14	15	16	17	18
建構互動式三維點選系統	■	■	■															
撰寫轉換矩陣程式			■	■	■													
規劃視角程式				■	■	■	■	■										
修正最小均方及插值色彩程式						■	■	■	■	■	■	■						
測試程式、取景＋網格數貼												■	■	■	■	■		
探討均方程式對色彩修正之影響															■	■	■	
探討拍攝角度對重建品質之影響																■	■	■

圖 7-1　計畫時程甘特圖之示意

　　研究完成之後，結案報告書格式只要刪去計畫書內容中的具體工作項目與預期成果部分，並加強以下兩節的結果分析與討論部分即可。

㈥ 結果分析（Results and Discussion）

　　在結果報告或正式論文中，結果分析部分十分重要，本節主要在說明：

1. 研究得到什麼結果？
2. 用什麼分析手法？
3. 與別人做的結果比較起來如何？

　　在計畫書階段，研究結果若還不具體，則結果分析這一節就可以省略，但是，若研究已經有了初步成果，則本節可以酌情併入下一節之結論項目之下。

㈦ 結論（Conclusion and Future Works）與其他

正式結案報告、研究報告或是論文的結論，宜：

1. 重申研究的重點。
2. 指出研究結果的優點。
3. 說明研究的發現，並
4. 把缺點的部分以正向敘述的方式，置入未來可以繼續研究或改進的方向[11]。

如果只是計畫書的結論，則要只要強調該研究的重要性及目前已經做到的程度。

以下引用的範例是一個以英文寫作的結論，此結論寫得極為精簡、沒有長句和複雜的句型，只要認得單字就可以體會其中大意，屬於值得分享的佳作：

寫作項目	寫作範例
重申研究的重點	The detail optical ray tracing geometry of cylindrical curve based Fresnel lenses is the foundation of this research. The design equations provide the information about irradiance transmitting through the lens as well as concentration profile on the absorber plane. A computer program has been written according to the design formulation to illustrate details about the solar radiation distribution under the Fresnel lens concentrator.

---

[11] 意即，與其使用類似「本研究的缺點是……」的句型，不如用「未來本研究在……方面可以加強……」的句型。

寫作項目	寫作範例
強調研究的重要性	This paper lays out detailed optical ray tracing geometry of curve based Fresnel lenses to eliminate the trial-and-error in the lens design process. The design equations provide information of energy transmitting through the lens to the receiver with solar flux profile on the absorber plane. It help to achieve better lens production management via computer aided manufacturing.
研究的發現	This study has the following findings[12]: 1. The beam spread caused by the refracting prism widens as the prism location become closer to lens edge. Because a wider beam is more likely to partially miss the target, the facet width should be kept within at least one order of magnitude less than the absorber width of so that the major portion of the beam it spreads will fall within the absorber. 2. The majority of the transmission loss is incurred at the exit face of the serration. As the curvature of the lens increases, the loss becomes more apparent. 3. Cylindrical Fresnel lenses with the focal ratio falling between 0.5 and 0.7 have optimum performance and are better choices for solar concentrator systems. 4. By comparing the performance of the lenses with a variety of focal ratios, the model finds that the lens with 1.2 focal ratio tops the list of performance. The concentration profile of a lens starts to deteriorate noticeably as its focal ratio drops to below 0.9.

---

12 條列式的寫法能大量減少修辭的困擾，值得鼓勵以英文為第二語文的論文寫作者使用，因為它不但寫來比較容易，讀來也比較輕鬆，

寫作項目	寫作範例
目前達到的程度	The model determines the beam spread of radiation at each wavelength interval from each prism and the position of the beam on the focal plane. The program takes into account the transmission/refractive loss of each facet and the absorption of the lens material. Such losses are calculated for each refractive index interval. The contribution of each facet to the radiation intensity at each point on the absorber plane is summed to obtain the flux profile.
未來研究或改進的方向[13]	Some researchers like Luque and Lorenzo (1982) have found that lenses with elliptical shapes have some interesting properties. Eriksen (1982) has shown that one of them almost exactly duplicates the curvature required to achieve maximum transmission. Therefore, the next stage of this research is to explore the optical geometry of an elliptical based lens.
	Real prisms split white light into its color components and the refraction indices of the material are wavelength dependent. Therefore, in the next stage the lens design routine used in this study should be enhanced via the incorporation of
	The solar spectrum and the refractive indices of lens materials to analyze each spectral increment's chromatic aberration. Such enhancement will help to illustrate details about the solar spectrum distribution under the Fresnel lens concentrators. Also, the beam spread of radiation can be further determined at each

---

13　在計畫書階段，連目前研究都還不具體，那麼「未來研究或改進的方向」這部分自然可以省略。

寫作項目	寫作範例
	wavelength interval from each prism and the position of the beam on the focal plane in the next phase of the study. The refractive losses can be calculated for each refractive index interval as well as each facet. In addition, the contribution of each wavelength increment on the absorber plane can be treated separately to investigate the spectral distribution of the flux profile.

　　計畫書的最後要加上參考資料表,第 6.1 節「參考文獻表」提供了一般中英文參考資料表常用的格式,讀者可以參酌使用。

　　計畫書完成之後,應該就以下各點加以核校:

1. 仔細核對相關資料,務使準確無誤。

2. 研討部分乃是主體,應該占主要部分。

3. 標點符號宜恰當,文章轉折宜清楚。

4. 文意必須通順且符合文法。

5. 涵蓋的項目都應與研究的宗旨有關,無關的資料均應予剔除,也不要光只是堆疊一些摘要或引用語。

6. 摘要、引文、註腳、參考資料的格式須正確且前後一致。

7. 應該提出自己對該研究主題的貢獻、分析自己見解與其他研究的異同。

8. 應該敘述研究過程的全貌,並正確表達預期成果。

9. 對該研究所要解決的問題提出明確簡潔的討論或建議。

資源補充篇

本篇的重點在於補充前面各章的未盡事宜，敘述中文論文英譯的準則，以及提供市面中文書中可見的最完備的英文標點符號使用指南。

本 篇 大 要

第八章
論文的譯述

　　翻譯或校閱任何學門的論文，都需要對該學門有基礎以上的了解，不能率爾操觚，有些人誤認為只要找個價錢還可接受的通英文的英語國家人士，即可放心交付任務，這是絕大的謬誤，除非你自己的英文已經在水準以上，只是需要找個人來修正一般的文法錯誤，不然，這樣做可能只是自欺而已。

　　對於不熟悉的學門，譯者最好的做法是請原作者一起坐在電腦之前，邊譯邊與作者溝通其所想要表達的原意，這種做法極為繁重費時，但也是唯一負責的做法。

　　論文的翻譯絕對不要拘泥於逐字逐句的對譯，而是要以原文內容為重，因此，讀懂原文並消化之後再重新寫作的方式，除了不至於翻出中式英文或是西式中文以外，還可以加快翻譯的速度。

　　本章介紹一篇管理類論文的翻譯，供有需要英譯論文者參考。筆者順著論文中出現的瑕疵，按部就班，在註腳中詳細註解了論文寫作時應遵守的部分原則，並說明了翻譯時捨棄部分原文不譯的原因，除善盡了翻譯的責任，也在譯文中改良了論文原有的品質[1]，這一篇範例不只顧及文法的正確性，還顧到了論文的邏輯和修辭適當性，對於學習論文寫作和論文的英譯，都極有幫助。

---

[1] 當然，再好的譯者也沒有辦法從根解救論文的缺失，充其量不過是做個化妝與小針美容的工作，先天太過不足的論文是無法起死回生的。所謂 *garbage in, garbage out*，即此之謂也。

Cost of Quality Management 品質成本管理方法

原文	英譯
摘要 　　品質成本報導制（COQ, Costs of Quality）強調，藉由成本揭露與報告的模式，可以有效稽核管理品管相關作業並評估其績效，從而促成品質的經濟化與效率化，解決多年來企業無法兼顧品質與成本的困擾，因此，COQ 備受歐美產業界所重視，國內部分廠商對其亦加以注意，並且開始引進實施。本研究採實證研究的方式，調查了國內五百大製造業品質成本實施的模式及程度，得出其品質成本之 1) 制度推行現況，2)資料蒐集與彙整模式，與 3)管理體系執行現狀等調查結果，並分項探討之。	**Abstract** 　　"Cost of Quality Reporting" emphasizes that through "Cost Relevance Reporting" the quality management related operations are more suitable for the effective performance evaluation and audit management. This, in turn, helps to improve business efficiency while at the same time taking care of both the quality and the cost issues in business. The Costs of Quality (COQ)[2] system has long been recognized by the industries in Europe and the United States. Some Taiwan enterprises have also start to pay attention to COQ and its implementation. 　　This research uses the Empirical Study method to survey COQ implementation status in 500 local manufacturers. The study reveals the surveyed objects' COQ implementation status, COQ information collection and compilation as well as their COQ management system execution.

2　在使用論文專業範圍內的關鍵詞時，可在其第一次出現處用括弧將該關鍵詞之縮寫括在裡面，以利後文引用。

原文	英譯
一、前言　　在今日競爭益趨激烈的網路時代中，不僅交易模式丕變，企業管理模式與思維亦應隨之改觀，方能確保企業求創新求改進原動力的長存，而在諸多新興管理手法中，[3]「品質成本管理法」因強調企業在提升品質的同時亦可降低成本，一改傳統高品質即高成本的迷思[4]，而獲諸多歐、美企業的青睞與驗證，結果發現，企業導入品質成本後確可達成品質提升、同時降低成本的顯著成效。　　相較國外產學界多年來在實際執行品質成本制度所累積的豐富經驗，國內[5]學術界	一、**Introduction**　　Cost of Quality management system stresses that a business is able to reduce its cost without suffering a quality loss. This emphasis breaks the traditional thiniking of "high quality means high cost" and wins the hearts of many European and American enterprises.　　Internationally, there have been many researches about COQ implementations. The academia in Taiwan has also contributed local research effort in this area and has provided local enterprises with the results that can serve as references for COQ implementations. Compiled in Table 1 are the international research findings about the COQ implementation status. This research team uses questionnaire to conduct a wider and deeper

[3] 原文到此之前全是應酬性的敘述，與論文宏旨無關，不論是中文或英文，加上此段都使論文鬆散，為求紮實，盡可略去。

[4] 迷思有成為 myth 標準中譯的趨勢，誰曾經證明「高品質即高成本」的說法是一種迷思呢？如果確有所本，就該標明出處，若沒有出處，不如將「迷思」一詞改成較中立的「想法」。

[5] 「國內」或「我國」等詞屬於第一人稱，從國際化的眼光來看，應該避免，因為，在國際性的期刊及討論會中，讀者及聽眾讀到或聽到文中的「國內」，還要搞清楚文中說的到底是新加坡、臺灣、中國，還是其他使用華文的國家，故應以國家名稱代替。

原文	英譯
在此領域的發展亦不遑多讓[6]，成果亦多已提供國內企業於導入品質成本制時作為參考。表一即列示國內外產學界歷年來針對品質成本實施程度調查之結果。 二、文獻回顧 ㈠品質成本報導制之理論探討 　　本節主要將說明品質成本制的內涵與本問卷研究架構的產生背景。 　1.品質成本定義 　　吾人[7]若以消費者與生產者兩個不同的層面來看品質成本的定義，大致可區分出 Juran 的消費者觀點，以及 Morse 等人所提出生產者觀點的兩種看法，除此之外，Ortreng（1991）另提出運用附加價值的觀念，可將品質成本視為企業分配資源工具的主張，	survey regardingcurrent COQ implementation status among top 500 manufacturers in Taiwan. 二、**Literature Review** ㈠ **COQ Reporting System** 　　This section describes the contents of COQ and the structure of this questionnaire survey. 　1. **The Definition of COQ** 　　In addition to Juran's consumer aspect COQ and Morse et. al's provider aspect COQ, there is Ortreng's added value COQ. This added value COQ can be deemed as a business's tool for resource distribution. When comes to added values, except for the prevention cost that can add value to the business, all the other costs such as those induced by assessment, internal failure, and

---

6　類似「不遑多讓」等無關宏旨的泛泛評論，不宜出於學術論文之中，宜略去。

7　中文句子中的主詞往往可以省略，不用強加「吾人」這個不文不白的怪異產物。作者可能誤以為「吾人」並非第一人稱，因而用它來取代「我們」，其實「吾人」這個早就可以淘汰的怪物，產自五四白話運動時期，正是一個進退失據的第一人稱。

原文	英譯
因之，除預防成本屬於有附加價值的成本外，其餘評鑑、內部失敗，及外部失敗成本，都是無附加價值的成本。	external failure have no added value [Ortreng, 1991].
2. 品質成本的功能	2. **The Functions of COQ**
由於品質成本的功能為本研究欲驗證的主要命題之一，故在廣泛蒐集眾學者對品質成本功能的說法後，彙整而得學者認知暨品質成本功能交叉比較表（如表一所示）。本研究所歸納之多位學者認定品質成本應具有的功能，共可分為兩大構面、四項分類，本研究的目的之一，即為驗證企業導入品質成本後，是否真能顯著提升這些指標。	The research team compiled a matrix (Table1) that illustrates various researchers' understandings of COQ Functions. This matrix helps to conclude that the functions of COQ can be classified into four categories within two phases. One of the purpose of this research is to verify whether the goals in this matrix are achievable with the implementation of COQ
㈡國內品質成本問卷研究結果彙整	㈡ **The Result of Local COQ Questionnaire Survey**
問卷調查法為實證研究的一種，由於具有普遍性與一般性的特點，往往用來檢定研究對象所報導之品質成本金額之間的關聯性 [Chauvel and An-	Questionnaire Survey is often used to verify the connectivity among COQ values reported by research objects [Chauvel and Andre, 1985], [Plunkett and Dale, 1988], [Krishnamoothi,

原文	英譯
dre, 1985], [Plunkett and Dale, 1988], [Krishnamoothi1, 1989], [Ponemon, etc.[8], 1994], [Ittner,1996]，並探討這些不同的品質成本項目間是否存有相互抵換的關係，不過在這方面的實證分析尚未有一致的結果。由於本研究目的在整合現有問卷調查結果，彌補現有研究結果的不足，故本研究擬進一步詳細說明現有問卷研究之調查結果，彙整如表二所示，以作為本研究架構形成背景之說明。	1989], [Ponemon, et. al., 1994], [Ittner, 1996]. It is also used to explore whether different COQ categories are mutually substitutable, although the empirical analyses in this regard have not reached a common conclusion. This research put together the available survey results in Table 2 and aims to fill in the gap left by previous researches.
三、研究設計與方法	三、**Research Design and Method**
本節將就本研究施測工具、研究架構、問卷變數設計與抽樣方法等相關內容依序說明如下：	This section describes the tools used in this research in addition to research structure, questionnaire variable design and sampling method.
㈠施測工具	㈠ **The Survey Tool**
為配合本研究期望獲得具普遍性、一般性之影響企業	The researchers decided that question naire survey is the best tool for acquiring 1)[9]

8　論文有三名以上作者時，若只列出第一作者，應使用 *et. al.*（而非使用 etc.）以表示尚有其他作者，見表 6-1。

9　括號通常都是用一對，但在用「i, ii, iii…」、「a, b, c…」或「1, 2, 3…」等項目符號與編號分條列舉大綱或分段時，可以只放括號的右半邊「）」在各該項目符號與編號之後。

原文	英譯
實施品質成本制之主要因素，與企業實施品質成本制後所能獲得之效益的實證結果，決定採用問卷作為本研究之驗證工具。 (二)研究架構 　　為達成本研究建構企業「品質成本系統參考指標」之目的，故設計本研究架構如圖一所示。 (三)問卷變數設計 1.企業經營體質調查 　　設計此變項之目的，主要用以探討『何種企業』較易／適合導入品質成本制。而此變項之內涵，則源自於彙整 (1) 國內、外文獻資料之所得，及分析 (2) 國內相關實證研究結果而得（見表五），茲分述本研究操作化構面如下文所示： (1)資訊化程度之差異 　　此變項設計理念主要來自於國外學者[10][Sullivan, E.,	universal and general factors that affect the COQ implementation, and 2) the proof of benefits for business to implement COQ. (二) **Research Structure** 　　For the purpose of constructing a COQ System Reference Indicator, this research is structured as shown in Figure 1. (三) **Questionnaire Variable Design** 1. **Business Management Quality** 　　Business Management Quality is a variable that identifies the type of businesses fittest for COQ implementation. The contents of this variable is 1) compiled from international literatures and 2) extracted from the local empirical surveys (Shown in table 5). (1) **Informationization Extent** 　　The concept of Informationization Extent comes primarily from Sullivan

---

[10] 學術無國界，不用作此強調。

原文	英譯
1983], [Tsiakals, J.J., 1983]，提及利用電腦資訊系統，除可簡化現行會計系統流程，尚可用於協助品質成本系統之構築與導入，因此將其視為影響企業是否容易導入品質成本制的重要因子。	[1983] and Tsiakals [1983], which indicates that using computerized information system not only simplify the current accounting system workflow, but also help in COQ construction and implementation. Therefore, the informationi-zation extent is deemed an important factor that affect the COQ imple-mentation.
此操作變項之設計，主要參考國內學者[11]劉○○所提資訊系統五大發展階段予以設計：①啓始運作階段；②系統規劃階段；③系統整合階段；④網路連結階段；⑤經營革新階段〔劉○○ 1996〕[12]。	The operation variable is designed as per five development stages of an information system: ① Initial Operation Stage ② System Design Stage ③ System Integration Stage ④ Network Connection Stage ⑤ Operation and Renovation Stage
⑵ 成本會計執行系統之種類　　此變項設計理念則主要來自 Plunkett and Dale 1988 針對歐、美地區所作之論文回顧，其中特別強調「品質成本制	⑵ **Cost Accounting System Category**　　The concept of Cost Accounting System Category comes primarily from Plunkett and Dale [1988], in which the authors, after reviewing related papers published in Eu-

---

11 學術無國界，不用作此強調。

12 資訊系統五大發展階段為早已存在之理論與實務，並非始自 1996 年該學者之論文。

原文	英譯
度」實施順利與否，端視於品管部門如何與會計部門合作，針對公司既有會計系統進行適當之調整，以簡化品質成本資料之取得程序[Plunkett and Dale, 1988]。 　　至於此變項之操作化設計，則主要參考蔡○○與江○○針對管理會計系統之彈性程度所作之歸類，並參考相關成本會計文獻，將成本與管理會計系統分為〔蔡○○與江○○ 1997〕： 　①傳統成本法：包括分步、分批及標準等成本法。 　②改良式成本計算法：含括歸納、逆溯及變動等成本計算法。 　③革新型成本計算法：計有作業基礎成本制、目標成本法、生命週期法。 ⑶品管意識成熟度／TQM執行水準 　　此變項之設計，則因獲	rope and the US, emphasize that the success of COQ implementation is dependent upon how a company's QC department cooperates with its accounting department, and how they make proper adjustment to the current accounting system to simplify COQ information acquisition. 　　The operation variable is designed, primarily, as per [Tsai and Chiang, 1997], in which the authors, after reviewing cost accounting literatures, grouped the cost and the management accounting systems into the following categories: ①**Traditional Costing Methods** (e.g. Step Costing, Batch Costing, Standard Costing, etc.) ②**Improved Costing Methods** (e.g. Induction Costing, Regression Costing, and Dynamic Costing, etc.) ③**Revolution Costing Methods** (e.g. Activity Based Costing, Target Costing, Life Cycle Costing, etc.) ⑶**QC Awareness Maturity / TQM Execution Standard** QC Awareness Maturity/TQM Ex

原文	英譯
國內陳○○與邱○○二位學者的實證研究證實，品質成本與 TQM 的實施的確存在顯著的正相關，故將之置入自變項當中〔陳○○1993〕，〔邱○○1999〕。 　　因本研究尚欲區分出何種品管執行程度，方達需導入「品質成本」之需求，故又將之區分為以下兩個構面： 　　品質內在重視度：包含品質主管位階、品質意識成熟度與 TQM 執行程度。 　　品質外顯成熟度：指標包括是否通過 ISO 認證、其他系統、產品認證，以及是否獲頒品質相關獎項等。 2. 企業品質成本實施現況 　　此變項之衡量方式，主要利用 ASQC[13]協會所頒布之	ecution Standard is being used as an independent variable for it has been verified by [Chen, 1993] and [Chiou, 1999] via an empirical study, which indicates that the implementation of COQ and the execution of TQM are positively relevant. This research also aims to identify, within a company, the extent of QC execution that will call for the COQ implementation. So the variable is further divided into two phases: 　　Internal Value of Quality (including the rank of quality manager's position, the maturity of quality awareness, and the extent of TQM execution.) 　　Explicit Maturity of Quality (including whether or not pass the ISO or any other certification, whether or not awarded with quality related award) 2. **Business COQ Implementation Status** 　　The measuring of Business COQ Implementation Status is based on the

---

13 有些人動輒使用英文字縮寫，認為只要寫出來就該有人認得，事實上即使是專業人士對自己專業中使用的專用縮寫也不見得能夠完全清楚，因此，在論文中使用任何縮寫時，應該在題目、摘要或關鍵詞中至少出現一次全稱。作者雖可以自己擴充縮寫詞，但也必須在該縮寫詞第一次出現時用括弧將全稱括在裡面。若縮寫字實在很多，最好建立一個縮寫字參照表（nomenclature），以供讀者閱讀時參考。

原文	英譯
品質成本分類辦法，在列示出所有的成本項目後，並利用流程型品質成本模式預先予以歸類，再請填答者依該公司實際執行狀況，利用李氏五點量表予以填答之。	COQ classify standard issued by American Society for Quality Control (ASQC). The research team lists all the cost items and classify the items with cost of process COQ model. And then, ask the survey participants to answer the questions based on his or her company's practical execution status using a fivepoint Likert Scale.
㈣抽樣方法	㈣ **Sampling Method**
針對商業週刊所載之「1999 臺灣地區 1000 大製造業」之前五百大廠商，進行全面性的問卷普查，共發出 500 份問卷，並預定區分為以下六大產業： 1. 積體電路產業 2. 電腦周邊產業 3. 電子、電機產業 4. 塑膠、石化產業 5. 鋼鐵、機械產業 6. 汽、機車產業	The questionnaires are distributed to the top 500 manufacturers (as per Business Week's "1999 Top 1000 Manufacturers in Taiwan") for a comprehensive survey in the following six major industries: 1. Integrated Circuits 2. Computer Peripherals 3. Electrics and Electronics 4. Plastics and Petrochemicals 5. Steal and Machineries 6. Automobiles and Motorcycles
㈤資料分析方法	㈤ **Data Analysis Method**
本研究計畫使用 SPSS（Statistical Package for Social	This research uses SPSS（Statistical Package for Social Science）and Excel for

原文	英譯
Science）統計軟體與 Excel 進行分析。並以敘述性統計之方式將所蒐集到樣本廠商基本資料作整理、分析。	data analysis. The basic information gathered from the surveyed manufacturers are also compiled and analyzed with descriptive statistics.
四、研究結果	四、**Study Results**
相較國外產學界多年來在實際執行品質成本制度所累積的豐富經驗，國內產學界在此領域的成就亦不遑多讓，成果並多已提供國內企業於導入品質成本制時之參考，並於其後[14]依序說明本調查所得現今企業在品質成本制度上的實施情形，內容包括：品質成本制度之推行現況；品質成本資料之蒐集與彙整模式；品質成本管理體系之執行現狀。	The results of this study as presented in the followings include: COQ implementation status in Taiwan The patterns of COQ information gathering and compilation Current execution status of COQ management system.
㈠品質成本制度之推行現況	㈠ **COQ Implementation Status in Taiwan**
本次調查主要針對臺灣五百大企業在品質成本制度上的實施情形，其中將依序介紹：受訪廠商品質成本的實施	This research is concentrated in the study of COQ implementation status among top 500 Taiwan Enterprises. For the Surveyed businesses, this paper will discuss:

---

14 本段已在前文出現過，若欲重複，應以不同之寫法出之，不宜用寫作新聞稿充篇幅的方式原文照錄。譯文中已將此段漏去不譯。

原文	英譯
現況、品質成本制度實施目的、企業未能推行品質成本的原因、品質成本制度的推行模式、品質成本體系的主導單位、品質成本年度目標值的決定依據，以及企業推廣品質成本時對教育訓練所做的投資等項目。[15]	their COQ implementation status, their purpose for implementing COQ, their reasons for not implementing COQ, their COQ implementing patterns, the department that conduct their COQ implementation, the basis for their annual COQ goal , and the amount they invest in COQ-oriented education and trainings.
1. 汽、機車產業較為傾向實施品質成本制	Finding 1.: The automobile and motorcycle industry tops the list in implementing COQ.
表六中列示依產業別所做之品質成本實施現況之彙整結果，在所有產業回收樣本中，若以產業別來作區分，可發現汽、機車產業的廠商表現較佳，其次則為電機、電器產業以及食品、飼料生化產業，其實施率的表現亦高於一般水準，而傳統產業中的鋼鐵、水	Table 6 illustrates the COQ implementation status by industries. It shows that the automobile and motorcycle industry scores top in implementing COQ, followed by electrics and appliance group and then food, animal feed, and biochemical group. The steal, cement, and machinery group has the lowest implementation rate among traditional industries.

[15] 內容可以分成數點來陳述時，使用「列舉」的表達方式會比較清楚。如果所陳述的每一點都自成段落，則各點可以用段落方式分列，並在每一段落前使用數字或符號標示。因為論文本身有固定的難度，寫作者不妨以「文字表情」（例如較佳的版面排列、使用黑體、斜體、加底線等方式）來增加其易讀性。又，對英文較無把握者在寫作英文論文或英譯論文時，使用列舉的表達方式可以省去不少文字轉折之間的修辭困擾，值得多多考慮使用。

原文	英譯
泥與機械產業之 COQ 實施率則最低。	
2. 內部需求為企業實施 COQ 的主要動力	Finding 2.: In-house demand is the major driving force for businesses to implement COQ.
一般企業導入品質成本制的目的，不外乎為因應內部高層主管之要求、品質改善之需要、績效評估與區別成本間之等級與特性等需求，表七即列示受訪企業實際填選品質成本推行目的之彙整結果，以「對有效管理品質水準之自我要求」與「尋求製程的改善機會」占最高的填答比例，至於公司外部主管機關或單位之要求與為區別成本間之等級及特性此兩點原因，則僅有少數廠商填選。此即表示品質成本在臺灣廠商的認知當中，多為解決實際品質問題而導入，而非受外部主管機關或單位之要求，而宣稱自己有實施，此點所蘊含的深意在於：品質成本制在臺灣廠商確實有其實用價	When a business implements COQ, most likely it is trying to meet the demand from its higher management, to improve the production, to evaluate performance, or to classify the cost levels and characteristics. Table 7 lists a business's purposes for implementing COQ. Among these purposes, "to voluntarily maintain an effective management quality standard" top the list, followed by "to improve the production." "To comply with the authorities" and "to classify the cost levels and characteristics" fall on the bottom of the list. This ranking indicates that business in Taiwan implement COQ to resolve practical quality issues instead of being demanded by authorities or just wanting to claim the title of having the COQ. This finding implies that COQ system does have its practical value for Taiwan

原文	英譯
值，方能吸引廠商主動使用，未來若能克服不易導入的障礙，相信此制度將更能為一般廠商所接受。 3.「缺乏一套有系統的導入模式」為實施 COQ 的主要障礙 　　本調查針對尚未實施 COQ 之企業，調查影響其未能實施此制度所可能遭遇之阻礙（如表八所示），可發現「缺乏對此工具的了解（占 35.71%）」、「資料蒐集不易（占 33.33 %）」、「界定品質成本不易（占 30.95%）」、「缺乏有力的單位來推行此活動（占 30.95%）」以及「現有成本制度足以找出有效改善品質的方法（占 28.57%）」此五項原因，為影響品質成本制度實施的主要因素。 　　其中「缺乏對此工具的了解」、「資料蒐集不易」、	business and the acceptance of COQ is expected to increase once the implementation difficulties are overcome. Finding 3.: The primary barrier for COQ implementation is the absence of a systematic implementation mechanism. 　　Among the factors that keep a business from implementing the COQ system, as shown in Table 8, "without sufficient knowledge of COQ" top the list (35.71%), followed by "information gathering difficulty" (33.33%). Right after them, "difficulty in classifying COQ" (30.95%) and "the absence of an influential promoter" (30.95%) go side by side. Then, "current system is capable to identify effective quality improving methods" takes a share of 28.57%. Among these top five, "without sufficient knowledge of COQ," "Difficult to gather information," "difficult to classify COQ," and "the absence of an influential promoter" can be collectively placed under the category of "in need of a systematic implementation mecha

原文	英譯
「界定品質成本不易」以及「缺乏有力的單位來推行此活動」等四項理由，均可歸因於「缺乏一套有系統的導入模式」，導致企業評估導入此系統時，產生建置過程不易順利進行以及費用將甚為昂貴的判斷，再加上企業對於「現有成本制度與品質系統足以找出有效改善品質的方法」的過度自信，自然造成目前品質成本制度推行不彰的現況。	nism." For a business that is evaluating its COQ implementation feasibility, "a systematic implementation mechanism" tends to imply that the process could be problematic and the cost could be high. In addition, some businesses are impractically confident about their current system. They thought their cost and quality system is sufficient for them to identify effective quality improvement measure. To these businesses, COQ becomes a tough sale.
4. 多數企業目前仍傾向採取自行開發的方式導入品質成本制	Finding 4.: Most businesses tend to develop their COQ system in-house.
有鑑於表八中彙整樣本廠商未能實施品質成本制的原因，以「缺乏一套有具體可行的導入模式」為目前所面臨到最嚴重的問題點，而在本調查中亦針對那些宣稱已實施品質成本制度的廠商，進行該制度導入模式之現況蒐集，問卷結果如表九所示，其中	For those businesses that claim to have implemented COQ, this research surveys theirCOQ status and compiles the results in Table 9. Table 9 shows that "using a system developed in-house" takes a share of 77.78% to top the list. As for the pattern generally agreed to be more feasible, "purchasing an off-the-shelf software package," barely make the list. This finding indicates that industry and academia should be up to speed

原文	英譯
亦以「自行發展出的系統」為填答比例最高的項目（約占 77.78%），至於一般人認為較可行的導入模式「購買資訊公司所提供之套裝軟體」竟僅占全體已實施 COQ 廠商的 5.56%，再次突顯「品質成本資訊系統」的開發，實乃當前產學界責無旁貸且已刻不容緩的任務[16]。	in development of a proper COQ information system.
5. 品質成本的推行多為品管部門所主導	Finding 5.: Within a company, the unit that first carries out the COQ is usually its QC departments.
品質成本制的導入與實施就如同推行任何系統一般，在引進初期應先挑選一個單位或部門試行，待試行成熟後，方能再套用在全企業的組織與部門。根據過往學者的調查，咸認一般企業在引進階段大多由品管部門主導，由表十的彙總結果中，吾人不難發現此理論	The implementation of COQ should start small. The system should be initiated and tested within a unit or a single department in the company and not to be applied to the entire organization until it reaches its maturity. Previous researches show that QC department is usually the unit that carry out the COQ within a company. This research

---

16 「責無旁貸……刻不容緩」云云，非論文用詞，用於新聞寫作則無可厚非，用於論文則過於「濫情」，本句可改寫成「當前產學界實宜加速品質成本資訊系統」之開發工作，並已依此英譯。

原文	英譯
再次獲得證實，共有 69.44% 的已實施品質成本制樣本廠商，交由品質部門主導整個品質成本制之運作；此外，亦有 19.44% 的廠商是由會計部門負責。然而美國會計學者 Atkinson 表示[17]，品管部門與會計部門的合作仍為 COQ 的最佳推行模式，隨著品質成本制度運作的益趨成熟，會計部門即應逐步負起制度推行的重任，以確保此制度的運作效率，並融為公司整體成本管理系統中的一部分。	found that 69.44% of the businesses that have implemented COQ have their implementation conducted by QC department, which confirms the previous findings. Other than that, the accounting department, which take a share of 19.44%, has a role as well. Nevertheless, Atkinson [19＿] stated that the joint force of QC and accounting is still the best partnership for carrying out COQ. As the operation of COQ become more mature, accounting department should assume the duty to carry out the system and integrate it to the company's overall COQ so as to assure its efficiency.
6. 品質成本年度目標值仍受企業高階主管所主控	Finding 6.: COQ Annual Goal is still controlled by the company higher management.
品質成本年度目標值主要可作為品質成本管理計畫方針展開的達成目標之一，表十一顯示：國內目前因缺乏一套具公信力之品質成本年度金額標準，故在決策方式上，大多仍	COQ Annual Goal can be used as a COQ management plan measuring criterion. Among surveyed businesses, this goal is either set by their higher management (47.22% of the surveyed) or is not explicitly set (30.56% of the surveyed). This is mainly be-

---

[17] 此處宜舉出原文出處。有了出處就沒有必要加上「美國會計學者」云云，英譯部分已修正，維原文出處待填。

原文	英譯
仰賴高階主管之主觀認定（占整體已實施 COQ 受訪企業之 47.22%），或如其中的 11 家廠商一般（占整體已實施樣本之 30.56%）雖並未設立明確的年度品質成本金額目標水準，但以類似 SPC[18]管制圖的理念，套用於管理公司的品質成本上：只要品質成本推移圖表現落在合理能解釋的範圍內，就不採取改善的措施；至於較為客觀的參考同業水準，則可能因資料不易取得，導致僅有 2 家廠商使用此法（占全體之5.56%）。	cause the annual COQ amount has not been standardized in Taiwan. For those businesses that have not set their annual target, they use something similar to Statistical Process Control (SPC) charting techniques to measure their COQ. As long as the amount falls within a reasonable range, these companies will not take any measure for improvement. Only 5.56% of businesses choose to refer to the standard set by same business. That the COQ amount is considered confidential by some companies and therefore is difficult to obtain might be the reason for such a subjective method not being more widely used.
7. 企業在品質成本教育訓練的　投資仍嫌不足 　　品管大師 Dr. Juran 曾道：「品質始於教育，終於教育」，可見[19]品質的觀念實	Finding 7.: The business's investment to COQ-related training still falls at the lower end. 　　Table 12 shows that less than 60% of the surveyed businesses conduct regular

---

18 又是一個英文縮寫驟然出現的例子，請參照本文第 3.3.2 節「企業品質成本實施現況」中 ASQC 項之註腳。英譯中已修正。

19 事實的真相不會由一個人的說法就足以證明，類似「由某人的說法得知……」或「由某人的說法可見……」這類的語法，應該盡量用「某人的說法旨在表示……」、「某人的說法表達了……」或「某人的說法意在指明……」等方式取代。又，此段敘述既未引出處，又與論文的宏旨無關，英譯文中已予刪除。

原文	英譯
與教育、訓練與實踐等息息相關，由表十二中可看出目前企業在品質成本制的投資仍然不足，僅有不到六成的廠商會定期實施品質成本教育訓練，且由於受矩陣式組織管理制度之影響，制度之推行多以專案方式進行，品質成本制教育訓練之參與對象，亦僅限於各部門參與專案之人員（占30.56%）；而教育訓練之實施方式，則並未有顯著之特定方法，不論是「派員至專業單位或公司受訓（占 25%）」、「由公司內部之品管專才自行訓練（占19.44%）」以及「禮聘外界專家來公司演講授課（亦占 13.89 %）」三者之間並未存有顯著差異[20]，但相信隨著網際網路之興起，將大幅影響企業對於此制度的教育訓	COQ trainings. This means over 40% of the businesses surveyed disregard that the quality is deeply related to education and training and simply do not invest enough money in such aspect. The participants of COQ trainings are mostly limited to COQ-related project personnel (30.56%), which indicates that the industry is influenced by the concept of matrix organization management system and consider the COQ implementation a project rather than a program. The statistics also shows that among the surveyed businesses that provide their staff with COQ-related trainings, 42.86% of the them choose to have their staff trained outside by professional training organizations. The remaining two training options are both in-house, which add up to 57.14%.[21] There is a reason to believe that the web-based training will prevail as time goes by.

---

[20] 25% 與 13.89% 間之差異超過 50%，焉可謂「未存有顯著差異」？譯文中已將之除去不譯。

[21] 譯文之百分比以「定期實施品質成本教育訓練之廠商」為基底，而原文中之百分比則為以「所有受訪廠商」為基底，故兩者有所不同。

原文	英譯
練方式與比重。 (二)品質成本資料之蒐集與彙整模式 　　品質成本資料的蒐集與彙整模式，實乃決定企業導入品質成本制後，能否長久順利執行的關鍵所在，本調查即針對臺灣五百大企業中已成功實施品質成本制度之企業，依序介紹其在品質成本資料蒐集與彙整之主導部門、資料歸類方法與資料彙整之運作模式等項目上之做法，期能提供有志導入COQ廠商之參考。 1.品管部門仍多主導COQ資料蒐集與彙整 　　會計相關資料的蒐集彙整，似乎都應由會計部門主導，然而在品質成本資料上似乎不然（如表十三所示），大部分的廠商是由品管部門負責此制度的運作（占52.78%），其次方為會計部門	(二)COQ Information gathering and compilation 　　The pattern of COQ information gathering and compilation is the key that assures a business to succeed in COQ execution after its implementation. For the survey businesses that have success fully implemented COQ, this survey explore their: 1) COQ cost compilation organization, 2) COQ categorization methods, 3) COQ information compilation operation patterns. 　　Hopefully, the following findings will serve as a good reference for the business that intends to implement COQ. Finding 1.: QC department is still the leading organization that gather and compiles COQ cost information 　　As shown in Table 13, 30.56% of the surveyed companies use their accounting department to collect and compile COQ information, while for 52.78% of the businesses, their QC department is responsible for information gathering. This seems to

原文	英譯
（占 30.56%），造成如此違背常理的背後主因，不外乎是由於品質成本制度的運作，往往需要一專責單位來主導，然而在傳統會計制度中，並未含括此一領域，近來方有若干成本與管理會計學者，主張將品質成本等相關作業資訊成本，納入整體管理會計系統中，身處這種情勢下，會計部門在參與品質成本導入計畫的過程中，應即應逐步主動擔負起品質成本實施與執行的重任，以確保品質成本資訊的正確性與效率。	defy the usual practice in which the accounting department are put in charge to gather and compile cost related information. Such uncommon practice might have been caused by the reason that the area of COQ is not covered by the traditional accounting system. There have been cost and accounting specialists who suggest to integrate the information cost of the COQ-related operation within the accounting management system. This will allow the accounting department to gradually pick up the responsibility of the COQ implementation and execution so as to assure the accuracy and the efficiency of COQ information.
2. 傳統品質成本四項分類法仍為廠商彙整 COQ 資料時之主要模式	Finding 2.: The traditional COQ 4-class Classification is still the primary mechanism for compiling COQ information.
品質成本彙整模式（如表十四所示），主要會影響品質成本資料之呈現方式，若以傳統成本分類法進行資料彙整，報表將會以四個分類成本項目（預防、鑑定、內部失敗與外	How the COQ information is classified will certainly affect the way how OCQ information is presented. If the information is compiled via standard COQ classification, the report will present four cost categories (e.g. prevention, assessment, internal failure

原文	英譯
部失敗成本）作為主要成本彙集與歸類依據（91.67%），此法無疑亦為現今較普遍的做法：若以會計科目分類法區分之，則報表將以一般作業項目為主，當需要分析整體品質成本資訊時，才會再由會計資訊系統中抓出彙整項目加總；品質損失法則在強調利用製成品質資訊，建構外部失敗成本估算模式；流程品質法，則主要藉由公司整體品質作業流程的架構，在每一處的品質相關成本發生點，將品質成本予以區分為「符合成本」與「不符合成本」兩大類，最後再予以加總與彙整的成本會計制度，目前較少為被廠商使用的制度（僅占全體之 2.78%）。 3. 多數廠商仍維持有需要方從會計資訊系統中擷取 COQ 資料之做法 　　在品質成本實施模式的最後一個調查項目，則針對已	and external failure costs). This is undoubtedly the most prevailing (91.47%) method as illustrated in Table 14. If the information is classified using Accounting Subject Classification, then the report will present the general operation items. The system will retrieve and sum up the required items from accounting information system only when an overall COQ information analysis is required. Quality loss method uses product quality information to construct external failure cost estimate model. The cost of process method, which is little used (only by 2.78% of the surveyed businesses), is a cost accounting system that categorizes COQ into two classes (i.e. cost-effective and non-cost effective) via company's overall quality operation process structure. The two classes are then summed and compiled as needed at wherever the quality related costs incurs. Finding 3.: Most businesses still acquire their COQ related information from accounting information system on needed basis. 　　For the businesses that have imple-

原文	英譯
實施品質成本樣本廠商之資料彙整模式作一調查，問卷結果顯示（如表十五所示），大部分廠商由於缺乏整體的管理資訊系統與架構，仍僅能藉由會計資訊系統擷取相關資料（占27.78%），而「傳統人工報表作業」與「利用辦公室自動化套裝軟體輔助資料彙整」，則同時位居第二高位的填答項目（均占 22.22%），表示品質成本資訊系統化的步調可能必須加快，方能跟上現今資訊化與自動化的腳步。	mented COQ, Table 15 illustrates the survey results of their information compilation pattern. As shown in the table that 27.78% of the businesses surveyed have to acquire related information from accounting information system when needed. Side by side with the "traditional manual reporting operation" is "use only the office automation software for information compilation", which takes a 22.22% share and falls in the second place. Summing up these three items to reveal a fact that 72.22% of the businesses with COQ do not have an integrated management information system suitable for compiling COQ information.[22] This finding indicates that the COQ information systemization is yet an area to work on.
(三)品質成本管理體系之執行現狀	(三) **Execution Status of COQ Management System**
品質成本管理體系的好壞，實乃決定品質成本資訊在企業中扮演何種角色的關鍵因子，唯有具備良好的品質成	The quality of COQ management system is the key factor that decides the role the COQ information plays in the business. Only when a business is equipped with a

---

22 本句是譯者自加以強化論文所要表達的邏輯。

原文	英譯
本管理體系之企業，方能善用品質成本資訊，有效改善企業品質文化、降低不當浪費，以達企業競爭能力的顯著提升。因此，本調查亦針對已實施品質成本，依序調查其在舉行品質成本跨部門檢討會之間隔期間、品質成本金額比例以及導入 COQ 之關鍵成功要素等項目上的實際做法、表現與觀念，以作為企業導入品質成本後，如何提升品質成本資訊效益時之參考。	well suited COQ management system can it use the COQ information to improve the quality of business culture, cut the wasteful operation, and thereby enhance the competency. This research surveyed the businesses that have implemented COQ to identify their: interdepartmental meeting frequency COQ-to-sales ratio key success factors for COQ implementation The following findings should help business to benefit more from its COQ information.
1. 多數企業舉行 COQ 跨部門檢討會之間隔週期為「一週」 　在回收問卷的企業訪查樣本中，有 10 家（占 27.78%）表示尚未建構定期舉行跨部門會議的機制（如表十六所示），而有 18 家廠商（占全體之 50%）表示已建立「每週舉行」的機制，而根據文獻報	Finding 1.: For most COQ business, their interdepartmental COQ meeting frequency is weekly. 　Although 27.78% of the companies surveyed indicate that they have not establish a mechanism for interdepartmental COQ-related meetings, 50% of them have establish a schedule to meet weekly, if it is not an overkill. As literatures point out, monthly or weekly meetings of such kind are necessary

原文	英譯
告[23]指出，品質成本跨部門研討會，應在初期引進與推行品質成本制度的前幾年，方需一個月甚至一週即召開一次檢討會，以達落實品質成本制度之目的，然而隨著制度的逐步落實與學習效果的反映下，檢討會舉行頻率便無須如此密集，而可改為一季或半年召開一次檢討會即已足夠。	only during the first few years of COQ implementation. As the system reaches its maturity and as the learning curve of thesystem become less steep, the meeting frequency can be reduced to quarterly or semiannually. The quarterly or semiannual meetings will be sufficient to fulfill the function of COQ system.
2. 臺灣已實施 COQ 的企業在品質成本的維持上足以媲美歐美廠商的表現	Finding 2.: The COQ businesses in Taiwan perform equally well as their Europe and the US counterparts when it comes the COQ maintenance.
由於本研究進行品質成本實施現況分析的最主要目的，即是得到一「臺灣地區」品質成本分析指標之參考資料（如表十七所示），並提出與美國既有之報告數據作一比較，以分析目前臺灣廠商在品質成本制度上的表現如何。	This research has fulfill its primary objective of obtaining reference materials to serve as the COQ analysis indicator for Taiwan area business (Table 17). Via comparing the data in Taiwan with what have been reported in the US, this research also helped to find, in the COQ performance aspect, where Taiwan business stands.

---

23 應提供出處。

原文	英譯
3.「高階主管之重視與支持」為成功推行 COQ 制的不二法門	Finding 3.: Support from Higher Management is the key factor for a successful COQ Implementation.
由表十八中，可看出本研究所獲品質成本推行成功關鍵因素之分析結果，可發現「高階主管的支持（獲 171 之高分）[24]」，其次則為「各部門之配合（尤以製造部門與會計部門為主，占 163 分）」，至於眾廠商較不重視的部分，則為「具備與品質成本相關之專業知識」，表示樣本廠商之填答者多半皆已接受過「品質成本相關教育訓練」，而使樣本廠商認為專業知識避不重視的結果。	The key factors for a successful COQ-implementation is, no doubt, the support from higher management, which reaches a high score of 171. "The interdepartmental cooperation" (especially from production and accounting which incur a score of 163) is ranked the second. And "COQ related knowledge" is the factor to which businesses pay less attention.
五、結論	五、**Conclusion**
回顧本次調查結果，實不難發現目前臺灣企業對於品質成本制，不論是在重視度或	Despite the COQ research effort contributed by the academia, business in Taiwan has failed to match their European and the

---

[24] 百分比的計算方式可謂人所周知，不必多做說明，但是這些分數從何而來，在論文中卻未交代，它們只是無端出現，寫作者應該提供其計算公式或是計量標準，以資徵信。譯文中雖予譯出，但也只是履行翻譯任務，論文本身的說服力仍待原作者補強。

原文	英譯
實施程度上，均未臻歐美企業之境，審視其因不外兩點：首先，由於目前仍缺乏一套完善的品質成本導入與實施制度，方造成品質成本觀念在推廣與散播上的不便；其次，外部誘因的缺乏（諸如類似 ISO-9000 系統認證制度的建構，或是政府主管單位的鼓勵推行等），亦為品質成本制度推廣不足的主因之一，以致多年來臺灣企業始終未能對品質成本這項管理工具，能有更進一步的認識。所幸 ISO-9000 系統認證 2000 年版，已將品質經濟原則（品質成本制的一項應用）列入其指導綱要當中，雖尚未列為正式條文，但已大幅提升其能見度，此點無疑將有助於品質成本制度在臺灣的推廣，當然 COQ 的成功案例亦會穩定增加，未來品質成本制度的道路亦終將寬廣。	US counterparts in either valuing or implementing COQ system. The possible reasons are:

the absence of satisfactory COQ implementation and execution guidelines (e.g. ISO-9000) the absence of incentive (such as government funding or encouragement) It is fortunate, however, the ISO 9000 series 2000 has integrated in its guidelines, the Quality Economy System (one of the COQ applications). This inclusion has greatly enhanced the visibility of COQ and will in turn endorse the implementation of COQ in Taiwan. With the number of COQ success stories growing steadily, the future of COQ in Taiwan will sure brighten. |

第九章
數字和標點使用法

本章提綱

一、數字（Numbers）的用法

二、標點符號（Punctuations）的用法

一、數字（Numbers）的用法

論文中可能出現時的數字包括阿拉伯數字、羅馬數字及科學記號，本節介紹它們的基本處理原則。

㈠阿拉伯數字（Arabic Numbers）

到底要用阿拉伯數字或直接把數用文字寫出來？這是個困擾了許多人的問題，在英文方面，一百以下或可以用兩個以下的英文字表達出來的數字不要使用阿拉伯數字，例如：

1. two hundred balls,
2. one million people,
3. twenty cars,
4. ten thousand bottles,
5. thirty-five degrees

一百以上數字可以用阿拉伯字表示，但是在句首出現的任何數字都應該用英文字寫出，例如：

誤：150 people showed up.

正：We can feed 150 people each day.

正：One hundred and fifty people showed up.

寫序號時不宜把英文字與阿拉伯字並用，例如：

誤：Number 1

誤：Number 123

正：Number one

正：No.123（No. 中的 N 恆為大寫）

誤：Phase 2 of the project...

正：Phase two of the project...

除了西元記年以及門牌號碼之外的四位以上阿拉伯數字，均應使用三位撇節號，以利判讀。

正：Columbus discovered America in 1492.

正：My home address is 12330 Fellowship Lane.

誤：This club has over 2200 members.

正：This club has over 2,200 members.

在中文方面，完整的數字應使用阿拉伯數字，例如：

12,350 匹、3,892 人

卷、期、頁等應採用阿拉伯數字，例如：

〔宋〕蘇軾：〈祭張子野文〉，《蘇軾文集》（北京：中華書局，1986 年），卷 63，頁 1943。

以下情況可表達出來的數字不要使用阿拉伯數字：
可用兩個以下的中文字表達者，例如：

十三行、廿五個、卅三支

尾數是零且可以用三個以下的中文字表達者，或千位以上整數之數字可用中文字表示者，例如：

四千雙、十七萬條、兩千萬人、七十億筆、二億三千萬

不完整之餘數應採用中文字，如：

參加人數二百餘人

部、冊、屆、次、項等應採用中文字，如：

> 第一部、全三冊、第二屆、第五次、三項決議

其他數字使用範例如：

誤	正
故本研究進一步以國內五個助人專業學（協）會之會員一二二五[1]名為對象，以自編之四六[2]題倫理信念、行為問卷進行調查，共回收了四二三[3]份有效問卷。	故本研究進一步以國內五個助人專業學（協）會之會員 1,225[4]名為對象，以自編之 46 題倫理信念、行為問卷進行調查，共回收了 423 份有效問卷。

　　中文和阿拉伯數字間也有些不宜並用的原則，例如年、月、日、星期、序數、約數等不宜中文和阿拉伯數字並用，成語中的數字部分當然絕對不可代以阿拉伯數字。

表 9-1　中文和阿拉伯數字使用範例

誤	正
第 1 號，第 5 位	第一號，第五位
1 石 2 鳥，7 上 8 下	一石二鳥，七上八下

---

[1] 以中文表達此數字之正確方式為一千二百二十五，非一二二五。

[2] 以中文表達此數字之正確方式為四十六，四六在傳統上為二十四，正如二八年華指的乃是十六歲。

[3] 以中文表達此數字之正確方式為四百二十三，這個數字與前二註的數字均無法用兩個以下的中文字表達，故皆應改用阿拉伯數字表示。

[4] 除了西元記年以及門牌號碼之外的四位以上阿拉伯數字，均應使用三位撇節號，以利判讀。

誤	正
3 月分，星期 4	三月分，星期四
7 千，20 多萬	七千，二十多萬
有 10 多人參加 5 月 9 日的聚會	有十多人參加五月九日的聚會

數學符號也不宜在內文的描述中與文字混用，例如：

誤：該期刊文獻在當年被引用數÷該期刊當年出版文獻篇數
正：該期刊文獻在當年被引用數除以該期刊當年出版文獻篇數

在一個句中出現兩個以上的數字時，不應有些使用英文字而另一些
則用阿拉伯數字，如果有一個以上的數字超過一百，則所有的數字都應
該以阿拉伯字表示，中文和阿拉伯數字間也有相似的原則，例如：

誤	正
I have two pens, three erasers, and 10 pencils.	I have two pens, three erasers, and ten pencils.
You gave me 20 clips, 150 push-pins, and three markers.	You gave me 20 clips, 150 push-pins, and 3 markers.
我有兩枝筆、三個橡皮擦和 10 枝鉛筆。	我有兩枝筆、三個橡皮擦和十枝鉛筆。
你給了我 125 枝筆、卅個橡皮擦和十枝鉛筆。	你給了我 125 枝筆、30 個橡皮擦和 10 枝鉛筆。

　　有兩個數字相隨時，**避免同時使用**阿拉伯數字，原則上應該把較短的數字直接拚出來，若不得已，兩數之間應以逗號分開，例如：

正：Give me five 50-cent stamps.

正：Give me 5, 50-cent stamps.

誤：Give me 5 50-cent stamps.

正：We sold 200 one-litter drink today.

正：We sold 200, 1-litter drink today.

正：On August 31, 2002, 5600 people joined the parade.

　　簡單的分數應以英文表示，但若分子或分母合起來不能以兩個字以下表示時則應使用阿拉伯數字，例如：

誤：He drank 1/3 of his milk.

正：He drank one third of his milk.

誤：He has completed twenty-two twenty-fifth of his journey.

正：He has completed 22/25 of his journey.

　　所有頁碼均應使用阿拉伯數字，例如：

誤：Turn to page ten.

正：Turn to page 10.

　　寫地址時，門牌號碼除**一號**之外，其他均應使用阿拉伯數字，例

如：

One Palm Avenue	3 Main Street	71 Elm Street

　　百分比應以阿拉伯數字及百分號表示，但如百分比出現在句首則應用文字表示，例如：

誤	正
The inflation is reaching a new high of eight percent.	The inflation is reaching a new high of 8%.
30% of samples are contaminated.	Thirty percent of samples are contaminated.[5]
50% 之受試者倫理信念不正確。	1.百分之五十的受試者倫理信念不正確。 2.有 50% 之受試者倫理信念不正確。
……在信念部分，僅有一題超過五十%之受試者顯示其倫理信念不正確；在行為部分，卻有十五題超過五十%之受試者顯示曾經發生不合倫理的行為。	……在信念部分，僅有一題顯示超過 50% 之受試者其倫理信念不正確；在行為部分，則有十五題顯示超過 50% 之受試者曾經發生不合倫理的行為。

　　為了免於混淆，表示百分比區間的時候，每個百分比均要加上百分號，例如：

5　此處用複數動詞，因為 30% 暗示一百個樣品中的三十個。

> 誤：The success rate was 10 to 15%.
> 正：The success rate was 10% to 15%.

在論文中的序數、比例或計數用的數字都要用阿拉伯數字表示，例如：

> The 3rd group contains 10 rats with a 3:2 male-female ratio.

㈡ 羅馬數字（Roman Numerals）

羅馬數字是古代羅馬人創造的，西元十三世紀以前，歐洲各國幾乎都是以羅馬數字記錄數字，沿用至今，雖已式微，但仍未完全被阿拉伯數字取代。

表 11-2 列出一些羅馬數字與阿拉伯數字的對照範例。

羅馬數字的記數法則如下：

一般數字由左至右由大至小排列，例如：

> CLXVI = 100 + 50 + 10 + 5 + 1 = 166
> MMCCLXI = 1,000 + 1,000 + 100 + 100 + 50 + 10 + 1 = 2,261

表 9-2　羅馬數字與阿拉伯數字對照表[6]

羅馬數字		阿拉伯數字	羅馬數字		阿拉伯數字	羅馬數字		阿拉伯數字	羅馬數字		阿拉伯數字
I	i	1	XI	xi	11	XXI	xxi	21	C	c	100
II	ii	2	XII	xii	12	XXIX	xxix	29	CI	ci	101
III	iii	3	XIII	xiii	13	XXX	xxx	30	CC	cc	200
IV	iv	4	XIV	xiv	14	XL	xl	40	CD	cd	400
V	v	5	XV	xv	15	XLVIII	xlviii	48	D	d	500
VI	vi	6	XVI	xvi	16	IL	il	49	DC	dc	600
VII	vii	7	XVII	xvii	17	L	l	50	CM	cm	900
VIII	viii	8	XVIII	xviii	18	LX	lx	60	M	m	1000
IX	ix	9	XIX	xix	19	XC	xc	90	MDCLXVI	mdclxvi	1666
X	x	10	XX	xx	20	XCVIII	xcviii	98	MCMLXX	mcmlxx	1970

6　羅馬數字中沒有零。

若 **I**、**X** 或 **C** 接在較其為大的數字之前，則 **I**、**X** 或 **C** 之值為負：

DCCXIV = 500 + 100 + 100 + 10−1 + 5 = 717

MCMLIX = 1,000−100 + 1,000 + 50−1 + 10 = 1,959

XM = 1,000−10 = 990　　IM = 1,000−1 = 999

因此不妨把 IV, IX, XL, XC, CD, CM 等各視為一字，分別為 4, 9, 40, 90, 400, 900。

㈢ 科學記號（Scientific Notations）

報讀或書寫很大或很小的數時，有時可能會多寫或少寫一個乃至幾個位數，因此我們常把這一類的數用科學記號法表示。科學記號統一了科學數字的表示法，所有的數字都用 10 的整數乘冪紀錄，有助於多位數字的表示。

科學記號的形式如下：

$$a \times 10^n$$

其中 $1 \leqq a < 10$，因此科學記號的小數點前需要有、而且只能有一位數，例如：

誤：63.3×10^{-24}　　　　　　0.633×10^{-22}

正：6.33×10^{-23}

表 9-3 列出常用科學記號的字根、中英縮寫和實例。

表 9-3　常用科學記號的字根、中英縮寫和實例

數字	字根	縮寫	實例
10^{-18}	atto	a	
10^{-15}	femto	f	
10^{-12}	pico	p	
10^{-9}	nano	n（奈）	nm（奈米）
10^{-6}	micro	μ（微）	μm（微米）
10^{-3}	milli	m（毫）	mg（毫克）
10^{-2}	centi	c（釐）	cm（釐米）
10^{-1}	deci	d（分）	dB（分貝）
10	deka	da	
10^{2}	hecto	h	
10^{3}	kilo	k（千）	kg（千克）、km（千米）
10^{6}	mega	M（百萬）	MB（百萬位元組）
10^{9}	giga	G（十億）	GB（十億位元組）
10^{12}	tera	T（兆）	TB（兆位元組）
10^{15}	peta	P	
10^{18}	exa	E	

二、標點符號（Punctuations）的用法

標點符號的重要性可以從下面這個例子看出來：

---

1. Will you please come and see me?

2. Will you please come and see me.

3. Will you please come and see me!

三個完全相同的句子因為標點符號的不同而有了不同的語氣，第一句旨在徵詢，第二句則屬於請求，第三句就成了命令，可見標點符號的功能不能小看，以下是一般英文寫作指導書籍裡少有的、系統化的英文標點符號介紹。

英文裡常見的標點符號有十餘種，其中用在句末的標點符號有**句號**（"." period）、**問號**（"?" question mark）和**驚嘆號**（"!" exclamation mark）；用來把完整句子分開的標點符號有**逗號**（"," comma）、**分號**（";" semicolon）、**冒號**（":" colon）和**破折號**（"-" dash）；而在句子中引述或插入別的敘述時使用的標點符號有**雙引號**（" " double quote）、**單引號**（' ' single quote）、**括號** [（ ） parentheses]和**方括號**（[ ] brackets）；另外還有**連字號**（"-" hyphen），用在一行字的末端把太長的字斷開，**撇節號**（" ' " apostrophe）則除用於表示所有格之外還表示省略。

現在將上述這些標點符號舉例在下列各節中詳細解說。

㈠句號、問號、驚嘆號

句號、問號和驚嘆號（又稱嘆號）都是用在句末的標點符號。

1.句號（"." period）的用法

句號是英文裡出現得最多的標點符號，只要多加幾個句號就能改善文字的品質，也就是說，把長句分成兩個以上的短句，就能使作品更明瞭、更容易閱讀。

句號除了用在一般完整句子的句尾之外，還可以用在一些縮寫的後面，我們姑且把這種句點稱為**縮寫點**，例如：

⑴Ph.D.（Doctor of Philosophy，哲學博士）
⑵*i.e.*（拉丁文之「亦即」，that is,）
⑶*e.g.*（拉丁文之「例如」，for example）
⑷*etc.*（拉丁文之「等等」，and so on）
⑸pp.（拉丁文之「某頁～某頁」，pages,）

另有一些比較不受注意的句號用法如下：

用三個連續的句點表示刪節號，一般用在引用他人的文字時刪節部分原文之用，例如：

This ion does not... until oxygen is totally dissolved.

若刪節號用在句尾，句子的句點還是不能免，因此在句尾使用的刪節點應該有四點，例如：

> The study has concluded that coffee is a carcinogen and ....

縮寫點與句點同形，不應連在一起使用，因此使用縮寫點作為句尾時，不可在句尾多加一句點，例如：

> The experiment will last until 5 p.m.

但是如果句子收尾時所用的不是句點，而是問號、驚嘆號甚或是逗號，則可以加上各該標點符號收尾，例如：

> ⑴Will you send it by 6 p.m.?
> ⑵The appointment was at 4 p.m., but you did not show up on time!

如果與引號同用，句號永遠需要放在引號之前，例如：

> He said, "we will leave home without you."

2.問號（"?" question mark）的用法

問號除了用在問句之後外，還可以用在事實並不明顯的時候，例如：

> I suppose it is seven o'clock in the morning in the US?

　　引用他人的敘述時，若引述的是問句，則問號應置於引號之內，否則應置於引號之外，例如：

(1) The manager asked, "has he arrived?"

(2) Did the manager say, "he is late"?

3. 驚嘆號（"!" exclamation mark）的用法

　　驚嘆號是個較少使用的標點符號，它多用在驚嘆句之後，但除了真正要表達驚嘆性質的句子外，它都可以用句點取代，例如：

(1) Wait! I have one more question.

(2) It's a wonderful lake!

　　引用他人的敘述時，若引的是驚嘆句，則驚嘆號應置於引號之內，否則應置於引號之外，例如：

(1) He exclaimed, "that's wonderful!"

(2) Don't use an exclamation such as, "dog ate my homework"!

　　在驚嘆性的字或詞後面也可以用驚嘆號，例如：

(1) Oh! My god!

(2) Good heaven!

(3) Hello!

㈡ 逗號、分號、冒號、破折號

　　逗號、分號、冒號和破折號都是把完整句子分開的標點符號，在某些用法上有些類似，除破折號外，其分開的效果依逗號、分號、冒號而漸強。

1.逗號（"," comma）的用法

　　使用逗號是種比使用句點要弱的斷句方式，下列是逗號的一般用法。

　　用逗號來分開句中提到的三個（或以上的）字，片語或短句，例如：

---

(1) The three qualities of a good worker are industry, honesty, and reliability.

(2) The store carries sweet potato, green onion, and red pepper.

　　在句中直接稱呼對方的姓名時應使用逗號，例如：

---

(1) It's our pleasure, Mr. Yeh, to have you here.

(2) Yes, Gary, we will be here until 10 p.m.

　　在引述他人的句子時可用逗號，例如：

---

(1) The waiter said, "I believe this is your order."

(2) "Close that door behind you", he said.

---

(3)"Close the window," said Barnaby, "the wind is blowing away my handwork."

　　西式人名寫法以姓在後、名在前為常態，若要將「姓」寫在「名」的前面，則必須以逗點把姓名分開，反之則否，例如：

(1)Clinton, Bill
(2)Bush, George

　　逗號在引述地址、稱謂及參考資料時的用法如下：

(1)地址（街、市、州、國間須以逗號分開）：1230 Main St., Edison, TX 75240, USA.
(2)稱謂：Naichia G. Yeh, Ph.D.; George Bush, the President
(3)參考資料：volume II, chapter10, page 114
(4)日期：May 10, 2002（日與年間以逗號分隔，月與日或月與年間則否）

　　同位語應以逗號分開，例如：

(1)Mr. Barnaby Yeh, our best student, will represent the school at the ceremony.（Barnaby Yeh 和 our best student 是同一人，屬於同位語）

(2) He is Alister Yeh, our best salesman.（Alister Yeh 和 our best sales-man 是同一人，屬於同位語）

(3) The staff, not the faculty, is on strike.（The staff 和 not the faculty 是同位語）

附帶問句前應使用逗號，例如：

(1) You will call me tomorrow, won't you?

(2) He is the best man we have, isn't he?

(3) You don't have a clue, do you?

以 **as, after, although, because, since, when** 等連接詞開頭的附屬子句後要加逗號，例如：

(1) When you finish your homework, you may go out and play.

(2) Because you are under age, you may not drink.

(3) Although I have a driver's license, I don't drive in Taipei.

以 **certainly, indeed, no, oh, surely, yes, well** 等開端字開頭的句子在該字後面要用逗號，例如：

(1) Certainly, I will follow the instruction.

(2) Indeed, he is very smart.

(3) No, I am not in the mood.

(4) Oh, what a terrible thing to happen.

(5) Surely, it is my pleasure.

(6) Yes, I will show up.

(7) Well, let me think.

逗號可以用作省略的符號，例如：

(1) The unemployment raised 1%; the inflation, 0.4%.

(2) This is the camp of the English; that, of French.

分號後面的子句裡以逗號分別代替了動詞「raised」和「the camp of the」。

名稱和 Inc., Sr., Jr. 等之間要用逗號分開，例如：

(1) Your Electronic House of publishing, Inc.

(2) Barnaby Yeh, Jr.

在句子中若有插入性的字詞可以用逗號分開，例如：

(1) Your situation, I believe, will get better in a few days.

(2) This case, however, will not affect my decision.

(3) My sons, for example, are very creative.

(4) John studied hard for, and came out first in, the test.

(5) Nancy, having spent all her money, return to her husband.

但是若句子很短,逗號也可以省略,例如:

正:He is, perhaps, busy now.

正:He is perhaps busy now.

2. 分號("``;``" semicolon)的用法

逗號和分號都可以把句子中對等的子句分開,但在使用逗號分離兩個對等子句時,必須要在逗號後面加一個連接詞(如:and, or 或 but 等),此時沒有連接詞的用法是錯誤的,例如:

正:Our sales department handles orders; our service department handles complaints.

正:Our sales department handles orders, and our service department handles complaints.

誤:Our sales department handles orders, our service department handles complaints.

所以「;」等於「, and」。

兩個對等子句中的任何一個若已使用逗號,則該兩個子句應以分號分開,以免導致混淆,例如:

> If you take a train, it will take you four hours; if you take a plane, it will take you only one hour.

要分開用 **also, accordingly, besides, consequently, for, furthermore, hence, however, in fact, likewise, moreover, nevertheless, otherwise, so, still, then, therefore** 等等所連接的子句時，應該用分號而非逗號，例如：

> 誤：Your order did not arrive in time, **otherwise**, we could have
> 　　shipped it today.
> 正：Your order did not arrive in time; **otherwise**, we could have
> 　　shipped it today.

事實上，上面所列的分號使用例子都可以用句號代替分號，把各該句子分成兩個獨立的句子，例如：

> (1) Our sales department handles orders. Our service department handles
> 　　complaints.
> (2) If you take a train, it will take you four hours. If you take a plane, it
> 　　will take you only one.
> (3) Your order did not arrive in time. Otherwise, we could have shipped
> 　　it today.

想將句子斷得乾淨就使用句號，否則，使用分號會比較流暢，分號能表示出兩個見解間的關係。分號的正確使用方法在於分開較短的獨立

子句，分號能將兩個有相互關係的想法分別指示出來，但不像句號一樣把句子完全分離。例如：

> 可：John drinks milk. Mary likes coffee.
> 較佳：John drinks milk; Mary likes coffee.
> 可：Milk is plentiful. It's inexpensive, too.
> 較佳：Milk is plentiful; it's inexpensive, too.

又「;」與「,」一樣，不可以使用於括號或引號內句子的句尾，若有必要，這兩種符號都要放在括號或引號外面，例如：

> Your order did not arrive in time (it is late for a day); otherwise, we could have shipped the order today.

3. 冒號（":" colon）的用法

用阿拉伯數字表示時間時，可以用冒號分開「時」與「分」，例如：

> (1) 8:40 am
> (2) 4:30 pm
> (3) 15:30

英文書信的開頭敬稱之後可以用冒號，例如：

(1) Dear Mr. Wong:

(2) Gentlemen:

(3) Dear Sir or madam:

敬稱若僅用及受信者的名或姓時，其後可用逗號，例如：

(1) Dear John,

(2) Dear Mother,

(3) Dear Jack,

在列舉一連串的項目時可用冒號，但在 **are** 或 **were** 後面千萬不能用冒號，例如：

誤：The items I need are: pencils, clips, and erasers.

正：The items I need are pencils, clips, and erasers.

正：Please bring me the following items: flash lights, a twoperson tent, and 150 bags of crackers.

但下面這種格式是可以接受的，因為在此例中各項已經變成表列式，而不是有如前例中的一連串項目。

The items I need are:

pencils,

> clips,
>
> erasers.

引述一段正式的敘述時可用冒號，例如：

> The owner of the store say: "The store will close at midnight, Friday, July 4 for the celebration."

請注意冒號前必須是個完整的句子。

4. 破折號（"—" dash）的用法

破折號乃是一長劃（—），不同於連字號的一短劃（-）。破折號可使用在文章中語氣有所轉折的時候，例如：

> ⑴Mr. Alister Yeh arrived yesterday afternoon—I forgot the exact time—to our Taipei office.
>
> ⑵The two rivals finally met-in a prison.

此句的「—」可用「,」取代如下：

> Mr. Alister Yeh arrived yesterday afternoon, I forgot the exact time, to our Taipei office.

同位語中的子句如果包括一系列的項目時，可以用破折號，例如：

> The principal of democracy—government for the people, of the people, and by the people—represents the ultimate goal of this nation.

注意：「—」的前後都不留空格，且不可和「:」或「,」連用。

㈢ 雙引號、單引號、括號、方括號

雙引號、單引號、括號、方括號是在句子中引述或插入別的敘述時使用。

1. 雙引號（" " double quote）的用法

雙引號「" "」用在引述他人或自己的敘述等，例如：

> On the date he wrote, "come to enjoy an evening with us."

引述歌曲名稱、詩、電影、書中的章名、雜誌中的文章名稱時，應使用雙引號，例如：

> ⑴"Moon River" is one of my favorite songs.
> ⑵"Enter the Dragon" is Bruce Lee's last movie.
> ⑶"How to Write Research Paper" is the title of my new book.
> ⑷The May issue of Times contains an article entitled "The art of Business Writing."

不同於「!」、「?」和「.」，若引號內的**句尾**有必要用逗號時，逗

號永遠要加在引號裡面，例如：

---

(1) "I am busy," he said.

(2) When speak of "office hours," I mean nine to five.

解釋或使用特殊名詞的時候應該用雙引號把該名詞標出來，例如：

"Tardiness" means one is late for the class by ten minutes.

---

2. 單引號（' ' single quote）的用法

單引號「' '」則使用在引述句中的引述句上，此外不單獨使用，例如：

---

(1) As he would say, "the term 'frequently' is used often today."

(2) I remember he said, "my mother told me, 'come home early tonight.'"

---

3. 括號 [( ) parentheses] 的用法

在文章中插入解釋、指示或補充說明時可使用括號：

This article (which was written by Mr. Barnaby Yeh on September 1999) is an excellent reading material for high school students.

在這類句子裡的括號可以用破折號或逗號來取代，例如：

⑴This article, which was written by Mr. Barnaby Yeh on September 1999, is an excellent reading material for high school students.

⑵This article-which was written by Mr. Barnaby Yeh on September 1999-is an excellent reading material for high school students.

到底哪一種標點比較好，沒有一定的標準，大體上，插入語很短時可用逗號分開，其他情形下則可以使用括號或破折號，例如：

This article uses a lot of references (see Appendix A) from (foreign) sources.

使用數字來覆述前面的文字時應使用括號，例如：

⑴The experiment requires two sets of fifty (50) beakers.

⑵We are sending you a check for twenty dollars ($20) .

⑶We are sending you a check of twenty (20) dollars.

使用序號來標明項目時，各序號應使用括號，例如：

The ingredient of this chemical are as follows: ⑴ carbon ⑵ sodium chloride (NaCl) ⑶ sodium hydroxide (NaOH).

括號通常都是用一對，但在用「i, ii, iii...」、「a, b, c...」或「1, 2, 3...」等項目符號與編號分條列舉大綱或分段時，可以只放括號的右半邊

「）」在各該項目符號與編號之後以代替一個句號。例如：

> My concerns are:
> a) Are you willing to work after hours?
> b) Is this the type of work you like?

　　在括號內使用任何其他標點符號的方法與各該標點符號在括號外的用法完全相同，但當括號內的句子屬於主句的一部分時，括號內的句尾不應出現句點，例如：

> He demonstrates outstanding management skills (see the attached reference) .

　　括號內的句子獨立於主句時，句點應該置於括號內：

> He has outstanding management skills. (He has a reference to prove such skills.)

　　注意，括號內的句尾絕不可以出現逗號，如有需要，逗號應打在括號外，例如：

> I like cream, sugar (preferably two) , or lemon in my tea.

4.方括號（**[ ] brackets**）的用法

　　括號內的補充性說明中若需要插入另一個補充說明，則可以使用方括號，例如：

　　The article (which was written by Barnaby Yeh [See Appendix B]) is a wonderful example.

　　方括號的另一項使用場合是在導出附註之用，例如：

　　A. Bohr [1934] discovered that the atoms of a water molecule vibrate in a frequency of ....

上例告訴讀者該項引述出自 A. Bohr 在 1934 年的著作。

㈣ 其他標點符號

　　還有兩個常用而未在前文加以分類的標點符號是「連字號」和「撇節號」。

1.連字號（"-" **hyphen**）的用法

　　連字號多用在一行字的末端，旨在把字斷開，一行的長度不足以把最後一個字完整納入時，可以用連字號把字斷開，使該字分列在兩行（即前行尾與後行頭）。斷字的規則敘述如下：

　　下列幾種字不應截斷而宜將整個字移到下一行，即：

(1) 單音節的字（如 drive, price, house 等）

(2) 單音節的字加上 -ed 所成的過去式及過去分詞（如 talked, pained, walked 等）

(3) 字首是母音的雙音節字（如 around, event 等）

(4) 字尾音節只有兩個字母的雙音節字（如：nearly, formed, thirty 等）

不可截斷屬於同一音節中的子音和母音，例如：

(1) principle 可以截成 prin-ciple, princi-ple 但不可以截成 princ-iple 或 pri-nciple 或 princip-le。

(2) international 可以截成 in-ternational, inter-national 或 interna-tional 而不可以截成其他任何形式。

字根型的字若字根在前則在字根後截斷，字根在後則應在字根前截斷，例如：

(1) collectible => collect-ible（ible 為字根）

(2) billing => bill-ing（bill 為字根）

(3) desirable => desir-able（able 為字根）

(4) missing => miss-ing（miss 為字根）

(5) running => run-ning（run 為字根）

字根型的字若要在其雙子音處截斷時，應自兩個子音節斷開，例

如：

---

(1) excellent => excel-lent

(2) omission => omis-sion

(3) shipping => ship-ping

已經有連字號的字只可在原連字號處截斷，例如：

---

(1) first-class

(2) long-standing

(3) well-organized

截成兩段的字中，每一段都至少要有一個母音，例如：

---

(1) Taichung's 可以斷成 Tai-chung's

(2) Chung's 則不可以斷成 Chu-ng's

問號使用在問句及連續性的問句後面，例如：

---

(1) Have you heard of his decision?

(2) I asked him "have you reached your decision?"

(3) What is the use of making a lot of money if you do not have good health? If you are not happy with your life? If you do not have someone you can love?

　　上例中第一個是簡單的直接問句，第二句是間接問句，而第三句則是個由三個句子組成的連續性問句，其中每個問句第一字都用大寫，句後都用問號。下面的例子是第三句的改寫，它成了一個句子，因此只需要一個問號。

> 　　What's the use of having a lot of money without love, health, and happiness?

　　注意，英文中若並肩使用兩個以上相同詞性的字，應該把最短的字排在最前面，最長的字排在最後面，例如：

> (1)He lives a happy, loving, and wealthy life.
> (2)His life is full of love, wealth, and happiness.

2.撇節號（" ' " apostrophe）的用法

　　撇節號除用於表示所有格（如 Joe's, Mr. Yeh's）之外還表示省略，例如：

> (1)it's = it is
> (2)wasn't = was not
> (3)can't = cannot
> (4)I'd = I would
> (5)Int'l = international
> (6)'99 = 1999

撇節號也用於表示複數，例如：

---

(1) He grew up in 1970's.

(2) I received three A's.

(3) There are many if's in the paragraphs.

(4) All who join the party are VIP's.

(五) 標點間的相對位置與關係

標點符號在絕大多數狀況下是單獨使用的，本節介紹在需要共同使用兩種標點符號時應注意的規則。

1. 破折號與逗號或冒號

冒號或逗號與破折號不要連用，冒號或逗號後面不可以緊連一個破折號，破折號後面也不可緊連一個冒號或逗號。

2. 破折號與句號、問號、驚嘆號

在縮寫字母的句號之後可以用破折號，例如：

His cooking is o.k.—he has been to a cooking class.

破折號所分開的文字如需要用到問號或驚嘆號時也可以使用，例如：

Our neighbor—is his name Yeh or Yeah? —said he would come to visit sometimes.

3. 括號與逗號

如果句子的結構上需要，可以緊跟在右括號之後使用逗點或分號，但絕對不可跟在左括號前後使用這兩種標點符號。例如：

I need paper, a pencil (the softer, the better), and an eraser.

緊隨右括號後面可用逗點，但在 **pencil** 和左括號間、左括號和 **the** 間以及 better 和右括號間，都不可用逗點。

4. 括號與句號、問號、驚嘆號

如果句號、問號、驚嘆號是屬於括弧內的片語或子句時，就要放在括弧之內，例如：

The sky is cloudless, the temperature is in mid-70 (What a beautiful day!) and suitable for an outing.

若括弧中的文字是原句中的一部分，而且是在句末，那麼句號、問號或驚嘆號就要放在括弧外面，例如：

It is not his fault (and nobody else's, either) !

　　但若括弧中的文字是獨立的，有加句號的必要時，應將句號寫在括弧之內。例如：

The new book by Dr. Gary Yeh covers what you need to know about punctuations. (The rules of punctuation are discussed at page 121.)

　　若一個完整的句子加了括弧嵌在原句中，就不可再用句號，例如：

The new book by Dr. Gary Yeh covers what you need to know (the rules of punctuation are discussed at page 121) thoroughly.

5.引號的位置

　　句號永遠是在引號之內。例如：

---

(1)Please do not use a double negative statement like "you don't know nothing."

(2)Dr. N. Yeh is the author of the book, "The Art of Business Correspondence."

　　冒號和分號一定要放在引號之外，例如：

Turn to the chapter entitled: "Consideration for Stock"; the reference is in the first paragraph.

　　問號和驚嘆號可以放在引號之內或外，端看全文的意思來作決定，例如下句並不是引述整個問句，所以問號在引號之外：

　　Is Dr. Naichia Yeh the author of the book, "The Art of Business Correspondence"?

　　下句中的驚嘆號也是所引用句子的一部分，所以要放在引號之內：

　　He exclaimed, "This is not my fault!"

　　除了「"」和「)」外，問號和驚嘆號後面不可以加任何標點符號。

6. 括號與分號

　　如果句子的結構需要，可以在括弧後面用一個分號。千萬不要在括弧前面用逗點或分號，更不可在括弧之內、文字之前用分號。

7. 標點的其他注意事項

　　逗點和分號後面要留一個字母空位。

　　句號、問號和驚嘆號之後要留兩個字母的空位，其後的任何字的第一個字母均需大寫。

　　冒號後首個英文字的第一個字母如果是大寫時，其後要留兩個字母的空位。

第十章
電腦輔助論文格式製作

本章提綱

　　一、目錄製作

　　二、註腳標示

　　三、索引製作

　　以電腦製作目錄、註腳、索引的方法簡單易學，目錄、註腳、索引製作完成後，不管論文的內容或頁數怎麼變更，藉電腦之助，只消按幾下滑鼠或鍵盤，就可以為目錄和索引重新編頁，為註腳重新編碼，這種一勞永逸的方法，實在值得任何論文寫作者一學。

　　本章旨在指導學者按部就班，學習用 MS-Word 製作目錄、腳註、索引，以增加論文寫作的效率。

一、目錄製作

　　目錄是論文的地圖，它提供了論文內容的結構，並且幫助讀者快速尋找特定的章節，瀏覽目錄可對論文主題有概略的了解。

　　目錄可以是簡單的章節標題清單，也可以包括數個標題或大綱階層，要是目錄的結構複雜有如本書，用人工建立目錄真的需要花許多勞力和心力，若能借重電腦，那就簡便多了。

　　目錄一旦製作完成，論文內容若有增刪而造成章節頁碼變更，重製

目錄只是按幾次滑鼠鍵之勞。

本節敘述如何使用 Word 一勞永逸地建立美觀正式的目錄。

建立目錄最簡單的方法是使用內建的**標題樣式**和**大綱層級**[1]格式：

㈠以標題樣式建立目錄

使用標題樣式的最大優點就是使用方便及快速，Word 有**標題** 1 到**標題** 9 等九種內建的標題樣式，使用內建標題樣式來格式化文件是標示文字的最簡單方法，只要使用九種預先定義的標題樣式的其中一種來格式化文字，然後建立目錄即可。

以標題樣式建立目錄有兩個步驟，**第一步**是在文件中**標示**想要列入目錄的文字，這部分工作需由手工完成。

標示欲納入目錄中文字的方法如下：

1. 在文件中手動選取欲列入目錄的文字（例如章節標題）；

2. 展開**樣式與格式**的下拉欄位，按〔**格式**〕工具列上的 凸 亦可將此欄位以工作窗格[2]的方式開啟於 Word 的右側；

3. 選取恰當的**標題樣式**。

4. 就每個要包含到目錄中的標題重複步驟 1 到 3。

---

[1] 大綱層級可以用來指定文件中的段落階層式層級（層級 1 到層級 9）的段落格式設定，指定大綱層級後，即可用大綱模式或「文件引導模式」處理文件。

[2] 工作窗格：Office 應用程式內的視窗，可提供常用的指令。其位置及小型尺寸即使仍在使用檔案也可使用這些命令。

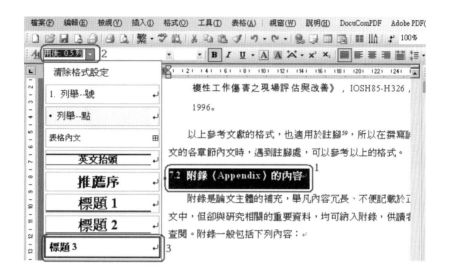

　　若在撰寫論文時寫到新的章節標題，立刻加以標示，事後便不必重新瀏覽整份文件，再一一標示須包含在目錄中的文字。

　　第二步是將標示的文字及其頁碼集中在指定的目錄所在地，這部分工作則由電腦代勞。首先，將插入點放在目錄應在的地方，通常是文件的開頭。接下來，在〔**插入**〕功能表上指向〔**參照**〕，然後按〔**索引及目錄**〕，再按〔**目錄**〕索引標籤。然後按〔**確定**〕以建立目錄。

㈡ 從大綱層級建立目錄

　　從大綱層級建立目錄的第一步，是建立文件大綱，其步驟如下：

1. 在〔**檢視**〕功能表上指向〔**工具列**〕，按〔**大綱模式**〕。

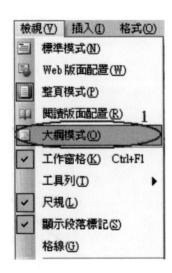

2. 選取目錄中要出現的第一個標題。

3. 在〔**大綱**〕工具列上選取相關的大綱階層。

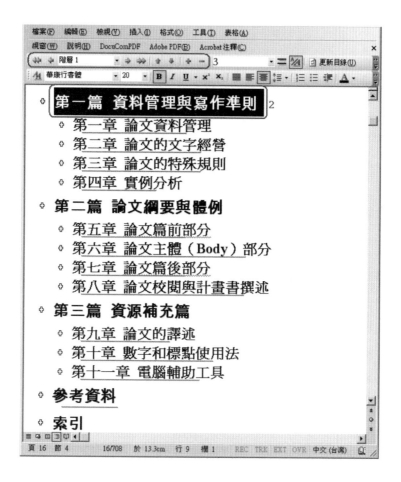

4. 就每個要包含到目錄中的標題重複步驟 2 和 3。

建立目錄

　　套用**大綱層級**格式或內建的**標題樣式**後，就可以直接進入預定要插入目錄的位置，再依序執行下列步驟：

1. 在〔**插入**〕功能表上指向〔**參照**〕，按〔**索引及目錄**〕。

2.按〔**目錄**〕索引標籤。

3.在〔**格式**〕下拉欄位中選定一個設計。

4.在〔**格式**〕欄位右邊的〔**顯示階層**〕欄位中選定要標出的層次數目（1
到 9）。

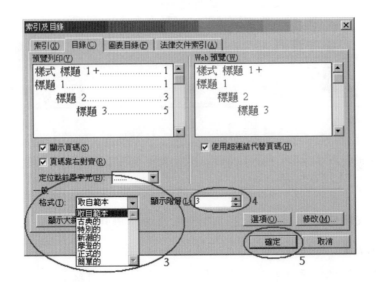

5. 選取需要的其他任何目錄選項，完成後按〔**確定**〕來正式建立目錄，此時 Word 會搜尋指定的標題，按標題層次對它們進行排序，並將目錄顯示在文件中。

(三)目錄檢視與更新

　　在 Word 中檢視文件時，若要快速瀏覽整個文件，可使用**文件引導模式**，此模式開出文件視窗左邊的垂直窗格，顯示文件標題的大綱，每個大綱項目都是超連結，可供點按，有利於快速瀏覽整份論文，並追蹤各標題在論文中的位置。

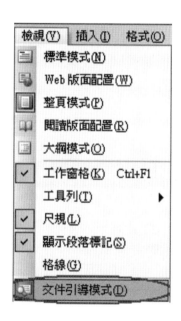

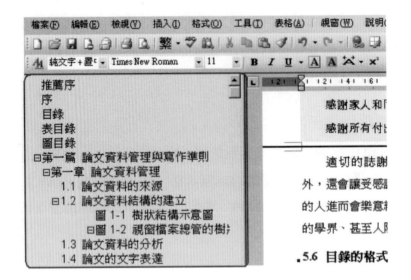

　　目錄建立後，如果在文件中加入更多標題，或只是增加更多內容，希望目錄能夠加入新的標題並顯示正確的頁碼時，就必須要更新目錄。此時可以選取目錄，然後按<F9>，開啟以下視窗，選擇更新整個目錄或只更新頁碼：

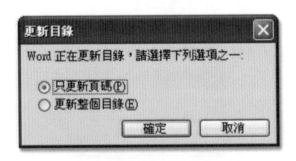

　　若未增加新標題，可選擇〔更新頁碼選項〕，如果已增加新的標題或已變更目錄中的任何文字，則選擇〔更新整個目錄〕。

　　目錄中的文字若需變更，不要在目錄中而宜在文件內文中編輯這些文字，然後按 <F9> 來更新目錄。

二、註腳標示

　　Word 的**註腳**及**章節附註**都是由**註解參照標記**[3]及對應的**註解文字**兩個部分所組成，**註腳**和**章節附註**兩者，均可用以顯示引用資料的來源、置入說明或補充的資訊，或甚至只是與本文中文字不連貫的離題註解，兩者之間的基本差別在於它們在文件中的位置，**註腳**位在頁面結尾，**章節附註**則是在文件或章節的結尾，它們都會以短水平線來與本文分開。

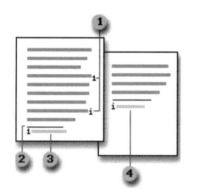

1 註腳及章節附註參照標記
2 分隔線
3 註腳文字
4 章節附註文字

　　註腳和**章節附註**的參照標記使用不同的編號系統，可以在同一文件中使用。不論在頁面底端或是文件結尾，註解文字的字型都會比本文小。

　　在來源資料或附加說明對閱讀內容很有幫助時，宜用註腳，因為註腳在頁面底部，可讓讀者在內文中查看。由於註腳的空間較小，因此若註解文字很長，或補充的資訊可在之後查看，那麼**章節附註**是較好的選擇。

　　將插入點置於希望註解參照標記出現的地方，然後在工具列的〔**插**

3　註解參照標記乃是數字、字元或字元的組合，用以指示註腳或章節附註中包含其他資訊。

入〕功能表上指向〔參照〕，再按一下〔註腳〕。

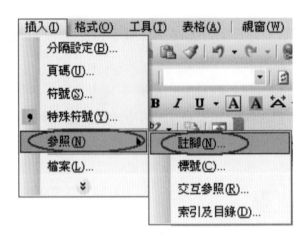

　　在〔註腳及章節附註〕對話方塊中，點選〔註腳〕或〔章節附
註〕，然後按一下對話方塊底部的〔插入〕按鈕。

　　此對話方塊關閉後，Word 會在插入點加入**註解參照標記**，且會自動編號。如果選的是〔**註腳**〕，相同號碼的註解參照標記會插至同頁底部；如果選的是〔**章節附註**〕，同碼的參照標記則會插至文件或章節結尾，等待使用者輸入註解文字。

　　新增下一個**註腳**或**章節附註**時，Word 會自動以正確順序編號，若稍後在此註解之前新增註解，Word 也會為新註解及文件中的其他註解重新編碼。

　　以上的步驟可以用快捷鍵來達成，在需要輸入**註腳**或**章節附註**之處，按<**Alt**>+<**Ctrl**>+**F** 就可插入註腳，按 <**Alt**>+<**Ctrl**>+**D** 則可以插入章節附註。

　　若要刪除註解，選取文件本文中的註解參照標記，然後按 <**Delete**>鍵。這樣就會刪除**註解參照標記**，以及頁面底部或文件結尾的文字。

刪除註解參照標記時，Word 會自動為剩餘的註解重新編碼。

三、索引製作

論文中的重要詞句、主題以及它們出現的頁碼，可以用 Word 的索引功能搜尋出來，列到適當的位置。要建立索引就得先標記文件中的**索引項目**[4]，索引項目的錯誤！尚未定義書籤。標記方式有手動與自動兩種。

(一) 手動標記索引項目

若要以手動標記索引項目，則選取欲置入索引的文字：

然後按 <<**Alt**>><**Shift**>+**X**，〔索引項目標記〕的視窗就會出現：

---

[4] 索引項目：標記特定文字，以將其包含在索引中的功能變數代碼。將文字標記為索引項目時，Microsoft Word 會插入格式設定為隱藏文字的 XE（索引項目）功能變數。

　　若單要標記該項目就按〔**標記**〕，若要將論文中此文字出現的每一次都標記起來，則按〔**全部標記**〕。

　　如要輸入自己的文字作為索引項目，則只要將游標插入索引項目的位置：

　　✓ 若要輸入自己的文字作為索引項目，則只要將游標插入索引
　　　項目的位置，再按<ALT><SHIFT>+X。

再按<<**Alt**>><**Shift**>+**X**。

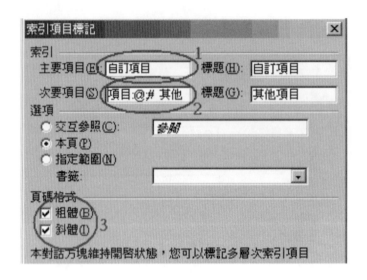

1. 欲建立主要索引項目，可在〔**主要項目**〕欄中鍵入或編輯文字，另外
   亦可建立次要項目[5]或指向其他項目的**錯誤！尚未定義書籤**。交互參
   照。
2. 若要包括第三層的項目，則在鍵入次要項目文字之後加上冒號（：），
   然後鍵入第三層項目的文字。如果要在項目中使用符號（如@），可
   緊接在符號後鍵入;#（分號後接數字符號）。
3. 欲選取索引中的頁碼格式，則核取〔**頁碼格式**〕之下的〔**粗體**〕或
   〔**斜線**〕方塊。

　　在〔**主要項目**〕或〔**次要項目**〕方塊中按滑鼠右鍵，再按〔**字型**〕
後可設定索引的文字格式：

5　次要項目乃是在較大範圍標題下的次項，例如，索引項目太陽系之下可以有火星、金星、土星與
　水星等次要項目。

　　欲標記其他索引項目，則重複本節步驟。

㈡以詞彙索引檔自動標記

　　詞彙太多的時候，若用手動標記的方式實在太過費事，Word 提供了自動標記**索引項目**的功能。

　　第一步是建立**詞彙索引檔**[6]，先開啟一空白文件，並在該新文件的**最頂部**插入一個兩欄的表格，然後在左欄中輸入要 Word 搜尋並標記為**索引項目**的文字，輸入的內容要與文件中完全一樣，然後在同列右欄中，鍵入左欄中的索引項目文字，重複此步驟以建立每一個索引參照和項目。如果要建立次要項目，請在右欄中鍵入主要項目之後，緊接著鍵入冒號

---

[6] 詞彙索引檔：索引中包含的詞彙表。在 Microsoft Word 中使用詞彙索引檔可以快速標記索引項目。

（：，如下圖中之 a, b 所示）：

SSCI	Social Science Citation Index：〔SSCI〕 a
Subject-specific Database	Subject-specific Database
Table	Table
Technical Report	Technical Report
Teleport	Teleport
Title	Title
Unit	Unit
WinZip	WinZip
人性化	人性化
口語化	口語化
大綱	大綱
內文列舉	內文列舉：列舉 b
公式	公式
分析	分析
分號	分號

　　要加速詞彙索引檔的建立，可同時開啟**詞彙索引檔**和論文，按〔**視窗**〕功能表上的〔**並排顯示**〕以同時查看兩份文件，將索引文字從主文件中一一複製到索引檔的左欄裡。製作完成後，記得儲存詞彙索引檔。

　　接著開啟主文件（即要編索引的文件），在〔**插入**〕功能表上指向〔**參照**〕後，按〔**索引及目錄**〕：

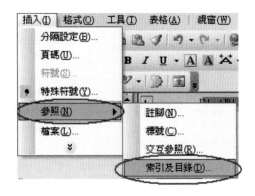

再點選〔索引〕標籤，然後按〔自動標記〕：

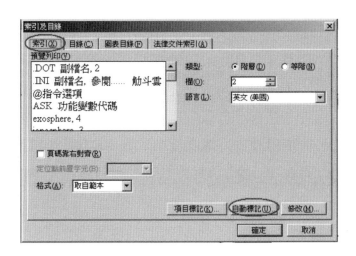

　　在〔**檔案名稱**〕方塊中輸入要使用的詞彙索引檔名稱後，按〔**開啟**〕：

　　電腦會在文件中搜尋每一個與**索引檔**左欄完全符合的文字，然後使用右欄的文字作為**標示項目**。Word 會標記每一個段落中第一個出現的目標，然後將它們根據英文字母或中文字筆畫順序排序，在你選定的索引預定處，列出**索引檔**中指定的所有詞彙及各該詞彙出現的所有頁碼。

　　Word 註明**索引項目**位置的**功能變數**[7]乃是 **XE 功能變數**，如果看不到 XE 功能變數，可在〔**一般**〕工具列上按 🔁 [8]，那麼原先隱藏的變數就會一一顯現出來：

7　功能變數：指示 Word 自動向文件插入文字、圖形、頁碼及其他資料的一組代碼。

8　〔顯示／隱藏〕鈕。

論文資料管理{ XE "論文資料管理" }結合了邏輯{ XE "邏輯" }概念和實際操作的過程，並形成一套為問題求解的技巧，一般而言，此套技巧有七個項目，分別為：資料取得、資料評估、資料整理、資料分析{ XE "資料分析" }、資料表達、資料保障、資料的協同運用。茲分別說明如下：

資料取得{ XE "資料取得" }：提問與回答、練習反覆搜索、利用電子圖書館的資料庫來查尋資料等，對資料的取得都很重要。資料的品質與資料取得的技巧有很大的關聯，附錄 C 提供會更詳盡的資料搜尋技巧介紹。

㈢ 刪除索引

若要刪除某**索引項目**，就要尋找該項目的 XE 功能變數，例如，選取整個功能變數（包括大括弧{}），再按 **<Delete>**鍵。欲編輯或格式化索引項目，則可用一般文字處理的方式直接變更引號裡面的文字。若要更新索引，就點選索引位置，再按 **<F9>**。

想要刪除許多**索引項目**時，就要一一尋找各該項目的 XE 功能變數，那未免耗費多功夫，此時不如以整體搜尋取代的方式把所有的**索引項目**通通除去。操作的步驟如下：

點選一般工具列上的〔**編輯**〕功能表：

點按〔取代〕帶出〔尋找及取代〕對話方塊：

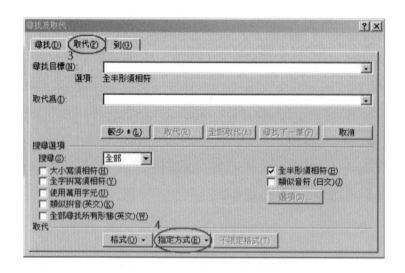

在〔尋找及取代〕對話方塊中，點選〔指定方式〕。

此時會出現一系列的方式供你選擇，請點選〔功能變數〕：

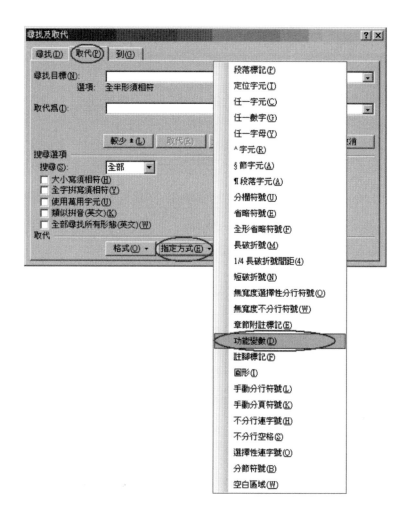

此時，〔尋找及取代〕對話方塊中的〔尋找目標〕欄中會出現 $\boxed{\textbf{^d}}$ [9]：

9　此即 XE 功能變數的搜尋代碼，你也可以直接鍵入「**^d**」。

　　將〔**取代為**〕之欄位保持空白，然後按〔**全部取代**〕鈕，電腦即會把所有的 XE 功能變數全數刪去。至此，你可以從新開始，用第 10.3.1 即 10.3.2 節的方式重新製作更滿意的索引。

第十一章
化冗贅爲簡潔

本章提綱

　　一、說得多不見得更有效

　　二、化繁爲簡範例

　　三、練習

　　我們且從身邊一些鬆散的句子中，找出某些作者無法精確表達的例證。*different* 常是不需要用的字，請看下面的原句，就算沒有了 ***different***，這句話也已經有了不同的意味，因此，去掉 ***different*** 並不會犧牲多少文意。

原句	修訂後
The committee raises three different issues.	The committee raises three issues.

　　有效改善文章的方法之一，就是刪除不必要的用字、用詞和用句。

一、說得多不見得更有效

　　一般人說話不打草稿，沒有多餘的時間可以潤飾，因此話的結構儘管鬆散些，也無可厚非。但是，寫作就必須比說話精確得多，因為，任

何端上檯面見人的作品，事前都已經有機會加以修飾，如果品質還是像不經心就脫口而出的話一樣，就有點不負責任了。

以下還有一些贅述及精簡後的例子：

原句	修訂後
at a temperature of 150°C to 200°C	at 150°C～200°C
at a high pressure of 5000 Pa	at 5000 Pa
at a high temperature of 900°C	at 900°C
discussed and studied in detail	discussed
has been found to increase	increased
specially designed or formulated	完全刪去

下例中的第一個句子不但有贅字，那多餘的部分還是被動式，第二句中刪去了贅字，也同時解決了被動式的問題，可謂一舉兩得：

原文	修訂後
This laboratory project has been done to evaluate pressure pulsing as an Enhanced Oil Recovery technique.	This laboratory project evaluates pressure pulsing as an Enhanced Oil Recovery technique.

下面的原文中，文字用得太繁瑣，顯得長而無力，修訂後把它們縮成一句反而更有力量：

原文	修訂後
It should be recognized that the distributed system and associated computation are not single entities. This contrasts with the other components in a management tool which are single entities.	Contrasting with other singleentity components in a management tool, the distributed system and associated computation are not single entities.

　　別以為英語系國家的人就能寫出完全合乎語法或文法的英文，君不見，我們這些華語系國家的人就不見得全都能寫出像樣的中文。像下例原文這種語意不完整的文字，在學術論文中比比皆是，而寫出這種論文的作者全是大學或研究所畢業，甚至有些還是為人師表者，所以也實在難以重責大、中，乃至小學生的作文程度低落問題。

原文	修訂後
……智力正常或一般水準以上，且沒有任何顯著的感官缺陷，但在閱讀或書寫的表現卻比一般學生落後很多，在語文學習方面比其他學科的表現有顯著落後的情形。由此可知，閱讀困難是排除智力、	……閱讀障礙[1]者的智力，一般均屬正常或在平均水準以上，這些人雖不見得有顯著的感官缺陷，但在閱讀或書寫時的表現卻不及一般學生，他們在語文學習方面的表現，比在其他學科方面有顯著落後

1　談到閱讀障礙，其實，寫作障礙是更普遍的問題，因為，寫作障礙者的閱讀能力可能正常，或在一般水準以上，但在寫作表達時卻縛手縛腳，無法達意。一般大眾若想體會閱讀障礙或寫作障礙，可以擬想自己在閱讀自己所不太熟悉的文字，或以自己所不太熟悉的文字（像英文）寫作時那種無能為力的情境。

原文	修訂後
環境及其他障礙之因素影響，而是本身閱讀傳輸上產生缺損問題，致使在閱讀文章時無法像正常人一樣。	的情形。也就是說，他們的閱讀能力與智力、環境及其他障礙因素較無相關，只在閱讀溝通能力上有所缺損，他們在閱讀時，無法像正常人一樣理解。

請比比看修訂後的文字，是不是容易了解得多了？

二、化繁為簡範例

本節中我們要利用一連串的例句來觀察英文中的某些冗贅片語，並把冗贅的例句一一改寫，以供讀者交互參照。

以下所舉的「冗贅」片語中，有些當然還是可以使用的，因此不見得要一概歸為冗贅而非要將之徹底改寫不可，我們之所以有限度地保留「冗贅」片語，是因為它們約定俗成地使用在一些特殊（如醫學、法律、政治等）文件中，而不是因為有好多英語國家的人士還是在使用。

英語國家的人不見得能寫出簡潔的英文，就像華文界人士不見得能寫出簡潔的中文，這一點再怎麼說都不為過。

冗贅	簡潔
It is of interest to note that	可略去（這一點很有趣）
It is of interest to note that the availability of these procedures also	The availability of these procedures also enables the selection of op-

---

2　*As to* 不算是很標準的用法，不如用 *about* 來得直截了當。

冗贅	簡潔
enables the selection of optimal issue policies for the case.	timal issue policies for the case.
Needless to say	可略去（不用說）
Needless to say, it could be very difficult to sell such a contradictory methodology.	It could be very difficult to sell such a contradictory methodology.
It is evident that	可略去
It is evident that the American marketplace supports a wide range of cost structure.	The American marketplace supports a wide range of cost structure.
as to[2] **having regard to** **in relation to** **in terms of** **with reference to** **with respect to** **with regard to**	**about, in**
The company has filed a complaint with the court and expects a decision later **as to** whether the court will launch a formal investigation.	The company has filed a complaint with the court and expects a decision later **about** whether the court will launch a formal investigation.

3　不論中英文，像「事實上」、「基本上」這些放在句首的發語詞都可以省略而無礙於文意。

冗贅	簡潔
The researchers have examined the physical and chemical properties **having regard to the said chemicals.**	**The researchers have examined the physical and chemical properties about the said chemicals.**
The result of this research discloses an overview of molecular forces **in connection to** protein structure.	The result of this research discloses an overview of molecular forces **about** protein structure.
Taiwan ranks the highest 37th in the world **in terms of** women's participation in politics.	Taiwan ranks 37th in the world **in** women's participation in politics.
This monthly report includes a list of frequently asked questions **with reference to** the corporate university.	This monthly report includes a list of frequently asked questions **about** the corporate university.
as a matter of fact	**actually, in fact**（事實上）
As a matter of fact, strikes were criminal acts in the martial law era during 1950's under the "National Mobilization Law".	**In fact**[3], strikes were criminal acts in the martial law era during 1950's under the "National Mobilization Law".
at the conclusion of **subsequent to**	**after**（在⋯⋯之後）
At the conclusion of the poster presentations, the participants will have gained increased knowledge of clinical research.	**After** the poster presentations, the participants will have gained increased knowledge of clinical research.

冗贅	簡潔
The objective of this paper is to investigate the aggregate behavior of the stock market immediately prior and **subsequent to** new stock market highs.	The objective of this paper is to investigate the aggregate behavior of the stock market immediately prior and **after** new stock market highs.
are of the same opinion	**agree**（同意）
The reviewers **are of the same opinion** that the advertising for this film is misleading.	The reviewers **agree** that the advertising for this film is misleading.
unanimity of opinion	**agreement**（意見一致）
There is no **unanimity of opinion** as to the effect of such procedures on the grading of coins although increasing experience in collecting may cause collectors to shun polished coins.	There is no **agreement** on the effect of such procedures on the grading of coins although in-creasing experience in collecting may cause collectors to shun polished coins.
despite the fact that	**although**（雖然）
Despite the fact that many American are unfamiliar with avian flu, majorities believe taking steps to prepare is important	**Although** many American are unfamiliar with avian flu majorities believe taking steps to prepare is im-portant
it is apparent that	**apparently**（顯然）
It is apparent that fetal growth can be maximized if the mother could	**Apparently** fetal growth can be maximized if the mother could have

冗贅	簡潔
have good living habits and reduction of stress during pregnancy.	good living habits and reduction of stress during pregnancy.
inasmuch as **insomuch as**	**as, for, since**（鑑於）
Insomuch as the United States is going to benefit both economically and militarily from the construction of the Seaway, the participation of the US is in the national interest.	**As** the United States will benefit both economically and militarily from the construction of the Seaway, the participation of the US is in the national interest.
as is the case	**as happens**（發生）
As is the case in every relationship, once in a while differences of opinion arise.	**As happen** in every relationship, once in a while differences of opinion arise.
forthwith now	**at once, promptly**（立即）
All the churches and chapels of every religion exist in Paris shall be closed **forthwith now**.	All the churches and chapels of every religion in Paris shall be closed **at once**.
cognizant of	**aware of**（知道；察覺）
Those who dream by day are **cognizant of** many things which escape those who dream only by night.	Those who dream by day are **aware of** many things which escape those who dream only by night.
on the part of	**among, by, of**
This resulted in a lack of business operation concepts and poor resource	This resulted in a lack of business operation concepts and poor resource

冗贅	簡潔
management **on the part of** participating schools.	management **among** participating schools.
Francis Oakley considers the charges aimed to higher education claiming a "retreat from teaching" **on the part of** faculty.	Francis Oakley considers the charges pointed to higher education claming a "retreat from teaching" **by** faculty.
Committees often treat bibliographies as a sign of seriousness **on the part of** the applicant.	Committees often treat bibliographies as a sign of seriousness **of** the applicant.
based on the fact that **accounted for by the fact** **because of the fact that** **due to the fact that** **for the fact that** **in light of the fact that** **in view of the fact that** **on the grounds that**[4] **owing to the fact that** **the reason is because**[5]	**because, since**[6]（因為）

---

[4] *On the grounds that* 沿用於法律性的文件，但若用在一般文書時，以 *because* 代之則較流暢易懂。

[5] *The reason is because* 雖然不乏人使用，但終究是積非成是的說法，像 *The reason he showed up late is because he didn't catch the train.* 就應改為 *The reason he showed up late is that he didn't catch the train.* 或 *He showed up late because he didn't catch the train.*

[6] 寫作論文可以不用挖空心思地講究花俏的修辭變化，因此，左欄中的每一個片語都可以用右欄中的任何一個字取代。

冗贅	簡潔
Those who want to become a lawful permanent resident **based on the fact that** they have US citizen relatives must go through a multi-step process.	Those who want to become a lawful permanent resident **since** they have US citizen relatives must go through a multi-step process.
This is **accounted for by the fact that** iron is easier to draw down from a lump by hammering on an anvil into rectangular sections than to any other shape.	This is **because** iron is easier to draw down from a lump by hammering on an anvil into rectangular sections than to any other shape.
This expectation is not surprising **because of the fact that** most search engines place their search field at the upper-center portion of their web page.	This expectation is not surprising **because** most search engines place their search field at the upper-center portion of their web page.
Ice over the ocean is melting much faster than expected **due to the fact that** the temperature of the oceans is rising. Heated oceans can melt ice rapidly.	Ice over the ocean is melting much faster than expected **since** the temperature of the oceans is rising. Heated oceans can melt ice rapidly.
Ms. Johansson is responsible **for the fact that** the Ministry of Health and Social Affairs was not more active in supporting the Ministry for Foreign Affairs in its work with medical relief.	Ms. Johansson is responsible **since** the Ministry of Health and Social Affairs was not more active in supporting the Ministry for Foreign Affairs in its work with medical relief.
as a consequence of **on account of**	**because of**（因為）
The use of newlywed rather than longer-married couples to study antici-	The use of newlywed rather than longer-married couples to study antici-

冗贅	簡潔
pated dissolution **as a consequence of** infidelity has several advantages.	pated dissolution **because of** infidelity has several advantages.
Several benefits may be provided to an officer who retires from or leaves the service **on account of** injuries.	Several benefits may be provided to an officer who retires from or leaves the service **because of** injuries.
is of the opinion	**believe**（相信）
Ninety percent of respondents **are of the opinion** that scientific knowledge could improve one's ability to make decisions.	Ninety percent of respondents **believe** that scientific knowledge could improve one's ability to make decisions.
it may, however, be noted that	**however**（但是）
It may, however, be noted that the promotions is not applicable to the existing accounts.	*However,* the promotions is not applicable to the existing accounts.
no later than	**by**（在……之前）
The paper is due **no later than** 12/12/2010.	The paper is due **by** 12/12/2010.
by means of **through the use of**	**by, using, with** （由……；以……方法）
The federal copyright law applies to materials published or circulated **through the use of** computing resources.	The federal copyright law applies to materials published or circulated **using** computing resources.

冗贅	簡潔
referred to as	**called**（稱做）
Alcohol is often **referred to as** a source of empty calories, meaning it has no nutritive value other than providing energy.	Alcohol is often **called** a source of empty calories, meaning it has no nutritive value other than providing energy.
give rise to	**cause**（導致）
A group of researchers have found that certain brain activities in youth could *give rise to* Alzheimer's disease.	A group of researchers have found that certain brain activities in youth could *cause* Alzheimer's disease.
in close proximity to	**Close to, near**（接近）
The researcher conducts a survey of rural areas **in close proximity to** an industrial town.	The researcher conducts a survey of rural areas **closed to** an industrial town.
consensus of opinion	**consensus**（一致）
A defined probability measure is provided, allowing one to determine if an actual **consensus of opinion** exists.	A defined probability measure is provided, allowing one to determine if an actual **consensus** exists.
take into consideration	**consider**（考慮）
When thinking about switching schools, one should **take into consideration** several things as listed below.	When thinking about switching schools, one should **consider** several things as listed below.

冗贅	簡潔
on a daily basis	**daily**（每天）
Hundreds of CIA employees are directed **on a daily basis** to break laws in foreign countries.	Hundreds of CIA employees are directed **daily** to break laws in foreign countries.
contingent upon	**dependent on**（依⋯⋯而定）
The agreement is subject to approval by regulatory authorities and is **contingent upon** the closing of Boston Scientific's proposed acquisition of Guidant.	The agreement is subject to approval by regulatory authorities and is **dependent on** the closing of Boston Scientific's proposed acquisition of Guidant.
give an account of	**describe**（描寫；描繪）
This paper **gives an account of** the major factors affecting cell fate during development.	This paper **describes** the major factors affecting cell fate during development.
during the course of	**during, while**（在⋯⋯期間）
During the course of World War One, 11% of France's population were killed or wounded.	**During** World War One, 11% of France's population were killed or wounded.
at an earlier date	**earlier**（早先）
At the same time, it will help the UN Millennium Development Goals to be realized **at an earlier date**.	At the same time, it will help the UN Millennium Development Goals to be realized **earlier**.

冗贅	簡潔
Students in this program should determine *at an early date* the specific requirements of the school they wish to attend.	Students in this program should determine *earlier* the specific requirements of the school they wish to attend.
entirely eliminate	**eliminate**（排除，消除）
The mineralizing of the wastewater sludge allows to *entirely eliminate* other systems used in sludge management techniques to date.	The mineralizing of the wastewater sludge allows to *eliminate* other systems used in sludge management techniques to date.
absolutely essential **important essentials**	**essential**（必要的）
There are a few *important essentials* of bodybuilding that are often left out of the picture.	There are a few *essentials* of body building that are often left out of the picture.
regardless of the fact that	**even though**（即使；雖然）
Office parties are still business events *regardless of the fact that* they are guised as social events for rewarding employees	Office parties are still business events *even though* they are guised as social events rewarding employees
with a possible exception of	**except**（除……之外）
Some researchers are not aware of the needs and requirements of typical teachers, *with a possible exception of* those in the computer science domain.	Some researchers are not aware of the needs and requirements of typical teachers, *except* those in the computer science domain.

冗贅	簡潔
fewer in number	**fewer**（較少）
A series of second weighting devices equal to or ***fewer in number*** than the first weighting devices weights the remaining output of the branching means.	A series of second weighting devices equal to or ***fewer*** than the first weighting devices weights the remaining output of the branching means.
for the purpose of **with a view to**	**for**（為了）
Council of Europe issued a recommendation to member States on action against trafficking in human beings ***for the purpose of*** sexual exploitation and explanatory report.	Council of Europe issued a recommendation to member States on action against trafficking in human beings ***for*** sexual exploitation and explanatory report.
The paper reviews the existing communication links ***with a view*** to upgrading and improving these links.	The paper reviews the existing communication links ***for*** upgrading and improving these links.
an example of this is the fact that	**for example**（例如）
An example of this is the fact that marijuana use typically starts during the ages of 15 to 20.	***For example***, marijuana use typically starts during the ages of 15 to 20.
completely full	**full**（滿）
The refugee camps are now ***completely full*** and if any more refugees	The refugee camps are now ***full*** and if any more refugees arrive, they

冗贅	簡潔
arrive, they will have to sleep out in the open under plastic sheeting,.	will have to sleep out in the open under plastic sheeting,.
to the fullest possible extent	**fully**（完全；徹底）
The school administration office should cooperate *to the fullest possible extent* in providing capacity building assistance.	The school administration office should cooperate *fully* in providing capacity building assistance.
in case **in the event that** **should it prove the case that**	**if**（假如；如果）
In case the main office becomes inoperable, the firm will shift its operations to its designated back-up facility.	*If* the main office becomes inoperable, the firm will shift its operations to its designated back-up facility.
In the event that allegations relate to a Student Member, the Proctors may take further action under the terms of Statute XI.	*If* allegations relate to a Student Member, the Proctors may take further action under the terms of Statute XI.
in a very real sense	**in a sense**（就某意義說）（可略去）
In a very real sense, people who have read good literature have lived more than people who cannot or will not read.	*In a sense*, people who have read good literature have lived more than people who cannot or will not read.

冗贅	簡潔
is defined as	**is**（是）
A user interface *is defined as* a collection of commands that users can use to interact with a particular CAD system.	A user interface *is* a collection of commands that users can use to interact with a particular CAD system.
Large in size	**large**（大）
The rooms within cottage style properties are **large in size** and have a tropical ambience.	The rooms within cottage style properties are **large** and have a tropical ambience.
at some future time	**in the future, later** （將來；往後）
American thinking might turn in this direction **at some future time**.	American thinking might turn in this direction **in the future**.
a decreased amount of **an increased amount of**	**less**（減少） **more**（增加）
The second mortgage effects were reflected on **a decreased amount of** returns perceived.	The second mortgage effects were were reflected on **less** returns perceived.
have the appearance of	**look like**（看起來像……）
There are techniques for coating articles to *have the appearance of* wood, leather or other natural materials.	There are techniques for coating articles to *look like* wood, leather or other natural materials.

冗贅	簡潔
It is generally believed	**many think**（許多人認為）
It is generally believed that the purpose of a newspaper is to state the facts about what is going on in the world.	*Many think* that the purpose of a newspaper is to state the facts about what is going on in the world.
It is crucial that	**must**（必須）
It is crucial that the international community, led by the industrial countries, conclude the current trade negotiations.	The international community led by the industrial countries **must** conclude the current trade negotiations.
the great majority of	**most**（多數）
The great majority (95%) **of** the papers express congratulations upon America's conduct throughout the war.	**Most** (95%) of the papers express congratulations upon America's conduct throughout the war.
at no time **on no occasion**	**never**（不該）
On no occasion should a student bring skateboards or roller blades to school.	**Never** should a student bring skateboards or roller blades to school.
It is worth pointing that **It should be noted that**	**note that**（注意）（或略去）
It is worth pointing that using *computer monitors* for a long period can cause visual problems and headaches.	Note that using *computer monitors* for a long period can cause visual problems and headaches.

冗贅	簡潔
at the present time **at this point in time**	**now, presently**（現在）
At the present time, it has an enrollment of about 12500 students who are studying and doing research in 16 colleges and research institutes.	**Presently**, it has an enrollment of about 12,500 students who are studying and doing research in 16 colleges and research institutes.
in many cases **it is often the case that**	**often**（常常；時常）
The president has intervened **in many cases** to undercut longstanding environmental rules for the benefit of business.	The president has **often** intervened to undercut long-standing environmental rules for the benefit of business.
on the basis of	**on**（在……之上）
These departments are also evaluated *on the basis of* the quality of their teaching.	These departments are also evaluated *on* the quality of their teaching.
in the possession of	**possess**（持有）
The total property **in the possession of** the contractor increased by $1.1 billion during the contract period of 2008.	The total property **possessed** by the contractor increased by $1.1 billion during the contract period of 2008.
within the realm of possibility	**possible**（可能）
Everything in this movie is **within the realm of possibility**.	Everything in this movie is **possible**.

冗贅	簡潔
militate against	**prohibit**（禁止）
By 2010 the uncertainties which *militate against* changes in policies might be resolved.	By 2010 the uncertainties which *prohibit* changes in policies might be resolved.
make reference to	**refer to**（提到；談論）
One can *make reference to* the guiding principles and take steps to develop a set of *green procurement* guidelines.	One can *refer to* the guiding principles and take steps to develop a set of *green procurement* guidelines.
presents a picture similar to	**resembles**（類似；像）
Scotland **presents a picture similar to** Ireland in landownership and cultivation of the soil.	Scotland **resembles** Ireland in landownership and cultivation of the soil.
in a satisfactory manner	**satisfactorily**（令人滿意）
If a certified company does not rectify arisen deviations **in a satisfactory manner**, the authority may revoke its certificate.	If a certified company does not rectify arisen deviations **satisfactorily**, the authority may revoke its certificate.
with the result that	**so that**（結果）
The mold is open at both ends, **with the result that** the hot air can stream through the cavity of the mold during baking.	The mold is open at both ends **so that** the hot air can stream through the cavity of the mold during baking.

冗贅	簡潔
in a number of cases **in some cases** **more often than not**	**sometimes**（有時）
In a number of cases new governments did not start reforms successfully after taking office.	*Sometimes* new governments did not start reforms successfully after taking office.
More often than not the forensic evidence was presented in a false or misleading manner.	*Sometimes* the forensic evidence was presented in a false or misleading manner.
at an early date **in the not-too-distant future**	**soon**（不久；很快）
In the not too distant future broadband will be established as an additional mode of television.	Broadband will *soon* be established as an additional mode of television.
place a major emphasis	**stress**（強調）
Some therapies in the west **place a major emphasis** on low sodium, high potassium foods.	Some therapies in the west **stress** on low sodium, high potassium foods.
engage in a study of	**study**（研究）
The team has been *engaged in a study* of race relations in India, South Africa, South America and other multi-races culture.	The team has *studied* race relations in India, South Africa, South America, and other multi-race cultures.

冗贅	簡潔
the result seems to indicate	**the result shows**（本結果表示）
The result seems to indicate that knowledge-intensive companies Manage their knowledge in different, unique ways.	**The result shows** that knowledge-intensive companies Manage their knowledge in different, unique ways.
incline to the view **be of the opinion**	**think**（認為）
Fifty percent of those surveyed *incline to the view* that the era of cold fusion will arrive in the near future.	Fifty percent of those surveyed *think* that the era of cold fusion will arrive in the near future.
Commission **is of the opinion** that such contract is not contrary to the public interest.	Commission **thinks** such contract is not contrary to the public interest.
as of this date **in this day and age**	**today**（今日；現今）
Many believe that eople must not ignore computer literacy which goes beyond traditional literacy *in this day and age*.	Many believe that people must not ignore computer literacy which goes beyond traditional literacy *today*.
until such time as	**until**（到……為止）
The commissioners serve *until such time as* they are replaced or reappointed.	The commissioners serve *until* they are replaced or reappointed.

冗贅	簡潔
of great theoretical and practical importance	**very important**（非常重要）
To study the trade barriers between China and the US *is of great practical and theoretical importance*	To study the trade barriers between China and the US is **vey important**.
is desirous to	**wants to**（想要）
The Chinese housing industry *is desirous to* build a market-based home building environment in its capital.	The Chinese housing industry *wants to* build a market-based home building environment in its capital.
ways and means	**ways**（或 **means**）（辦法）
Changing **ways and means** enables the researcher to work for a better result.	Changing **ways** enables the researcher to work for a better result.
determination was performed	**was determined**（決定）
The new car structure *determination was performed* by comparing the experimental data with simulated data.	The new car structure *was determined* by comparing the experimental data with simulated data.
in a situation in which **on those occasions in which** **during the time that**	**when**（當）
The difficulty lies **in a situation in which** the demands of plot require that the reader classify discourse as either true or false.	The difficulty lies **when** the demands of plot require that the reader classify discourse as either true or false.

冗贅	簡潔
On those occasions in which the subject matter is too sensitive to put on paper, the committee will discuss it at the meeting.	**When** the subject matter is too sensitive to put on paper, the committee will discuss it at the meeting.
This occurred **during the time that** the Roman Empire ruled parts of Italy	This occurred **when** the Roman Empire ruled parts of Italy
the question as to whether	**whether**（是否）
The central issue here is **the question as to whether** the passage of fluid across the membrane is a process of filtration.	The central issue here is **whether** the passage of fluid across the membrane is a process of filtration.
in the absence of	**without**（沒有）
In the absence of rapid worldwide transformation of energy supplies to low carbon sources, climate stability is unlikely to achieve with a global population of more than 2 billion.	With a global population of over two billion, to achieve climate stability is unlikely *without* rapid worldwide transformation of energy supplies to low carbon sources.

三、練習

　　熟能生巧，本節提供近百個習作例句，請依 11.2 節的範例修改這些冗句。

1. **It is of interest to note that** this refraction boundary forms a surface that has essentially the same radius as the boundary between the totally shielded matter and the normal unshielded matter.

2. **Needless to say**, Einstein's Theory of General Relativity has a profound influence to modern physics.

3. **It is evident that** there are many people on AB who in the past few years, lost the love of their lives in death.

4. Missing black holes give clues **as to** how galaxies evolve.

5. The authority will re-value the dwelling **having regard to** all the physical factors as they existed at the date of demolition.

6. Where there is a proposed change **in relation to** a carrier licensee, any interested person may apply in writing to the Authority.

7. Wikipedia comes close to Britannica **in terms of** the accuracy of its science entries.

8. The United Nation has established a framework for assessing fisheries **with respect to** ecologically sustainable development.

9. The investigator discusses problems **with regard to** Taiwan's radioactively contaminated buildings.

10. **As a matter of fact**, Thursday trading action had confirmed the validity of the "profit taking" scenario.

11. Researchers must sign out at the reference desk **at the conclusion of** this conference.

12. In the year **subsequent to** the earthquake a maximum of at least 20 cm of displacement occurred on a 30 km section of the San Andreas fault.

13. They are all **of the same opinion** that aggression is totally unnecessary.

14. With astonishing **unanimity of opinion** and clarity of voice, respondents pointed to digital collection development as their single greatest challenge.

15. **Despite the fact that** many industries have begun to appreciate added value by design, the significant profit of OEM/ODM production or even counterfeiting has created disincentives that discourage many enterprises from investing in value-added design.

16. **It is apparent that** such segregation has long been a nationwide problem, not merely one of sectional concern.

17. **Inasmuch as** human oncogenes and tumor suppressor genes are often components of growth factor signaling pathways, mTOR is a potential target for anti-cancer chemotherapy.

18. **As is the case** with lots of aging miners, addiction to pills began in a doctor's office, not a back-alley drug deal.

19. Both the principal sum and interest shall become due and payable **forthwith now**.

20. Teachers must be **cognizant of** their beliefs about children who come from low socio-economic backgrounds and culturally diverse homes.

21. **In light of the fact that** Taiwan has lost all diplomatic recognition in the United States, people-to-people diplomacy is of the utmost importance.

22. This litigious storm which sweeps through the USA can be **accounted for by the fact** there are more lawyers here than in any other country.

23. Ms. Johansson made a mistake by not remaining in service throughout the period, **in view of the fact that** she is the minister responsible for health care issues.

24. Trading standards officers have ordered the Black Mountains Smokery to

change the name of its Welsh Dragon sausages **on the grounds that** they are made with pork, not dragon meat.

25. **Owing to the fact that** the workers have gone on strike, the company has not been able to fulfill all its orders.

26. Hillary Clinton won overwhelmingly and **the reason is because** she has a plan to inject stimulus into the system and turn the economy around.

27. As spouses successfully negotiate their marital expectations, conflict generated by the negotiation process diminishes, as does the likelihood of dissolution **as a consequence of** such conflict.

28. **On account of** the pleasant Gulf breezes many strangers were residing temporarily near the beach.

29. Professor Yeh **is of the opinion that** consensus does not have to be a prerequisite for such action.

30. Details of suitability as a guide of each type of extinguisher is shown in Table I. **It may, however, be noted that** this is only for guidance and does not cover certain special cases.

31. Formal applications must be received **no later than** May 2, 2008.

32. The genes identified **through the use of** these approaches represent potential targets for designing agents capable of regulating ovarian physiology

33. The hostility that America continues to express against the Muslim people has given rise to feelings of hatred **on the part of** Muslims against America.

34. This information does not imply any opinion **on the part of** the Food and Agriculture Organization.

35. This is about an awareness **on the part of** some smart young people starting

their business careers.

36. There is an interesting reason why a psychiatrist are commonly **referred to as** a shrink.

37. The question whether certain laws can **give rise to** a Section 1983 violation remains an unstable area in civil rights law.

38. The developer offers investors the opportunity to purchase a spacious two bedroom apartment **in close proximity to** the central city.

39. They accelerate the diffusion process and thus speed up the process by which a **consensus of opinion** is reached.

40. There are additional drawbacks people need to **take into consideration**.

41. They sow rumor and disinformation **on a daily basis** in order to discredit critics of the government.

42. The employment is **contingent upon** drug test and background check.

43. This page provides the prophecy of the coming judgment where everyone will **give an account of** their lives.

44. This study analyzes in detail antibody responses against A60 components **during the course of** tuberculosis.

45. The Defense Department is taking the lead in handing over wartime operational control **at an earlier date,**

46. To work out **at an early date** a new international statute banning arms race in the outer space tops the agenda in the disarmament field of the international community.

47. A new congressional transportation appropriations bill will **entirely eliminate** some $600 million worth of annual federal funding.

48. After scouring hundreds of random spam-filled websites, newsgroups and forums, The researchers have settled on the following list of **absolutely essential** software.

49. Mineral deposits which are embedded in the land shall belong to the State, **regardless of the fact that** private individuals may have acquired ownership over such land.

50. There is no other language **with a possible exception of** Sanskrit that a language is written in so many scripts.

51. Although far **fewer in number** than their western relatives, mountain gorillas have had a profound effect on both the public and the naturalists who have encountered them.

52. This report identifies issues and research needs for interpreting bioaccumulation data **for the purpose of** assessing sediment quality.

53. The government should take immediate steps **with a view to** reducing the risk of accidental or unauthorized use of nuclear weapons. **An example of this is the fact that** the boiling point of water is lower on the top of a mountain where the air pressure is lower.

54. Hotels in this area are **completely full** during the flower season.

55. Rehabilitation Services help people with disabilities to develop their physical, mental and social capabilities **to the fullest possible extent**.

56. **Should it prove the case that** consumers are unwilling or increasingly unable to pay higher retail prices, retailers are likely to once again face a setback.

57. **In a very real sense**, even very small children are responsible for the care of their own child-sized environment.

58. The model coordinate system **is defined as** the reference space of the model with respect to which all the model geometrical data is stored.

59. The recent consolidation, though **large in size**, changes only slightly the degree of concentration in the entire industry,"

60. The cause of the loss was an oversized bet on where certain natural gas prices would be **at some future time**.

61. It initiates a chain reaction leading to **a decreased amount of** crops in a harvest as well as **an increased amount of** diseases and plague.

62. The smartest thing to do is to **have the appearance of** doing something to claim political credit but without having any actual responsibility or doing any work.

63. **It is generally believed** that children may not be able to differentiate an exciting and unusual experience from reality.

64. **It is crucial that** Taiwan establish effective communications with the U.S. to promote mutual understanding.

65. **The great majority (80%) of** the Marine Park is still relatively pristine when compared with coral reef systems elsewhere in the world.

66. **At no time** will the administrator of the "Recruitment System" release personal information to anyone other than the experimenter conducting the session.

67. **It should be noted that** all of these air bags protect people's heads in the event of a collision.

68. The market **at this point in time** has devalued the dollar, which is contrary to the US policy.

69. Catastrophic events can have a substantial impact on a species' population,

because **it is often the case that** such interruptions can affect the results of competition within that species.

70. Rankings of economics departments **on the basis of** faculty research productivity also produce outcomes that are lop-sided at the top.

71. The club **is in the possession of** a club premises certificate covered by the provisions for late night refreshment.

72. It is **within the realm of possibility** that man may impact the earth to a degree that the earth becomes uninhabitable to human and other species.

73. Waste having a solid content high enough to **militate against** its disposal as sewage is typically disposed of by burning or dumping.

74. When **making reference to** someone's work in the report, remember to indicate where that reference came from.

75. Research on social dominance in young children **presents a picture similar to** that existing in animal research.

76. The licensee should install, calibrate, maintain and operate **in a satisfactory manner** a device to monitor the. exhaust gas temperature.

77. That point has largely eluded the press, **with the result that** most people think this is a new phenomenon.

78. **More often than not**, the fast food places take basically good food and turn it into bad.

79. The shortage of fossil fuels **in the not-too-distant future could. seriously affect the activities of all walks of lives**

80. The Administration should **place a major emphasis on** negotiating nuclear disarmament.

81. **The researchers have been engaged in a study of** the Christian origins

and of the doctrinal development in the apostolic age.

82. **The result seem to indicate** that the inhabitants of the regions in which vaccination has been practiced are in a state of immunity against yellow fever virus.

83. Some scientists incline to the view that the space-time is not infinite.

84. The Panel is **of the opinion that** the molecular characterization of the DNA insert does not raise safety concerns.

85. **As of this date**, the verification is delayed and time consuming due to inadequate system and communications.

86. A non-resident student who is a member of an ROTC unit will be required to pay non-resident tuition rates **until such time as** the student has signed a proper contract.

87. The author concludes that such an evolution will be of great **practical importance** to the enhancement of the relevance of APEC.

88. The study on industrial competitiveness is **of great theoretical and practical importance**.

89. Israel **is desirous to** have good, peaceful and neighborly relations with Lebanon.

90. This paper discusses **ways and means** to reduce flood risks in arid zones.

91. The selenium **determination was performed** using an atomic absorption spectrophotometer.

92. **In a situation in which** nationalism in China is awakening, Taiwan should avoid a direct nationalist confrontation.

93. As small children, they were chastised **on those occasions in which** they were unwilling to share.

94. There was no definitive record of a bright nova appearing in the sky **during the time that** biblical historians believe the Magi made their journey.

95. Eating when exposed to large portions of palatable foods **in the absence of** hunger may cauxe overweight.

96. Associated with this was **the question as to whether** library and information science should be a discipline in its own right from bachelor degree onwards.

附錄

一、研究報告字體及字型配置

　　長篇論文裡的章節標題宜用不同的字體來分別，這種做法不但在視覺上有美化效果，也可以明顯呈現出論文整體的層次，使閱讀者更易理清論文的理路。

　　行距指一行文字底端到下一行文字底端的距離，在 MS-Word 中以點數表示行距，內文行距應為字高的 1.5 倍，內文字高若為 12 點，則行距應為 18 點。

　　每一段起首時，通常要留空三至五個字母，段與段之間要多留半行空位。每個段落第一行應空二格，段落的左右邊緣應對齊，盡量避免呈鋸齒狀，段落與段落之間應空一行半的距離，以求容易閱讀。

　　論文中應用的字體、字型雖沒有絕對硬性的規定，但還是有一定的準則可循，附表 1-1 簡明地陳列了一般論文中字體及字型的配置原則。

附表 1-1 論文章節圖表各級標題的字體及字型配置

表 1-1

文字	體例	字體		字型大小
		中文	英文	
章標題	第二章 資料管理	細明體	**Times New Roman**	**16p**
一級節標題	2.1 私人知識的管理	細明體	**Times New Roman**	**14p**
二級節標題	2.1.1 知識獲取及累積	細明體	**Times New Roman**	**12pt**
三級節標題	2.1.2.1 檔案維護與搜尋	細明體	Times New Roman	12pt
圖表標題	圖 2-1 樹狀結構示意圖	細明體	**Times New Roman**	**12p**
內文	每段起首要留空三至五個字母，段與段間…	細明體	Times New Roman	12pt
參考文獻	Yeh, Gary, "Waste Management Decisions," InDyne, Rep. TR22, 1990.	細明體	Times New Roman	12pt

二、長字及其清晰有力的代用字表

附表 2-1

長字	簡潔的代用字	中譯
abundance	plenty	豐富；充足
acquire	get, gain	獲得；取得
apprise	inform, tell	通知，告知
advantageous	helpful	有利的
advise	say, tell	勸告；告知
aforementioned	this, these	上述的
alternative	another course	二中擇一
anticipate	expect, look for	預期；期望
approximate	about	近似；接近
ascertain	find out	查明；確定
assistance	help, aid	援助；幫助
attitude	feeling	意見；看法
available	ready	可利用的
commence	begin, start	開始；著手
competent	able	有能力的
compliance with	according to	合於……
comprised	made up of	包括；包含
concerning	about	關於
conclusion	end	結論；結束
confined	limited	被限制的

長字	簡潔的代用字	中譯
cursory	short	疏忽的；草率的
demonstrate	show	顯示
deprive	keep from	剝奪；阻止
desire	want	慾望；渴望
determine	decide, find out	裁定
difficult	hard	困難的
effectuate	cause	原因；導致
efficacy	effectiveness	有效
efficient	able	有能力的
eliminate	leave out, omit	消除；除去
elucidate	explain	解釋
employ	use	應用
endeavor	try	努力
esteemed	respected	受尊敬的
eventuate	happen	發生
exceedingly	very	非常地
expedite	hasten	促進
explicit	clear, plain	明確的；清楚的
exterior	outside	外部
fabricate	make	做；製造
facilitate	help	幫助；有助於
finalize	end	結束

長字	簡潔的代用字	中譯
furnish	give	供應；給與
henceforth	after this	今後
impact	affect	影響
inform	say, tell	告知
initial	first	最初的
initiate	begin, start	開始
institute	begin	開始
interior	inside	內部
lenient	easy	寬厚的
necessitate	need	需要
negligent	careless	粗心的
participate	share	參與
perform	do	做
peruse, perusal	study	閱讀
possess	have	擁有
preserve	keep	保持
previous	before, former	先前
procure	get	獲得
prominent	leading	突出的
provide	give	提供
pursuant	according to	根據；依照
quantify	measure	量化；測量

長字	簡潔的代用字	中譯
reconcile	make agree	使符合
relinquish	give up	放棄
render	give	給予
request	ask	要求
require	need	需要
restrict	limit	限制；約束
retain	keep	保持
secure	get	獲得
solution	answer	解答
sufficient	enough	足夠的；充足的
terminate	end	結束；終止
transpire	happen	發生
ultimate	final, last	最終的，最後的
utilize, utilization	use	使用

三、論文檢索系統

　　為了方便論文的檢索，降低因為文獻快速增長而在搜尋資料時所造成的困難，有些資訊組織應運而生，它們將原始文獻的主要內容摘錄出來，做成文獻，並出版檢索期刊。由於摘要種類、編輯方式、檢索方法等等的不同，檢索期刊種類也是多樣化，從而形成**資訊檢索**（Information Retrieval）這種專門的領域。

㈠ 知名的國際文獻檢索系統

　　較知名於國際的文獻檢索系統有：

1. 社會、經濟及管理類：***ABI***[1]（Abstract of Business Index）和 ***SSCI***（Social Science Citation Index）。

2. 科技類：***EI***（Engineering Index）、***ISTP***[2]（Index to Scientific & Technical Proceedings）和 ***SCI***（Science Citation Index）

　　以上五種指標可供國際學人判斷列名期刊之特色、屬性及重要性。以下介紹華人學術界在論文排名、研究基金申請、個人職稱晉升等競爭中最倚重的三種指標。

EI

　　EI 於 1884 年創刊，在 1892-1906 期間名為 Descriptive Index of Current Engineering Literature，1906 年以後改為 Engineering Index。

　　EI 每年約收錄二十萬筆工程與技術方面的文獻摘要。收錄主題範圍包含有航空、生物、電腦、通訊、能源技術、材料科學等工程與技術方

1　收錄商學暨企管期刊文獻及報紙新聞之資料來源（citations）及摘要（abstracts），主題涵蓋銀行、金融、政府、會計、稅法、基金管理、經濟等。

2　譯為「科技會議錄索引」，彙集了包括專著、叢書、抽印本以及源自期刊的會議論文等多學科的會議論文資料。

面的資訊。每年約收錄 4,500 種期刊、2,000 種會議論文集，外加學會出版品、技術報告、標準、圖書專論等等。

EI 初期為年刊（EI Annual），自 1962 年起，開始出版月刊本（EI Monthly），之後陸續有顯微膠卷、磁帶等型式，1969 年以後則有 COMPENDEX（Computerized Engineering Index）資料庫的建立，使用者欲檢索其資料庫，可透過多重管道，例如：CD-ROM（光碟）、DIALOG（國際百科）、STICNET（科資中心科技網路）等檢索系統檢索。讀者可依 Engineering Index、EI Annual（紙本式）、COMPENDEX 光碟資料庫、COMPENDEX Reference Database 三種不同的型式進行檢索。

SCI

SCI（科學摘錄索引）是 ISI（Institute for Scientific Information，美國科學資訊學會）[3]發行的期刊文獻檢索工具，SCI 收錄全世界出版的理、工、醫、農、天文、地理、環境、材料、技術及生命科學等各類期刊數千種（數量每年均有增減），其出版形式包括印刷版期刊、光碟版、線上資料庫和 Internet 版資料庫。ISI 以嚴格的選刊標準和評估模式，使 SCI 收錄的文獻涵蓋全世界最重要、最有影響力的研究成果，這些成果的文獻資料大量被其他文獻引用。

SCI 設置了 Citation Index，透過先期文獻被後期文獻引用的頻率，來說明文獻之間的相關性，及先期文獻對後期文獻的影響力，這種做法，使 SCI 不僅成為一種文獻檢索工具，而且成為科技及工程研究評價的一種依據。學術研究機構被 SCI 收錄的論文總量反映了該機構的研究水準；個人的論文被 SCI 收錄的數量及被引用次數則反映其個人研究的

---

3 網址：http://www.isinet.com。

水準，國內高等教育界研究者升等考核便與 SCI 息息相關。

SSCI

　　SSCI（社會科學引文索引）也是 **ISI** 的學術論文檢索工具和資料庫，是以收錄社會科學的論文為主，於 1973 年創立，其構想係根據 Bradford's Law[4]而來。SSCI 收錄的主要是社會科學的論文，覆蓋的領域包括社會、經濟、金融、教育、心理、管理、法學、哲學、歷史、政策及其交叉學科等等，至今收錄社會科學類五十餘個學科，共有近兩千種學術期刊，同時也收錄科技期刊中與社會科學相關的論文，因此 SSCI 收錄的文章與 SCI 收錄的文章部分是重疊的，不少 **SCIENCE** 和 **NATURE** 的文章也被收入 SSCI 中。論文刊登在 SCI 和 SSCI 所認證的期刊上，代表該研究已獲得國際的肯定。

　　ISI 之期刊選錄標準相當嚴格，它持續對 SCI 和 SSCI 之期刊進行排名，定期評比與汰換，各期刊以被選錄為榮，它們遂成為期刊品質之認證。SCI 和 SSCI 的排名變化，多少象徵了期刊品質的消長，因此，榜上期刊多本著學術界公認之原則來選審稿件，以期提升排名與學術聲譽。

　　ISI 對於期刊的評比，成為期刊審稿時的良性的刺激，它維護與提升了學術期刊的品質，所以 SCI 和 SSCI 已被學界公認為評量學術刊物之水準及地位的有效指標。

　　ISI 每年還出版了 **JCR**（*Journal Citation Reports*，期刊引文報告），JCR 是期刊評鑑的必備參考工具，且是唯一提供期刊引用文獻（Citation）數據的來源，收錄範圍涵蓋全世界六十多個國家，七千多種學術期刊。

4　該定律與 1.5 節所述之 80/20 法則似乎異曲同工，認為大部分的重要科學研究成果，僅在少數期刊刊載，在社會科學類此少數期刊即為 SSCI 期刊，而這些期刊就是社會科學學術研究文獻的基礎。

(二) Impact Factor（影響點數）

指標中最為華人學界所熟悉的，就是 Impact Factor **影響點數**[5]，一種刊物的 Impact Factor 越高，代表其刊載的文獻被引用率越高，說明這些文獻報導的研究成果影響力大，也反映該刊物的高學術水準。圖書館可根據 JCR 提供的資料，制定期刊引進政策，論文作者也可根據期刊的 Impact Factor 排名，而決定投稿方向。

透過 JCR 可得知其所收錄的期刊中：

1. 最具影響力的期刊
2. 最熱門、最常被引用的期刊
3. 出版量最大的期刊
4. 某期刊點數及立即引用率（Immediacy Index）的高低
5. 某期刊的引用及被引用的情形
6. 某期刊的詳細出版資訊及刊名沿革

JCR 以其大量的期刊統計資料及計算的 Impact Factor 等指數，成為一種權威的期刊評價工具。一般人使用 JCR 索引某期刊之總排名，或該刊在某學科之排名，因此 JCR 最常被參考的數據是各學科的期刊點數及排名。若要查詢某文章被引用的情形，則需利用 SCI 或 SSCI 等引用文獻資料庫為之。

JCR 中定義了下列四項指數：

1. Impact Factor（文獻影響點數 I_F）
2. Immediacy Index（文獻立即引用指數 I_X）
3. Cited Half Life（文獻被引用半生期 L_D）
4. Citing Half Life（文獻引用半生期 L_G）

---

[5] Impact Factor 即引用率，國內通稱「點數」。

今將各項指數的計算方法解釋於下：

影響點數 I_F（Impact Factor）

某期刊的文獻影響點數 I_F，為該期刊在出版年之<u>前兩年被引用次數</u>的總和除以<u>前兩年的該期刊出版文獻之總篇數</u>，即：

$$I_{F2016} = （C_{2014} + C_{2015}） / （P_{2014} + P_{2015}）$$

其中

I_{F2016} = 某期刊 2016 年的 Impact Factor

P_{2015} = 2015 年出版的文獻數 = 1,037 篇

P_{2014} = 2014 年出版的文獻數 = 1,054 篇

C_{2015} = 2015 年出版的文獻在 2016 年被引用的次數

　　　= 24,189 次

C_{2014} = 2014 年出版的文獻在 2016 年被引用的次數

　　　= 25,170 次

因此

$$I_{F2016} = （24,189 + 25,170） / （1,037 + 1,054）$$

$$= 23.605（次 / 篇）$$

例如：某刊 2014 及 2015 年共出版 181 篇文章，而在 2016 年共被引用 210 次，則 Impact Factor 為：

$$210 ÷ 181 = 1.16$$

立即引用指數 I_X（Immediacy Index）

某期刊的文獻立即引用指數 I_X，為該期刊在出版當年被引用次數總和除以當年該期刊出版文獻之總篇數，即：

$$I_{X2016} = C_{2016} / P_{2016}$$

其中

I_{X2016} = 某期刊 2016 年的 Immediacy Index

P_{2016} = 2016 年出版的文獻數 = 1,095 篇

C_{2016} = 2016 年出版的文獻在 2016 當年被引用的次數

　　　= 5,297 次

因此

I_{X2016} = 5,297/1,095 = 4.837

　　例如：某刊 2014 年共出版 89 篇文章，而在 2014 年共被引用 72 次，則 Immediacy Index 為 72 ÷ 89 = 0.809。

文獻被受引半生期 L_D（Cited Half-life）

　　某期刊的**文獻被受引半生期**（L_D），乃是該刊論文受引用平均年限的指標。L_D 越小即表示：該刊論文近年被引次數較昔年高出越多。

　　L_D 的計算是以年為單位，由該期刊最新出版年回溯十年，統計該刊論文被引用之次數，於多少年內達到該刊十年間被引用總數的 50%[6]。

　　以 2016 年統計某期刊被引用的狀況為例：

出版年	2015	2014	2013	**2012**	2011	…	十年累積
2016 年被引用次數	5,297	24,198	25,170	**23,762**	20,697		191,696
累積百分比（%）	2.76	15.39	28.52	**40.91**	51.71		
年數（L）	1	2	3	**4**	5		

　　累積百分比最接近 50%（2012），且再加一年（2011）即超過 50% 的年數 L = 4

　　L_D = L +（50 − 40.91）/（51.71 − 40.91）= 4.84（年）

6　在最新出版年之被引用次數低於 100 者不被列入，另外若十年以上其數字仍未達 50%，以 > 10.0 表示。

這表示該期刊在 2016 年的文獻受引半生期為 4.84，即，在 4.84 年內，該刊論文受引用之次數就達其十年受引總數的一半。

文獻引用半生期 L_G（Citing Half-life）

某期刊的文獻引用半生期（L_G），乃是該刊所引論文篇次之成長率的指標。L_G 越小即表示：表示該刊近年所引論文篇次較昔年高出越多。

L_G 的計算也是以年為單位，由該期刊最新出版年回溯十年，統計該刊所引論文之篇次，於多少年內達到該刊十年間所引論文總篇次的 50%[7]。

以某期刊 2016 年統計的引用狀況為例：

出版年	2015	2014	2013	**2012**	2011	…	十年累積
2016 年引用次數	2,792	6,678	5,553	**4,352**	3,240		39,958
累積百分比（%）	6.98	23.69	37.59	**48.48**	56.59		
年數（L）	1	2	3	**4**	5		

累積百分比最接近 50% 並於次年即超過 50% 的年度是 2012，該年至 2015 的年數 L = 4

$L_G = L + (50 - 48.48) / (56.59 - 48.48) = 4.19$（年）

這表示該期刊在 2016 年的文獻引用半生期為 4.19，即，在 4.19 年內，該刊論文所引用論文之篇次就達其十年引用總篇次的一半。

7　在最新出版年之引用次數低於 100 者不予列入，另外若十年以上其數字仍未達 50%，以 > 10.0 表示。

中文

1. 葉乃嘉：《中英雙向翻譯新視野》，臺北：五南圖書出版公司，2007 年 3 月。

2. 葉乃嘉：《個人知識管理的第一本書》，松崗圖書公司，2007 年 7 月。

3. 葉乃嘉：《研究方法的第一本書》，臺北：五南圖書出版公司，2006 年 7 月。

4. 葉乃嘉：《中英論文寫作綱要與體例》，臺北：五南圖書出版公司，2005 年 1 月。

5. 葉乃嘉：《知識管理實務、專題與案例》，臺北：新文京開發出版公司，2005 年 8 月。

6. 葉乃嘉：《知識管理》，臺北：全華科技圖書公司，2004 年 2 月。

7. 葉乃嘉：《知識管理導論與案例分析》，臺北：全華科技圖書公司，2006 年 9 月。

8. 葉乃嘉：（2002），《商用英文的溝通藝術》，臺北：新文京開發出版公司，2002 年 12 月。

英文

1. Alley, Michael. (1996). *The Craft of Scientific Writing (3rd ed.).* New York: Springer-Verlag.

2. Becker, Howard Saul. (1986). *Writing For Social Scientists : How to Start and Finish Your Thesis, Book, Or Article.* Chicago: University of Chicago Press.

3. Booth, Wayne C., Gregory G. Colomb & Joseph M. Williams. (2003). *The Craft of Research (2nd ed.).* Chicago: University of Chicago Press.

4. Chin, Beverly Ann. (2004). *How to Write a Great Research Paper*. Hoboken, N.J.: John Wiley.

5. Kamil, Michael L., Langer, Judith A. & Shanahan, Timothy. (1985). *Understanding Reading and Writing Research*. Boston : Allyn and Bacon.

6. Lester, James D. (1999). *Writing Research Papers: a Complete Guide* (*9th Ed.*). Glenview, Ill.: Scott, Foresman.

7. Meyer, Michael. (1985). *The Little, Brown Guide to Writing Research Papers*. Boston: Little, Brown.

8. Murray, Rowena. (2002). *How to Write a Thesis*. Buckingham [England] ; Philadelphia, PA: Open University Press.

9. Paltridge, Brian. (1997). *Genre, Frames, and Writing in Research Settings*. Amsterdam, the Netherlands; Philadelphia, Pa. : John Benjamins Pub.

10. Seech, Zachary. (2004). *Writing Philosophy Papers. 4th ed*. Belmont, California: Wadsworth.

11. Turabian, K. L. (1996). *A Manual for Writers of Papers, Theses, and Dissertations* (*6th Ed.*). Chicago: University of Chicago Press.

12. Veit, Richard. (1998). *Research: The Student's Guide to Writing Research Papers* (*2nd Ed.*). Boston, Mass.: Allyn and Bacon.

13. Walker, Melissa. (1984). *Writing Research Papers : a Norton guide*. New York: Norton.

14. Watson, George. (1987). *Writing a thesis: a Guide to Long Essays And Dissertations*. London; New York: Longman.

Note

Note

Note

國家圖書館出版品預行編目資料

論文寫作的第一本書——中英論文及研究計畫
綱要與體例／葉乃嘉著. 一 三版. 一 臺北
市：五南, 2016.09
　　面；　　公分.--
　　參考書目：面　含索引
　ISBN 978-957-11-8690-0（平裝）
　1. 論文寫作法
811.4　　　　　　　　　　　105011739

1X2D 論文寫作系列

論文寫作的第一本書
——中英論文及研究計畫綱要與體例

作　　者 — 葉乃嘉（323.2）

發 行 人 — 楊榮川

總 編 輯 — 王翠華

主　　編 — 黃惠娟

責任編輯 — 蔡佳伶 卓芳珣

封面設計 — 陳翰陞

出 版 者 — 五南圖書出版股份有限公司

地　　址：106台北市大安區和平東路二段339號4樓

電　　話：(02)2705-5066　　傳　　真：(02)2706-6100

網　　址：http://www.wunan.com.tw

電子郵件：wunan@wunan.com.tw

劃撥帳號：01068953

戶　　名：五南圖書出版股份有限公司

法律顧問　林勝安律師事務所　林勝安律師

出版日期　2005年1月初版一刷
　　　　　2011年1月二版一刷
　　　　　2016年9月三版一刷

定　　價　新臺幣450元